Six Concepts f

SF Concepts for the End of the World

Part of the Goldsmiths Press Unidentified Fictional Objects Series

Six Concepts for the End of the World

Steve Beard

Goldsmiths
Press

© 2019 Goldsmiths Press
Published in 2019 by Goldsmiths Press
Goldsmiths, University of London, New Cross
London SE14 6NW

Printed and bound by TJ International, UK
Distribution by the MIT Press
Cambridge, Massachusetts, and London, England

A CIP record for this book is available from the British Library

ISBN 978-1-912685-09-7 (pbk)
ISBN 978-1-912685-10-3 (ebk)

www.gold.ac.uk/goldsmiths-press

for Victoria

Contents

Acknowledgements

Six Concepts for the End of the World is an unidentified fictional object. Any resemblance its characters have to persons, living or dead, is purely accidental. The actual persons who deserve the author's thanks are as follows:

Victoria Halford for coming up with the idea on which this book is based – a film about the end of the world. Steven Bode, Caroline Smith and Film and Video Umbrella for shaping the idea into a creative proposition. Stephen Foster and John Hansard Gallery for support and encouragement.

John Armitage and Ryan Bishop for consultancy on Paul Virilio and the meaning of his fragmentary and elliptical writings about the end of the world.

Nick Jennings at the University of Southampton for providing access to the Electronics and Computer Science research on autonomous drones. Alex Rogers, Luke Teacy, Victor Naroditskiy, Gopal Ramchum, Trung Dong Huynh, Nadia Pantidi and the rest of the ORCHID team for their compelling thoughts about end-of-the-world scenarios. Angela Westley for scheduling interviews and much else.

Leverhulme Trust for an Artist in Residence grant.

Sarah Kember and Goldsmiths Press for publishing the book. Jeff Noon, Tony White and various anonymous peer reviewers for their feedback on the first draft. Adrian Driscoll, Michelle Lo, Sue Barnes and Adriana Cloud for helping to produce the book.

Intro: Field Notes on a Residency

Haubenstock was driving along the south coast of England towards the port of Southampton. He had his camera equipment in the back of the Mini Cooper. I was next to him in the passenger seat. It was autumn 2013 and we were going to do an artists-in-residency at Solent City University.

We'd got a grant from Unilever, the Anglo-Dutch multinational, to sit in with a team of the university's computer scientists. They were building algorithms for what they called 'autonomous aerial vehicles'. Robot drones, in other words. The scientists claimed in a press release that autonomous drones would be able to make their own decisions about how to conduct surveillance operations. The drones would fly over earthquake zones, plane crash sites and other large-scale disaster zones and be able to recognise debris, oil spills and refugees without any need for human oversight. Search-and-rescue teams would find them invaluable. So the press release said.

I'd talked to Jenkins, the head of the computer science team at Solent City University, when I was putting together the Unilever application. Garlanded with awards and fellowships as he was, Jenkins had been a polite, almost demure, presence on the phone. He said that having an arts project attached to his drone research programme would be good PR as far as his institutional and corporate backers were concerned. He mentioned British Red Cross. He mentioned British Aerospace.

Jenkins had told me his team of drone scientists were working with a disaster scenario that was already out of date. It involved the site of the London 2012 Olympics being flooded as a result of a terror attack on the Thames Barrier. Fires and stampedes also featured in the scenario. I suggested he needed a new disaster scenario and he agreed. It was then that it had hit me. Surely the ultimate disaster zone, the absolute worst-case scenario to consider when testing the feasibility of any drone algorithms, was the end of the world. What might that look like? Not a bad question, said Jenkins.

So here Haubenstock and I were months later, bowling along the M27 from Brighton to Southampton. Unilever had contracted us to work with the Solent City University drone scientists on generating at least three end-of-the-world scenarios for them to test their algorithms against. Haubenstock would video our collaborative activity for the university archive. I'd write up the scenarios. And then together Haubenstock and I would go away and make a short experimental art film about the Apocalypse, based on one of the scenarios. It all looked good on paper.

As Haubenstock drove further towards Southampton, however, he began to pick apart the terms of the residency. He was unhappy with the fact that one of the sponsors of the drone team was British Aerospace, an arms manufacturer. It's obvious that search-and-rescue could be swapped out for search-and-destroy in the final application of the computer algorithms, he said. Bombs could easily take the place of cameras. He clenched his fist. Which meant that the two of us were probably being treated as a couple of useful idiots. What would happen to any film we made? It could easily end up in the Imperial War Museum as an exhibit in some godawful show-and-tell about the British Army's so-called humanitarian interventions in the Middle East. He was fuming.

I reminded Haubenstock that we had creative control over the residency. We'd been in this situation plenty of times before. We'd filmed *Stalker II* with the radiation protection technicians at Hokkaido in Japan and *Zero Gravity/Zero Gender* with the cosmonaut trainers at Star City in Russia. We'd made *Voodoo Science Park* with mechanical engineers at the industrial accident testing range in the old mining district of England. And in each case we'd been free to thumb our noses at institutional sponsors if they didn't like the films we'd made.

What I didn't say was that we'd been able to be a little cavalier in those days because there had been plenty of public funds sloshing around the art world. Things were very different now there was an austerity government in power. Alienating the people at Unilever or Solent City University might well put a block on funding for any future residencies by us. But no matter. I suspected our art career was in terminal decline, anyway.

By the time we drove through the outskirts of Southampton, the mood in the car was sombre. I was staring out of the window. The fast food outlets, hairdressing salons and computer repair shops went by. We drove past the elegantly formed modernist slabs of the Whitlock Gallery. A publicly funded exhibition space, it had a modest reputation in the art world for showing experimental work, though it struggled to attract critics from London. I'd made a point of attending the gallery's summer party a few months previously.

There had been a marquee on the lawn at the back of the gallery. The guests were eating hamburgers from paper plates. I'd managed to corner Farmer, the gallery director, next to the barbecue grill. He was a genial fellow whom I'd known, on and off, for a number of years. The man listened to my news of the Unilever application in between pricking the sausages with a fork. He said the Whitlock would be happy to make a provisional commitment to showing any film that came out of the Solent City residence, circumstances permitting. He handed me a hot dog.

It was later during that same afternoon on the lawn that I'd first met Angleton. He had cut a solitary figure against the Sun, standing to one side of the makeshift bar, sipping his Pilsner from the bottle. I opened a can of Coke and we exchanged pleasantries. He said he was a professor of media studies at Chilton School of Art, just a short drive up the M3. Farmer popped up at that moment to say that Angleton was being far too modest. He was also the world's leading expert on the French theorist Paul Virilio. Angleton smiled, shyly. We shook hands. Farmer wiped his greasy fingers on his apron and disappeared.

When I told Angleton I was planning to make an art film about the end of the world, he wasn't fazed. He said that Virilio was always writing about the Apocalypse. He'd be a good person to have in the film. Except that he never gave interviews. He was retired, in fact. Seeing out the end of his days on the Brittany coast in seclusion, a near-hermit at the edge of the continent. Angleton swirled the last remains of the beer in his bottle.

I'd heard of Virilio only vaguely but thought there might be something in his writings I could bring to the residency. Angleton was happy to talk about his specialist subject. Virilio was a Christian anarchist who'd written extensively about cities, military architecture, technology, geopolitics and war. He believed in the reality of angels and demons, though he had never really spoken about them in public. And he honestly thought that Armageddon was coming, complete with final battle between the forces of good and evil.

Virilio sounds like a bit of an odd character, I said. If he were so reluctant to speak openly about his faith, then how on earth could he write sincerely about the Apocalypse? Angleton side-stepped the question. Virilio started out as an architect, he said. In fact, he'd co-designed a Catholic church in the 1960s. Angleton had actually made the pilgrimage, to Nevers in the middle of France, to take photographs of the sacred edifice. The locals called it 'l'eglise bizarre'. Virilio had designed it as an almost Cubist version of a concrete bunker.

Interesting, I said. Yeah, said Angleton. Virilio had been obsessed with the bunkers of the Second World War. He saw his church as a kind of concrete survival shelter for the Christian faithful. A defence against the Apocalypse? I asked. Angleton squinted at the Sun. 'Apocalypse' was not a word Virilio used much. Instead, he preferred the term 'global accident'. I expressed my puzzlement. Angleton said this was one of Virilio's more cryptic phrases, attesting to an epiphany or perhaps even a prophecy. At over 80-years-old Virilio was tempted to despair of the state of the world. In fact, he was so depressed that he was speaking only to the Bishop of La Rochelle.

So, definitely no interviews, I said, looking down at the tops of my shoes. Angleton said he was sure I'd find a way round it. He promised to send me an early copy of his latest textbook, *Virilio: A-Z*. We parted on good terms.

Haubenstock was already driving us into the car park at Solent City University. Jenkins had phoned ahead and the car park attendant had our names on a list.

We had an appointment with Jenkins, but were a little early. So we sat in the car. I got out my laptop and fired up the PDF of *Virilio: A-Z* which Angleton, true to his word, had emailed me. I'd been studying it for the last month. I scrolled down the document until I found Virilio's definition of the 'global accident'. I read the words once again:

The global accident extends across continents. It propagates itself through chain reactions. It affects everyone on the planet at the same time. It integrates us all consciously even as it disintegrates us physically.

There was a strange metaphysical sub-text here, especially in the idea of being almost enlightened by one's own destruction. I thought of the torments of the Christian martyrs. Was this what Virilio was getting at? It was baffling.

Haubenstock and I left the car and ambled over to the computer science building. Jenkins was on the third floor. His office was well lit and offered a panoramic view of the campus. There were bound volumes of the *International Journal of Autonomous Agents and Multi-Agent Systems* on his shelves. We sat down and talked through the structure of the residency over the next few months.

I said I'd like to have six workshops with the drone scientists. Jenkins nodded. I went on to talk about the importance of Virilio and how his thinking could help us conceptualise the ultimate disaster scenario with great precision. Jenkins nodded, a bit more uncertainly this time. According to *Virilio: A-Z*, I said, there were six perspectives that could be extracted from Virilio's take on the world. Six ways of thinking about the world implied six ways of thinking about the end of the world. That was what I'd really like to get out of the workshops. Six global disaster scenarios. Three more than specified by Unilever.

Jenkins coughed. He wanted to know more about these six ways of looking at the world. I counted them off on my fingers. First, there was the sociological perspective, the everyday world where people went to work, came home and went shopping at the weekends. Then there was the world invented by technology, with its computers, phones and electronic networks. The world of the geographers came next, with its focus on logistics and globalisation. Then there were the various compulsions and disturbances that belonged to the world of psychology. Coming next was the theological perspective, with its thoughts on the Last Judgement, so important to Virilio the practising Catholic. Finally, there was the narratological perspective, with its linguistic separation of the world-of-the-reporter from the world-to-be-reported-on.

Jenkins drummed on the desk with his fingers. He said that he would perhaps be able to nudge four or five of his drone scientists into attending the workshops. But no more than that. They were busy people. Naturally, I said. Haubenstock promised to film the brainstorming sessions for the university archive. Jenkins said he would book out some dates.

As we walked back to the car park, Haubenstock complained about having to do the workshops and said he just wanted to get on with making the film. I said we had to be patient. I was already thinking about the stimulus material I would have to prepare to share with the scientists in the workshops. I wanted to push them into making some imaginative extrapolations from known circumstances so that in each of the six sessions, we arrived at a solid idea for an end-of-the-world scenario. I would then work up each idea into a brief piece of writing – whether in the shape of a report, a monologue, a short story or a creative treatment. So, six end-of-the-world narratives, one of which Haubenstock and I could turn into a film towards the end of the residency. Again, it was all looking good on paper.

Of course, said Haubenstock, as if reading my mind, no plan survives contact with the enemy. We slammed the car doors, one after the other.

1

Sociology: End of America

Field Notes on a Residency

For the first workshop, we'd been given a small meeting room with a bolted window. It was just after lunch on a Thursday. Haubenstock was setting up his Sony Z1 on a tripod in the corner. Jenkins was helping me to connect my laptop to the wall-mounted TV screen. I'd prepared a few PowerPoint slides – images, short videos, Paul Virilio quotes – to help stimulate discussion.

The drone scientists slipped into the room, sat down at the big table and flipped open their laptops. Jenkins said they were some of his finest postgraduate students. They introduced themselves, one by one.

Trinh said she grew up in the port city of Hai Phong during the years of economic liberalisation. Her eyes were watchful. Rausch was restless. He said he had been up all night writing code for swarming and flocking behaviours. Novichkov nodded graciously. His mind seemed elsewhere. Finally, there was Gupta. He looked up from his laptop and offered a smile. He said he was looking forward to the session.

I introduced myself and Haubenstock and explained the purpose of the day's session. We wanted to come up with an idea for an end-of-the-world scenario that was coherent from a sociological perspective. This would no doubt be a great help to the scientists in their drone research.

I tapped a key and the wall-screen lit up with an image of Turner's painting, *The Decline of the Carthaginian Empire.* It showed broken columns and shadows amidst the ancient classical architecture, people consoling each other, the debris of an imperial past. And at the centre of the picture, there was the sea meeting the sky in the glow of the setting Sun, an impressionistic dazzle of light.

From ancient times onward, I said, the world could always be considered – in a kind of cognitive shorthand – as the society of its dominant culture. Before Rome, there was Carthage. And before Carthage, there was Egypt. Don't forget Ancient Sumer, said Gupta. Or the Hittite Empire. What about the Olmecs? said Trinh. Everyone always forgets about them. There then followed a long digression as the scientists argued about which ancient people could lay claim to having founded the very first world culture to have emerged from pre-history. The discussion eventually petered out with jokes about Erich von Daniken and ancient astronaut theories.

I reminded the group that the rise and fall of world cultures was a subject that had fallen out of fashion in sociology. Toynbee was no longer read. But even in the fashionable sociology of Hardt and Negri, with all its talk of a new world order with no fixed power centre, an Empire without a Rome, it was still conceded that the moral leadership of the world had been taken up by one country – the United States of America.

This, I said, was something with which Virilio would not disagree. I flipped up another photo on the TV screen. It showed three young Japanese rockabilly guys in Yoyogi Park in Tokyo, posing in leather jackets and Ray-Bans, their hands delicately massaging their huge Elvis quiffs. Virilio argues that the United States achieved global dominance after the Second World War not by settling foreign territory, but by exporting its domestic way of life. The models of democracy, consumer capitalism and mass media entertainment developed in the United States have been adopted in large parts of the world.

To sum up, I said, the United States has remade the world in its own image, with its rather neo-primitive civilisation of cars, cinemas and supermarkets. All of which means that the world constituted by sociology is a world made in America. Do you see where I'm going with this? I asked the scientists.

A strong end-of-the-world scenario from a sociological perspective, said Trinh, is likely to have an American look and feel. Exactly! Here, I flashed up a photo of the vast, abandoned Packard Motors factory, with its rusted girders, rubble-strewn floor and dirty walls covered in graffiti. The industrial ruins of Detroit, I said, are no doubt a prophecy of the end of the American world order. They already have the melancholy aspect of decaying Mayan pyramids or weathered Polynesian totem poles.

The question from this perspective is quite simple. How would the American way of life collapse? I clicked on YouTube and played the *White House Down* trailer. There were flash-cut images of the White House in flames, menacing choppers riding the skies and black-clad mercenaries storming the Oval Office in search of nuclear launch codes. The digital special effects were thin and unconvincing and the situations were melodramatic. The scientists laughed.

I nodded in sympathy. I said that the film's director, Roland Emmerich, had form when it came to bad Hollywood movies about the end of the world. I listed a succession of movies and described their scenarios. *The Day After Tomorrow* – American white guy attempts to save son from global Ice Age and succeeds. *2012* – American white guy attempts to save family from global earthquakes, megatsunamis and floods. Again, he succeeds. Okay, last one. *Independence Day: Resurgence* – American white guy attempts to save Earth from invasion by aliens. Does he succeed? Of course he does. More laughter.

Hollywood loves happy endings, said Rausch. Even its disaster movies have happy endings. The end-of-the-world scenarios are plausible enough, though, said Novichkov. Climate change, terror attack. Maybe alien invasion, not so much. He grinned.

The scientists spent quite a bit of time discussing their favourite Hollywood disaster movies. They evaluated the plausibility of the various scenarios, commented on the performances of the actors and swapped memorable one-liners.

It's almost as if, said Jenkins, Hollywood were running disaster scenarios for the industrial-military complex. He shrugged. I said that was a good thought.

Gupta said that *Die Hard 4.0* was interesting. It imagines a three-stage hack attack on North America's digital infrastructure, he said. First, terrorists shut down the transport grid – traffic lights, railroad lines, subways systems and airports. Then, they disable financial systems – Wall Street, banks, financial data. Finally, they turn off the utilities – gas, electricity, telecoms and satellite systems. It's a scenario that could perhaps be applied to many parts of the world at the same time. A coordinated cyber-terror attack.

Denial-of-service attacks were the way to do it, said Novichkov. He remembered when this happened in Estonia a few years back. The big government ministries, media outlets and banks had been offline for three weeks as a result of coordinated cyberattacks. There was chaos. Political activists had finally admitted responsibility for overloading the targeted websites with spam messages. He forgot what the point of it all was.

Trinh spoke up. She said that when one of the big White House defence chiefs had left office a few years ago, he had written a best-selling book arguing that a cyber-terror attack could take out North America within 15 minutes. Is that really possible? she wondered. Gupta said that, if it were, it would make quite a short Hollywood disaster movie. He seemed pleased with his joke.

Jenkins said that the Pentagon was certainly taking these kinds of threats seriously. It had set up a cyber command at Fort Meade in Maryland only a few years after the fourth *Die Hard* movie had come out. Right, said Gupta. He'd found a photo online of the NSA building at Fort Meade. Two high-rise blocks of reflective blue-black glass squatting in a flat landscape. He turned round his laptop so everyone could see the screen. A Vatican City for computer geeks, he said. Well, it's certainly a very secretive institution, said Rausch. With some highly select protocols, said Gupta. This is where the world's data is targeted, pulled in from Google searches and Facebook profiles, assessed for its terror threat potential and then fed to the CIA and the FBI. According to ex-CIA whistleblower Edward Snowden, said Rausch. Let's get that right.

Jenkins said he thought this was a good time to end the session. He was tapping his watch. The scientists left the room. Haubenstock packed up his camera. I unplugged my machine.

The session had got me thinking. If Virilio were employed as a creative consultant in Hollywood, what kind of end-of-the-world disaster movie would he pitch? It was a good question. I would dream up some answers when I got back to the dorm.

Eight One-Pagers for a Hollywood End-of-the-World Disaster Movie

1 Particles

In this science fiction action thriller, special agent Hank Edwards is brought out of retirement by his old boss at the FBI to investigate a strange mass suicide. Six members of the religious sect TransEarth have been found dead in their Californian compound. The cult's literature indicates that they believe in the existence of a parallel world it's possible to enter through ritual suicide. Hank tracks down surviving members of the cult and finds that they expect the world to be destroyed by an asteroid collision. The six Californians saw themselves as an advance party scouting out an escape route for the rest of the cult.

The FBI wraps up the case. But then Hank is visited by Irene, a mysterious ex-employee of the cable TV station Impact Hazard News (IHN). The TV station takes NASA predictions about the orbital pathways of comets and asteroids, plots out possible collision courses with Earth and streams live TV news from the projected impact zones, complete with sensational predictions about floods and famines. Irene tells Hank that the TV station used TransEarth sect members around the world as news stringers. She says that the mass suicide is the starting signal for a much bigger and potentially devastating terror action by the cult.

The FBI is sceptical of Irene's story, but Hank is seduced by the young woman's charms. Together, they infiltrate the cult's London temple and discover that the Swiss branch of the cult has been ordered to stage a suicide bombing campaign against the world's biggest particle physics lab in Geneva. The cult believe that their bombs can help nudge the lab's particle accelerator into producing a worm-hole powerful enough to swallow the Earth. They plan to guide the world's transit through the worm-hole so that it re-emerges safely in another solar system. Hank and Irene fly to Geneva in an effort to head off the bombers. But they arrive at the lab too late. The final scene of the film sees a shadow falling across the Earth as, one by one, the stars are eclipsed in the sky.

2 Ilsa and the Gene Bomb

In this post-apocalyptic fantasy film, the Earth is divided into two groups of creatures. A caste of genetically engineered posthumans, known as Mesons, live a life of aesthetic pleasure in orbit above the planet. Meanwhile, in the ruined cities below, a discarded remnant of humans, known as Zebomites, scavenge for existence. A spaceship in the shape of a flying saucer is used by the Mesons to spread an airborne contraceptive virus across the planet. The Zebs worship the flying saucer and are eager to prostrate themselves before it. As the Zebs die out, the Mesons return to Earth. They harvest the corpses, fix them with preservatives and transform them into mammoth tableaux that re-enact the great wars and massacres from human history.

One of the Zebs, named Ilsa, is immune to the virus. She hijacks the spaceship and sexually humiliates its pilot in an extended rape and torture scene. At the point of exhaustion, he reveals to her that the spaceship is powered by a giant crystal. Ilsa finds the crystal and bathes in its glow. She discovers that one of its hidden properties is that it can magnify the energy of her orgasms and resurrect the dead. She has a marathon sex session with the spaceship's crew and forces the pilot to fly around the planet so that its population of dead humans can receive the reanimating effects of her bioelectromagnetic radiation.

In the final scenes of the movie, the human corpses that have been so artfully arranged by the Mesons stir themselves and come back to life. Zombie armies of Roman centurions, Nazi storm-troopers and Native Americans overwhelm the Mesons and con-sume them in an orgy of cannibal violence. Ilsa is borne aloft by the armies and crowned queen of the world.

3 Lost in Algospace

In this dystopian science fiction adventure film, a teenage maths prodigy from the slums of an Indian city is offered a life-changing job as a trader at an investment bank. The girl, Maisie, is taken to a concrete bunker. Inside, there is a vast floor kitted out with financial trading platforms and high-speed brainwave readers. There are flashes and disturbances on the viewing screens. Stacks of bunk beds hold the comatose forms of VR-equipped traders. Maisie is told that their minds are working too fast for their bodies to stand. They have been injected with a psychoactive drug that enables them to enter a dimension where time has slowed down. Here, they are able to outwit the trading algorithms of the bank's competitors and make big profits.

The only downside is that the traders return from their adventures as prematurely aged men and women. It is their bodies that pay the price for the mental transfer between dimensions. Maisie is told that she is young and, so long as she doesn't spend too much time in algospace, she will come back a rich woman. Maisie needs to pay for a transgender operation for her kid brother. So she agrees to the terms of the bank's contract. At that point, the true nature of her mission is revealed.

The bank's analysts have noticed a series of unpredictable blips in trading activity. It's probably nothing. But it could be a sign that a monster global stock market crash is on the way. Maisie is given the task of identifying the cusp catastrophe the bank thinks will trigger the upcoming crash. She takes the drug and enters algospace, a videogame-like world of stacked realities, with deserts situated next to icescapes and dark corridors crumbling into nothingness. As she approaches the cusp catastrophe, she discovers it's taken the form of a huge snake encircling a hill, a dragon breathing fire. She radios for back-up, but there's only silence. She will have to defeat this monster on her own.

4 Planet Earth Has Fallen

In this science fiction action movie, a heroic CIA agent named Megan battles to prevent a global terror attack from creating panic in North America and Europe, undermining governments and spreading civil war. A psychotic criminal mastermind named Rashid operates out of a hidden cave in the mountains of Afghanistan. Using old Soviet mind control technology, he has embedded sleeper agents in the major airports of the world and plans to active them on a sacred day in the calendar. When he sends out the trigger word, Rashid expects each of his followers to hijack a plane and fly it into the nearest tall building.

When Megan discovers that a renegade faction of her own agency is in league with Rashid, hoping to plunge the United States into profitable new wars in the Middle East and North Africa, she designs her own plot to foil them. Once Rashid receives images of the great iconic buildings of the Western world – the United Nations skyscraper in New York, the Houses of Parliament in London, the Louvre Pyramid, the Sydney Opera House – collapsing into dust, he is convinced that his plans have been successful. He comes out of hiding and contacts his CIA allies. They are shocked and surprised. It turns out that Rashid has been fed hoax images manufactured by Megan from a secret TV studio.

In a climactic face-off in the Afghan desert, Megan defeats Rashid and exposes the traitorous machinations of her CIA colleagues. The film ends with the injured agent accepting a medal from the first female president of the United States.

5 Goodnight, Sweet Detroit

In this post-apocalyptic road movie, an auto repairman in 1950s America builds a time-travel machine from the debris in his Detroit back-yard. He plans to travel to the future to find a cure for cancer and return with it to heal his sick wife. When Joe opens the door of his timeship 40 years into the future, he discovers that the device has been damaged in transit. He's also shocked to find that his native city now lies in ruins and has been largely abandoned.

Thinking that there must have been some kind of nuclear accident, Joe wanders the industrial wastelands of Detroit in search of the tools and parts he needs to rebuild his time machine. Along the way, he falls into the company of a glamorous, disfigured woman, an artist who makes sculptures from junk. Joe thinks she may be his wife, Tess, grown old. Like many people in Detroit, the woman's memory has been damaged by what she calls the 'Event,' an unspecified disaster that happened some years ago. She admits that one good thing about the Event is that it has somehow wiped out many human diseases.

Joe suspects that the Event – which may or may not have a nuclear origin – is somehow linked with a cure for cancer. He is now determined to unlock the mystery of the Event so he can return home, heal his wife and save his city from devastation. At the climax of the film, Joe enters the mysterious ghost tunnels of Michigan Central Station. What he discovers on the other side is that he is merely a test subject in a psychosocial experiment. Researchers at an entertainment company are planning the next generation of theme parks and have settled on disaster as an exciting new concept. Joe's memories of the 1950s have been implanted. He must now battle to recover his true identity and rebuild his world.

6 *The Legend of Alice D Apocalypse*

In this retro hippy exploitation movie, a young heiress to a coffee fortune is kidnapped by Satan's Holy Rollers, a militant Californian religious cult. Alice is stripped naked, forced to drop acid and guided by the cult's African-American leader on a shamanic vision quest. The trip sequence features found footage from old movies – porno films, cowboy films – as well as drive-by visuals of Hollywood's Sunset Strip. Alice hallucinates that she meets Crazy Horse, the old Lakota warrior, panhandling on the street. He tells her that she must use her fortune to unite Native Americans, blacks, homosexuals and teenagers into a liberation army, use it to overthrow the United States government and introduce a new global society of liberty and equality.

As Alice recovers from her ordeal, she is sexually assaulted by the cult leader, but fights back and manages to kill him with her bare hands. She takes over leadership of the cult and uses her fortune to buy vast truck-loads of acid, which her followers dump in the biggest lakes and reservoirs of California. As the acid finds its way into the water supply of Los Angeles, Alice cuts an album of psychedelic rock songs and blasts them out over the FM airwaves. She is an instant pop sensation.

Alice's songs contain hidden messages inciting blacks to kill whites, women to kill men, teenagers to kill their parents and gays to kill straights. As the Los Angeles population gets high on acid, they begin to follow Alice's instructions and slaughter each other. The movie has a few gore scenes, but most of the story at this stage is told in the form of radio news bulletins. The state governor calls out the National Guard, but, disorientated and demoralised, they desert and join Alice's hippy army. By the end of the movie, Satan's Holy Rollers have taken over the Californian government and declared an independent republic. As the final credits roll, Alice's acid trucks are seen rumbling out over the freeways of Oregon, Nevada and Arizona, ready to contaminate the reservoirs of the rest of America.

7 *Claustropolis*

In this science fiction art film, a spaceship crash-lands on a planet light years from Earth, having travelled for many decades. It's been a risky flight. The crew of two men and one woman wake from their cryogenic sleep, exhausted and fractious. They are on a test mission to discover whether this new planet, originally detected telescopically, is capable of supporting life. Earth is no longer fit for human habitation. Its atmosphere has overheated to produce a dying fog planet.

The three astronauts explore the vast grasslands of the new planet. There is permanent cloud cover, the light is dim and there are high winds. The three argue about philosophy and religion and have sex to pass the time. Eventually, they stumble upon a population of large tortoises. It is clear they have never seen creatures like these before. The woman, Elena, places her hand on the shell of one of the older tortoises. Elena is a telepath. The tortoise informs her that this planet is the original home of humanity's ancestors, who evacuated it millions of years ago in order to colonise the stars. Elena is unable to find out why people decided to leave or how their world came to an end. All the tortoise can tell her is that humans don't belong on this planet any more.

As the astronauts' quest continues, Elena begins to pick up faint telepathic signals. There are moans and roars, the strangest of voices. Are people still alive? They come to the ruins of an old spaceport, with rusted gantries, huge rocket stages lying in the sandy grass and sunken concrete blockhouses. Entering one of the blockhouses, they find that it opens up into a vast underground set of tunnels filled with thousands of bones. Is this a burial place? Or the remains of a lost prison? Elena is overwhelmed by the voices inside her head. The men run their fingers over the carvings on the walls – seals, elephants, horses, bison – marvelling at the strange images. They begin to collect the bones. It will take them years to assemble the skeletons. But the one thing they have is time.

8 Ark of Uriel

In this science fiction thriller, an expeditionary spacecraft draws alongside the remnant of an old space hulk. Its hull has been blown open. A team of astronauts, fully suited up and breathing oxygen, enters the ancient ship. It seems empty and has obviously been drifting in space for many years. The leader of the expedition, Wardour, checks the log and discovers the ship was originally sent out from Earth as an interstellar ark, designed to support a population of migrants who would live and die on the ship for successive generations until it reached its destination.

The expedition reflects on the pathos of their find. They themselves come from Tau Ceti Delta, a local planet colonised by Earth people just 80 years ago, after the invention of faster-than-light space travel. The derelict starship had been launched many centuries before that, in the expectation that it would take many long slow years of sub-light speed travel to reach the Tau Ceti star system. The ship is now a museum piece. More than that, it is a space wreck. Wardour decides to explore the ship in an effort to find out what happened to the apparently missing occupants. The astronauts pass through the ruins of several artificial ecosystems – a forest of burned-up trees, a dry ocean bed, an empty desert. Soon, they are lost.

Wardour's rival, Costello, calls for a halt to the expedition. After a violent struggle with Wardour, he heads back with most of the team. Wardour and his remaining followers press on. Finally, they open an airlock to discover artificial blue skies and a field of corn. They remove their helmets to breathe the thin air. Here is an ecosystem that has somehow survived. They stumble through the tall green leaves, only to be shot and killed by painted warriors, armed with bows and arrows. The warriors drag the corpses of the astronauts back to their village and strip them of their oxygen tanks. Then they each take a hit from one of the looted tanks, pass round the sacred tribal oxygen mask, and tell stories of their latest victory.

2

Technology: Global Accident

Field Notes on a Residency

We had the second workshop in the same small meeting room in the computer science department as before. Haubenstock had his camera set up in a corner. I was checking the running order of the PowerPoint presentation on my laptop. The drone scientists slipped into the room, one by one. Gupta, with his friendly grin. The moody, self-contained Rausch. Trinh, with her books and electronic devices, her anxious charm. The pampered and slightly vacant Novichkov. And, of course, Jenkins, the affable head of department.

I got into it straightaway. From a technological viewpoint, I said, the world is a huge synthetic environment, a planet whose surface has been almost entirely manufactured, one way or the other. On the large TV screen behind me, I showed a video still of a huge metal orb floating in outer space. It was the Death Star, the planet-sized fortress from the *Star Wars* movies. Everyone except Rausch grinned. The Death Star had a self-destruct button, I said. So imagining the end of this particular technological world was quite easy. I released the video, enabling it to play out its ten second explosive fantasy. Boom! A cloud of smoke billowed across the screen. Gupta cheered.

Next I flipped up an old newsreel image of Rotterdam after it had been bombed flat by the Nazis during the Second World War. No building was left standing except for the old medieval Christian church. The city was an empty landscape of roads and canals, depopulated, with no cars, no homes. I said that Paul Virilio, the French theorist whose ideas underpinned our workshops, was only a child when he saw Nantes undergoing similar devastation. The Nazi blitzkrieg of 1940 was something he'd never forgotten.

But what about us? I said. Virilio thinks we have in fact forgotten about the wholesale destruction of European cities which took place only 70 or so years ago. Here, I showed a contemporary tourist image of Rotterdam city centre, with its dense tangle of skyscrapers, motorways, bridges and billboards. The old church was barely visible. The Dutch didn't reconstruct their old medieval city, I said. They built a completely new city from scratch, using the latest design and media technologies to come out of the war.

Our technological world in general is largely a product of our collective experience of the Second World War, I said. But, according to Virilio, we've either forgotten this or not fully accepted it. And that means we're still haunted by it, unconsciously. Maybe, said Rausch. But creation always follows destruction. It's the dialectical method. He shrugged.

Okay, I said. But Virilio makes a further point. War is the mother of invention. I flipped up an old press photo of General Patton, who had led the US Third Army into Nazi Germany at the end of the Second World War. Holstered at his waist was an ivory-handled Colt .45. Here's an example, I said. The Colt six shooter, with its revolving cylinder of chambers, was a model for the development of the Kodak 24-exposure camera, with its two rotating spools. Rausch nodded. The Colt was loaded with bullets, he said. Just as the Kodak was loaded with a roll of film. Exactly, I said. In fact, the designer of Kodak's film-roll holder was William H Walker, who began his career as an apprentice at Colt's armoury in Hartford, Connecticut.

Maybe all media technologies have their origins in war, said Trinh, her eyes narrowed. After all, before Remington made typewriters, they made rifles. Sure, sure, said Jenkins. But maybe it's bigger than that. Maybe this guy Virilio is right and all technology, not just media technology, is a product of war. He mentioned how nuclear power plant technology had its origin in the Second World War's Manhattan Project.

I nodded. How many technologies we take for granted today can trace their origin back to the Second World War? I asked. The scientists shouted out their ideas. The jet engine, said Gupta. Hans von Ohain and the Messerschmitt Me 262. He beamed with pleasure. That was actually a British invention, said Rausch. His voice was low. Von Ohain found Frank Whittle's patent for the turbo-jet in the university library at Gottingen. Although, said Jenkins, all Whittle was really doing with the turbo-jet was taking existing steam engine technology and using air rather than water as the power source. The debate about the ins and outs of the jet engine continued until everyone agreed it was essentially a nineteenth-century technology.

What's the exact hypothesis we're testing, here? Novichkov asked. Is it that our contemporary technological world is entirely an outgrowth of the destructive capacities of the Second World War? If so, the hypothesis is surely disproved by the development of the internet, which was funded by the RAND Corporation in California during the Cold War. Specifically, said Trinh, during the American War in Vietnam. My grandfather helped to dig the thousands of miles of defensive tunnels under South Vietnam. The tunnels formed a huge decentred communications network, something the RAND guys in the States no doubt understood.

I don't know, said Gupta. Isn't the internet really a function of the computer? And wasn't the digital computer invented by Alan Turing at Bletchley Park during the Second World War? Of course it was, said Jenkins. The computer is simply a high-speed method of running algorithms.

The faster, the better, said Gupta. My older brother works for a stockbroking firm in New York. They depend for their success on one thing – getting their algorithms to execute trades faster than those of their competitors. Algorithms operate in microseconds. And that translates into feet and inches at the level of real estate.

Manhattan stockbroking firms have been creeping northwards from Wall Street for years. Why is that, exactly? Gupta asked. It's because they want to be closer to the old Western Union building on Hudson Street, where the cables come up from the Atlantic. It gives them a real competitive advantage when trading on the London stock exchange. Gupta sat back and grinned.

Novichkov said, okay, he'd let Gupta have the internet as a Second World War invention. But what about television? That was developed by John Logie Baird in the 1920s, way before the Second World War. Yes, said Gupta, but the war stopped Baird from going into production with his new invention. The British government banned television broadcasting, such as it was. They were worried about the BBC transmitter acting as a beacon for German bombers. Interesting, said Jenkins. I heard the government put Baird to work on various hush-hush projects. Television as a means of transmitting military maps at high speed. That sort of thing.

What about antidepressant drugs?, said Rausch. Psychoactive drugs, really, I suppose. They came out of the Second World War. I'm thinking of the Nazi experiments with mescaline in Dachau. It's an undeniable fact that a lot of present-day technology came out of the camps. His face was a mask. He spoke quickly. Wernher von Braun's rockets were built using a slave labour force. And Apollo programme life-support technology – space medicine in general, come to think of it – came out of experiments on Dachau prisoners sealed inside pressurised air cabins. There was silence in the room.

A bad business, said Jenkins. Of course, said Rausch. I hardly need mention Mengele's genetic engineering experiments in Auschwitz. Biotech, said Gupta. It's big business today. In fact, the demand for biotech company stocks has become so strong that NASDAQ has had to set up a separate index.

Jenkins said he was now wondering about nuclear tech. A look of mild concern was on his face. Was it actually a product of the Second World War? The nuclear bomb was, in essence, a chemical device used to blow things up. It was simply a bigger version of dynamite. Another nineteenth-century technology, said Trinh. Jenkins nodded.

Trinh leaned in close to the group. I've always loved rockets, she said, nodding to Rausch. In fact, I hope to work on the Vietnam space programme one day. Let me tell you that one of the images engraved on my mind, something I shall never forget, is the TV footage of the *Challenger* space shuttle exploding in a clear blue sky in 1986. That time when all the astronauts inside were incinerated.

It had been a cold morning in Florida on the day of launch, she reminded everyone, as if she'd been there. The rockets on the craft hadn't been designed to work at such low temperatures. The engineers had tried to point this out to senior management, but their evidence was so highly technical it had got lost in the shuffle of PowerPoint slide decks routinely used for internal NASA communication. Meaning that the failure of the American space programme was actually caused by the limitations of Microsoft software. Trinh sat back triumphantly. Gupta laughed.

A smiling Jenkins drummed his fingers on the table. He said, Of course, many lessons have been learned by NASA from the *Challenger* disaster. We shouldn't forget that. It's all part of what we call the disaster management cycle.

I asked Jenkins to explain. The professor cleared his throat. The disaster management cycle is composed of four phases, he said. The phase we're focused on at Solent City University is disaster response – we're building drone software to aid search-and-rescue operations on the ground. He fluttered his hands. But let's not forget the phase that comes directly before the disaster response phase. This is the disaster preparedness phase, with its training exercises and early warning systems. Nor should we dismiss the phase that comes directly after the disaster response phase, the disaster recovery phase, with its clean-up and recon-struction efforts. Jenkins paused. I motioned him to go on.

Jenkins said that often ignored was the fourth disaster management phase. Disaster mitigation. By that he meant coming up with measures that could reduce the risks or impacts of a potential future disaster. Flood-defence was the classic example. He mentioned the Thames Barrier.

The US government investigation into the *Challenger* disaster had generated useful recommendations, he said. Mainly to do with mitigating the low-temperature risk associated with the space shuttle's rocket design. NASA had implemented all the safety improvements and, within less than three years, its space shuttle programme was up and running again.

Everyone was nodding. I told Jenkins his comments were very illuminating. He shrugged. The *Challenger* rocket failure was a classic case study in disaster management, he said.

Our time was running out. I thanked everyone for their input and said it had been a useful afternoon. I flipped up one final black and white photo as a parting image. It showed a helmeted figure in a gas mask, holding a hydrochloric-acid pump in his gloved hand. This was the artist Gustav Metzger staging an industrial accident as a kind of prophetic early warning on London's South Bank in 1961. Beside him was suspended a nylon canvas, disintegrating, burned with great ragged holes due to being sprayed with acid. Visible through the aperture, on the other side of the Thames, was the much-painted London skyline, with St Paul's Cathedral still intact. Here was a sly performance that Virilio would no doubt have appreciated.

As the scientists gathered up their things, Jenkins took the liberty of summarising the session's findings. He said that it looked like a number of Second World War technologies had helped to shape our world. Rockets and space medicine. Biotech. Psychoactive drugs. Television. And computers, obviously. He said he wasn't quite sure if nuclear power and the jet engine quite fitted the research criteria drawn from Virilio's thinking. But they were certainly worth considering.

On the way back to our dorm room, Haubenstock was busy tapping his forehead, in a vain effort to relieve the stress. I don't like Rausch, he said. I sighed. Rausch and the other scientists have given us plenty to think about, I said. The truth was I was eager to read the *Challenger* accident investigation report mentioned by Jenkins. Something told me that the report would help to crystallise my ideas.

Back in the dorm room, I downloaded the 1986 Rogers Commission report on the *Challenger* disaster. Haubenstock left for the campus gym.

The report consisted of five volumes of documentation. One of the members of the commission was Richard Feynman, Professor of Theoretical Physics at Caltech, scientific educator and noisy advocate of plain speaking. Unlike other members of the commission, who'd paid extensive attention to NASA senior management and their vague utterances, Feynman had talked to the rocket engineers. He'd discovered that the failure of the rocket was due to a fault with the rubber O-ring seals. I scanned Appendix F of the report, which was personally written by Feynman:

The O-rings of the Solid Rocket Boosters were not designed to erode. Erosion was a clue that something was wrong. Erosion was not something from which safety can be inferred.

The tone of the criticism was laconic almost to the point of being sarcastic. The truly interesting thing, though, was that Feynman was prepared to state that there was a single cause of the disaster. I knew from a previous residency at a crash test lab that investigators were always keen to find the 'root cause' of any accident. It was fundamental to their discourse. Accident investigators typically worked backwards from the scene of a crash, plotting a sequence of cause-and-effect events on a timeline until they isolated a single material circumstance without which the crash could not have occurred. It was almost Aristotelian in its forensic rigour.

I remembered the British government report on the King's Cross fire on the London tube network in 1987. I'd read it some years ago, back when I was developing my taste for accident investigation reporting as perhaps the definitive example of Ballard's 'invisible literature'. The King's Cross fire report was an elegantly written 286-page document, authored not by committee but by a single man, a barrister. Desmond Fennell had traced the root cause of the fire to a single burning match dropped onto one of the escalators by a passenger lighting a cigarette. It was like something out of a morality play. One minor sin creating a hideous blaze which kills many innocent people.

I cast my mind back to another of the accident investigation reports I'd read, this time into the Potters Bar train derailment of 2002. In this case, the root cause had been identified as the working loose of some nuts that were supposed to bolt together a set of points on the rail track. The resulting weakness had allowed the points to fail as the train passed over them. One of the carriages derailed, flew through the air and hit the platform at the railway station. Seven people died and scores more were horribly injured.

I sat back and let my mind drift into reverie. I imagined a parade of these suspicious objects, found guilty by the magistrates of common sense. The guilty O-rings, a single guilty match, those guilty nuts and bolts. What singled them out? Was it some defect in their original manufacture? Or were they, perhaps, merely unlucky? Maybe Georges Bataille was right and there was always a margin of industrial production which had to be dedicated to destruction for things to work properly. A train wreck was a kind of offering to the gods of chaos.

Haubenstock was late returning from the gym. I passed the time staring out of the dorm room window, watching the Chinese students come and go.

That night, I had a strange dream. I saw Virilio at work in a vast echoing bunker on the Atlantic coast of Europe, somewhere at the end of the world. There were shadows on the stone benches.

Virilio's face was etched with lines. He sat in the corner, with a big, bulky two-way radio set on a table. Listening to the cries and alarms of the Apocalypse on his headphones, he was saying his prayers into the microphone, calling on God to send his only begotten son once again to Earth to purge it of evil.

I dreamt I was crouched at Virilio's side. The floor was scattered with sand and litter – torn packets of food, dead matches, scrunched-up newspapers, an old blanket. Virilio paused his mutterings. He was looking out at the bloody and smoking field of Armageddon through a narrow horizontal slit in the bunker wall. How has it come to this? I asked him. A stupid question, unworthy of this lonely seer's vigil, I suddenly realised. Did I really think there was a root cause of the Apocalypse? Virilio removed his headphones. His eyes were filled with pain.

The rocket crash was not caused by the worn-out O-rings, Virilio said. It was caused by the invention of the rocket. The train crash was not caused by the loose nuts and bolts on the line. It was caused by the invention of the railway. The old man paused. He leaned in close. An accident is not caused by any material imperfection in technology. It's caused by the invention of the technology itself. Wasn't this precisely what he, the prophet Virilio, had been saying, all these many years? His eyes burned with an unnatural brightness.

I woke with a start. The curtains drifted in the breeze. Haubenstock was sound asleep. The laptop was close to my bed. I switched it on and opened my electronic copy of *Virilio: A-Z*. I soon found the quote I was looking for:

The invention of any technology is simultaneously the invention of an accident. The shipwreck is the invention of the ship, the air crash the invention of the supersonic airliner and the stock market crash the invention of technologies of automated dealing.

I nodded in agreement. I loved that quote. It was such a simple but devastating insight. How could I have forgotten it?

I turned things over in my mind. When an accident investigator told the story of how a crash happened, they started with the root cause and they ended with the crash itself. If Virilio were telling the story of the King's Cross fire, he would certainly end with the fire. But he wouldn't start with the dropped match. He'd start with the invention of the railway. Yes, I thought. He'd write about the railway's shortening of travel times, its lengthening of urban sprawl, its hypnotic effect on the mind of the passenger looking out of the window. Virilio's report on the King's Cross fire would be an indictment of a whole technological way of life.

I drifted through the *Virilio: A-Z* document, trying to discover if Virilio had written anything about accident investigation. All I could find were a few scattered references to something he called the 'local accident'. He argued that a local accident – like the sinking of the *Titanic* – was an accident that happened to a specific group of people, at a specific place and time. The freezing waters of the North Atlantic at midnight, I thought, with the bodies sinking all around. Virilio contrasted the local accident to the 'global accident', which I knew was something he thought could happen to everyone on the planet, everywhere at once. I wondered if the local accident were something specific to older technologies, technologies that predated the Second World War and – like the *Titanic*'s steam engines – were not capable of having a global impact.

The computer was a technology with a global impact. It was certainly possible to theorise the possibility of a global internet failure. That would be one version of Virilio's 'global accident'. But what would it be like to experience? I wondered. And what about the other technologies mentioned in that day's brainstorming session with the drone scientists? Rockets. Space medicine. Biotech. Psychoactive drugs. Television. These were probably, each in their different ways, also global technologies. So, again, it was possible to speculate that each was capable of delivering its own version of Virilio's global accident.

It was getting light outside. I was still thinking. Maybe it was possible to imagine the global accident specific to the internet as a scaled-up version of some local internet failure, such as a stock market crash. But which stock market crash? And was a stock market crash even the best example of a local internet failure to consider in the first place? To answer this question, I realised I would have to go back to the invention of the digital computer.

How would Virilio do things, if he were commissioned to write an accident investigation report about the global computer accident? He'd begin with the military development of the computer during the Second World War, sketch out the civilian adoption of computer networks by postwar society, pinpoint the definitive instance of the local computer accident and then consider the subject at hand – the global computer accident – as a scaled-up version of the local accident. That would be his method.

I could do that, I thought. I could write an accident investigation report on the internet apocalypse – or the computer apocalypse, to be more precise. It would, at least in its final prophetic chapter, be an example of creative science fiction, a scaling of history into plausible futurology. But it was doable. In fact, it was also doable for all the other Second World War technologies that had come out of the brainstorming session. I could write an accident investigation report on the rocket apocalypse. On the space medicine apocalypse. On the biotech apocalypse, the psychoactive drugs apocalypse and the television apocalypse.

Six separate reports, I thought. Six separate versions of the global accident following the same four-phase logic of technological evolution in each case – military origin, civilian transfer, local accident, global accident.

I would do it, I thought. I would write myself into the bunker at the end of the world where I dreamt I had seen Virilio. I would offer him six separate panoramas of technological Armageddon through his viewing slit – like slides in a magic lantern. Six scenarios for the global accident. Six technological versions of the Apocalypse.

I got out of bed, careful not to wake Haubenstock. It was a twilight dawn.

Six Tech-Based Scenarios for the Global Accident

1 Bioengineering Apocalypse

In 2015, Chinese scientists in Guangdong said they had isolated the gene required for human memory formation. Over the next 15 years, the genetic modification of human characteristics became widespread not only in China but also in South Korea, Russia, Argentina and Chile. Gene therapists claimed to be able to boost intelligence, sexual endurance and physical appearance.

Over the same period, a black market in human embryonic stem cell treatments developed. Semi-legal IVF clinics sprang up in the new Chinese and Indian cities to meet the rising demand for human embryos. They attracted young migrant women from the country, who were paid in cash for a two-week course of egg-harvesting. Using sperm from donors, an IVF clinic was able to fertilise its eggs within hours, before freezing them for storage and shipment.

There were plenty of ageing rich people from the US, Europe and the Middle East only too eager to extend their lives with regular genetically modified organ transplants. They made pilgrimages to the black market clinics of South East Asia and South America and were featured in the pages of celebrity magazines showing off their brand-new eyes and teeth. Soon, those with less money were copying them by catching flights to the quick-fix genetic surgery clinics of eastern Europe and Russia.

Sensing they were missing out on a possible biotech boom, North American and western European governments deregulated experimentation on human embryos. The 2030s became the decade of the transhumanist philosopher-aesthetes, who danced their way through the media salons, arguing that *homo sapiens* had engineered its own obsolescence and a new human species had evolved.

The 2038 Rodriguez Act in the US recognised a new category of hominid, *homo aeternus,* or the 'Eternals', as they became known. In the process, it put into question all human rights legislation. A tiny transnational elite of financiers, government officials and tech entrepreneurs saw themselves as a species apart from the ten billion humans on the planet. They considered pregnancy a form of barbarism and selected their offspring from the aisles of the designer baby labs. They stopped having sex and contented themselves instead with the invention of hundreds of new genders.

The heirs to the great Silicon Valley fortunes invested heavily in human cloning. This was seen as the ultimate form of self-rejuvenation. But it came at the price of a temporary death. At first, there were few billionaires willing to make the jump. They looked at the sickly versions of themselves stumbling out of the cloning labs and shuddered. Only when the decision was taken out of their hands by power of attorney did they submit to the legal transfer of identity.

There were some accidents. In 2045, for example, there were two self-identified heirs to the Facebook fortune, each claiming to be Mark Zuckerberg II. Genetic testing could not distinguish them. In the end, they settled their dispute using the archaic method of trial by combat.

The Eternals called themselves the 'One Million'. They felt this was a good number for the size of their clan and each Eternal voluntarily adopted a one-clone-at-a-time policy. Meanwhile, their ecologists claimed that a good number when it came to the management of the remaining human population was actually about one billion.

The Eternals took no pleasure in human suffering. The culling of nine billion humans was simply a job to be done. The Eternals were just as ethically scrupulous about it as they were about other important jobs like rewilding the forests and replenishing the rivers. The planet's ecosystem was out of balance and the Eternals were determined to restore it. They had a responsibility to the wolves and the otters, as well as to the humans.

The first human contraceptive virus trial happened in West Virginia in 2045. The airborne virus was sprayed over the old coal-field settlements by US Air Force jets. Medical tests over the next year showed that 90 per cent of the human female population had stopped ovulating. Over the next ten years, military jets criss-crossed the planet, spraying the virus over Tokyo, New York, Sao Paolo, Lagos, Mumbai and other cities. It spread rapidly.

The Eternals introduced a lottery system for selecting the one in ten human females who would be given an antidote to the virus. Every five years, the global winners were announced. In each case, they had their ovulation restored and selected a suitable sperm donor from an online database of human males. Six months later, they were presented with a fantastically beautiful baby at a public ceremony sponsored by one of the big IVF clinics.

One of the most famous winners was White Toni, who documented every moment of her child's life, from birth onwards. She became a global TV star, inundated with toys and buggies and nappies by well-wishers and sponsors. In the end, she placed a selection of these gifts in a Museum of Human Childhood in Amsterdam.

The Eternals waited 100 years for the human population to decline. During the 'Long Change', as it was called, maternity wards and schools were demolished, amusement parks bulldozed and toy manufacturers shut down. There were fewer and fewer children, and more and more old people. The Eternals invested in retirement communities, hospices, funeral homes and crematoriums. Death became big business. There were euthanasia TV shows, ostentatious new funeral rites, fashions inspired by the Mexican Day of the Dead festival, a brief vogue for the Buddhist contemplation of the nine stages of death, and museums filled with plastinated human corpses reenacting the great massacres and famines of the past.

And so the world changed. In 2160, the Eternals announced the end of the Long Change. They reset the calendar to Year Zero. They promised to manage the planet responsibly for all of its inhabitants and creatures. There was, for one glorious interval, a kind of Heaven on Earth.

2 Computer Apocalypse

On March 1st 2011, the price of futures in cocoa slumped six per cent in just one second on the world's stock markets. Then it rebounded. It was just a glitch. On August 1st 2012, Knight Capital Group lost four times its annual income in minutes and nearly went bust. Another glitch. On August 7th 2020, the US dollar fell 21 per cent against the yen in less than a second before correcting itself on the world's stock markets. A trading algorithm was at fault.

These pings and flashes on the stock markets of the world became more and more common as the volume of high-frequency computerised trading increased. It was always possible for an algorithm to make a mistake. But, equally, it was always possible for an algorithm to find an unexpected short-cut to a successful trade. That was, after all, what they were designed to do.

'Switchbacks' anticipated market tops and bottoms, 'cross-dressers' identified trends in one market and projected them into other markets and 'randomisers' broke up large orders to make them less visible to competitors. Other algorithms – 'bait &

switch', 'bottom feeder', 'dummy run' – were more indecipherable still. They were created to distort price signals in the market and manipulate competitors.

Trades were happening so fast that it was impossible for the regulators to keep up. And the shadow markets – with their disguised money laundering, cross-product manipulations and last-minute close-outs – kept on growing. Even the auditors struggled to understand whether an investment bank had really made a profit or a loss for its clients. The world's stock markets were threatening to become an abstract mathematical space comprehensible only to algorithms. The human traders looked at the crazy signals racing across their screens and wondered whether they were the result of market manipulation, algorithms gone haywire or, on the contrary, algorithms accurately calculating the mathematics of complex dynamical systems.

By the early 2020s, flash crashes and unpredictable price hikes were happening all the time. Billions of dollars disappeared from one end of the market only to reappear at the other end. Tiny start-up banks became world players overnight and then crashed and burned the next day. After the global crash of 2025, only four big banks were left – Goldman Sachs, Credit Suisse, HSBC China and Stalinbank. The 'Great Correction', as it was also known, saw a change in the global balance of power. The Chinese yuan, not the US dollar, was now the world's preferred reserve currency.

Many things changed. The old high-seas trading routes in drugs, oil and weapons were still operational but subject to piratical skirmishes and sudden taxes. The Californian experiment in digital cryptocurrency began. People hoarded gold and Chinese bank notes. The vast majority of the world's population survived by resorting to barter and exchange.

In the slums and shanty-towns of the world, the role of the alchemist made a comeback. Old men able to juggle numbers preyed on the superstitions of the poor and desperate. They promised to make the ancient cash machines work and conjured vast fortunes behind the tiny electronic screens they held in their hands. These cunning men never lasted long in any district. Most were beaten with sticks and compelled to move on. Some were burned.

As for the Big Four banks – or the banks of the West, the North, the East and the Northeast as they were known – they continued to prosper. But they were highly secretive. The throw-downs on the electronic platforms of London, Zurich, Shanghai and New York were in any case mainly for show, said the street-corner players, as they blew on their dice. The money was shuffled around according to protocols agreed in Beijing. Others, better informed, who had travelled to the gambling meccas of Las Vegas, San Juan and Aruba, said the banks had been using drug-assisted technologies for years to stay one step ahead of the algorithms. It was all about leveraging quantum intervals, they whispered.

After the financial meltdown of the Bank of the North in 2042, it was revealed that traders had indeed been using a time-stretching drug, together with brainwave-detecting VR tech, to play the stock market. Leaked videos showed the Credit Suisse traders seated in the lotus position with their eyes closed, the electroencephalogram sensors trailing from their headsets, the trading screens flickering behind them, making millions of yuan a second. They were dead to the world and alive only in algospace, where they wrestled with fiendish equations among complex virtual geometries.

The remaining Big Three banks closed ranks quickly. Their trading systems were to remain mysteries, revealed only at harvest time to the young mathematicians they lured to their temples of finance. These initiates had the briefest of careers, their minds burning out rapidly on the latest versions of the time-stretching drug, their bodies curling up like dead leaves. At the end of three or four years, they were reduced to feeble wrecks, spinning out the ends of their pensions on the beaches of Necker Island and Las Alamandas, cackling at the moon.

There was one of these ancient traders, named Ren, who gained the reputation of being an oracle. She lived in the permanent darkness of a hotel room in the Bahamas. To those willing to make the pilgrimage, she claimed that the Big Three Banks secretly worshipped the Sun. The light passing through the fibre-optic cables connecting the internet was ancient sunlight, she said. And this was what the banks, who huddled so close to the planet's internet hubs and cable stacks, really wanted. The warmth of the Sun. She giggled.

It was always at that moment, opening her sightless eyes, that Ren made her prophecy. She said that one of the Big Three banks was destined to vanquish the Sun. At this moment, faster-than-light communication would become possible. The banks would crack open the infinite nexus of space-time. There would be parallel worlds to plunder and past lives to exploit. The signs were already there, she said. What were the stock market's flash crashes and sudden losses if not evidence that the banks were already reaching into the present from the future? Was there not an honest-to-goodness opportunity here for the right kind of investor? And at that point she held out her hand for coin.

3 Psychoactive Drug Apocalypse

In 2023, Apple University grad Ed Kalani started up the educational technology company K-Head. In his 'One World' manifesto, he said that he wanted to bring all peoples to a 'unity beyond borders, languages, colors, cultures, sexes, strategies and thoughts.' He spoke like a man possessed.

Kalani won a contract to pilot his education techniques in the US federal prison system. He brought together gang members from the Black Guerrilla Family, Mexican Mafia, Aryan Brotherhood and Mara Salvatrucha and got them to act out their differences with each other in group therapy sessions. He said he wanted to break down racist and sexist attitudes, make prisoners learn from each other and bring them closer together.

The prisoners resisted his techniques. So Kalani began to experiment. He hooked up women's prisons with men's prisons, he threw transgender prisoners into the mix. He invented gangs like the Mixed Bloods and the Male Lesbian Nation and hired actors to pretend they belonged to them in the group therapy sessions. Nothing seemed to work. The breakthrough came only when he persuaded the federal authorities to let him use psychedelic drugs in his sessions. The prisoners succumbed to his techniques quite rapidly after that.

Kalani published videos of sessions where prisoners renounced their gang affiliations in elaborate ceremonies of mutual forgiveness. They embraced each other and fell weeping to the floor. Of course, there were some reports of bad trips, psychotic episodes and unscrupulous manipulation. But Kalani was expert at brushing these aside. His stories of lives redeemed became widely popular.

The secret of Kalani's therapeutic success was to give prisoners the plant-based hallucinogen ayahuasca and turn their group encounter sessions into stage-managed vision quests. He replaced all his psychiatric counsellors with South American shamans and primed them with his 'One World' philosophy. In a typical group trip, the shaman would encourage participants to talk through their hallucinations as they were having them. He would then marshal the various individual visions of writhing snakes and crystal palaces and whirring robots into a shared group trip, effectively hypnotising participants into seeing and hearing the same things at the same time. The goal was to get prisoners to experience a transcendental unity.

Kalani documented all of the trips and spent months analysing the data. He saw that alongside the usual psychedelic snakes and robots, there were new kinds of bizarre images and mental curiosities he'd never seen reported before in the pharmacological literature. He began to name them. There was Pink Hitler and Malcolm Z, Virgin Mary-Jane and Smoking Cortes, Ugly Betty Coyote and Shark Missile. Furthermore, these archetypes – as Kalani was soon calling them – seemed able to cross from one group vision to another as if they had a life of their own.

Ever alert to commercial opportunity, Kalani trademarked his archetypes under the same laws that protected comic-book characters like Superman and Wolverine. In some interviews with the news magazines, he went further, claiming that the archetypes were inter-dimensional beings which his shamans – or 'consciousness engineers', as he now called them – were able to conjure and dispel. He began to talk of a higher plane of existence called 'Dimension K'.

It was not long before Kalani realised that his transformation of the federal prison system was only the beginning of a much larger mission. He had to remake the world. In 2027, he built K-Time, a social media network designed to rival Facebook. He said it was a 'body of dissimilar bodies and organisms living in deep and loving harmony and partnership in the best interest of all within the body'. The idea was that K-Time's members would sign up to models of responsible thinking and behaviour online which they would gradually migrate out into real life. The network was an incubator of behaviour change.

Kalani's cultural revolution proceeded step by step. K-Time was rolled out through student frat houses by Ivy League university administrators as a means of improving gender relations. European football leagues enrolled their players on K-Time to ease racial tensions. Banks and corporations experimented with the network as a means of improving collaboration between workers from different cultures. K-Time became fashionable.

Flame wars, hate speech, trolling and grooming broke out episodically on K-Time, as they did on any network. But Kalani had an ingenious solution to this age-old social media problem. He referred disputes among K-Time members to the informal body of case law established by his earlier prison experiments. The accounts of how angry encounters between gang members were mediated by a shaman's use of various archetypes set useful precedents for the interventions of a moderator on the network. Soon, arguments were being settled by appeals to Pink Hitler, Malcolm Z, Smoking Cortes and Flower Guevara.

K-Time's members soon realised they didn't need the moderators to regulate their behaviour. They could access the archetypes of Dimension K directly. All they had to do was take ayahuasca while on K-Time and conjure the network's ruling archetypes themselves. It wasn't long before the first mass panics and crowd anomalies began to show up.

There was the Phantom Flu pandemic of 2036, when hundreds of thousands of K-Time members across the world reported episodes of numbness, dizziness and vomiting. There were hospitalisations, mass no-shows at work and a wave of company bankruptcies. The source of the hysteria was traced to a bad batch of online Pink Hitler memes.

In 2037, there was the Next Level suicide epidemic, when thousands of K-Time members from different parts of the world tripped together online and killed themselves at the climax of a lunar eclipse. They believed this was a means for them to go to Dimension K and become deities. In a way, it worked. Their names are still remembered by K-Time devotees and they regularly show up in vision quests.

And then in 2038, there was the JM kill craze, when some K-Time members claimed that drug-assisted encounters with the notorious shadow archetype Jack the Mack had shifted catastrophically into real life. They reported seeing the demonic figure, with his top hat and tails, and flashing blade, loitering on street corners and following them at night. They blamed other K-Time members for bewitching them. There were several killings.

Kalani was dragged through the law courts by aggrieved K-Time members. Lawyers argued that as the founder of

Dimension K, he bore responsibility for what happened in its name. What K-Time users believed had happened to them through the medium of Kalani's archetypes was as true as what had actually happened to them through the combined mechanism of drugs, screens and internet routers. Psychedelic drug trips produced valid forms of testimony. Visions of the gods were admissible as evidence in court. It was a wild time.

Kalani's empire crumbled. But new drug-assisted media networks rushed in to take its place. There came a time when everything was potentially true and nothing was legally permitted. Guilt was reckoned in percentages. Nobody was ever completely innocent. The world's prisons emptied. Surveillance was everywhere. The Earth became a giant madhouse.

4 Rocket Apocalypse

One year after the ratification of the Paris Agreement on climate change by United Nations members, the Eiffel Tower was bathed in green lights and the hashtag #SmileForThePlanet was flashed around the world. It was November 2016.

The United States was the first country to withdraw from the agreement. Other nations followed suit. China, India, Indonesia and Nigeria were soon building new coal-fired power plants at the rate of one a week. Carbon dioxide emissions from smokestack industries climbed rapidly during the 2020s, trapping much sunlight in the Earth's atmosphere and retaining its heat.

The planet baked. As the oceans steadily evaporated, even more fogging vapour was trapped in the atmosphere. Plants and trees withered. 'Runaway climate change' was a phrase on everyone's lips.

There were some visionaries. Baron Rothschild shipped much of his banking industry into orbit. The Iranians launched manned satellites and prayer rooms into space from their Imam

Khomeini Spaceport. The old dotcom billionaire Jeff Bezos fired off thousands of rockets from the Florida Space Coast as he built his 'Las Vegas in the Sky' in the 2030s. Payloads delivered, the rocket stages dropped into the Atlantic Ocean, to be salvaged and reused.

The Zurich-based insurance giant Swiss Re reported a huge spike in storms, floods, droughts and wildfires round the world in 2039. People began to prepare for the melting of the Earth's ice caps. There were end-of-the-world parties.

The 2040s was the era of the great migrations from the South to the North, the wars between the East and the West, the pogroms, massacres and regime changes. It was also when the world's elite made the final move into Earth orbit.

There was a clamour among the mass of the world's left-behind population to be permitted access to the relative safety of what was called 'Skyland'. But the terrific expense of rocket travel meant that only billionaires and government officials could afford it. Shanty towns sprang up around the Kennedy Space Center in Florida, the Baikonur Cosmodrome in Kazakhstan and Jiuquan Satellite Launch Center in Mongolia. Every so often, some of the shanty dwellers were crushed by a falling rocket.

Cargo cults built replica spaceports from tin and cardboard at the Earth's equator, where it was agreed there was the best chance of using the planet's rotational speed to achieve lift-off. Pirates scoured the shrinking seas hoping to find jettisoned rocket stages and sell them on the black market. Singapore, Kuala Lumpur and Nairobi installed zero gravity chambers in their public squares, boasting of their value first as training centres, then as grief-counselling centres.

The rockets burned brightly in the night sky for many years. Oil and gas were pumped out of the ground at an astonishing rate to fuel the rocket trade. The Middle East oil fields had long ago burned themselves out in the serial Gulf Wars. Daqing, Texas and Siberia were now the world's oil states.

In 2051, the Skylanders placed a total ban on Earth emigration to its orbital palaces and hotels. But they still wanted soybean, rice and wheat from the planet's farms. They wanted fish from its oceans, beef from its stockyards and alcohol from its breweries. They ordered up vast quantities of materials, more than they could ever need. And, in return, they rained down on the planet the only things they had to give – their garbage and their money.

The warlords who protected the Earth's oil fields and spaceports grew rich from the rocket trade. They spent their wealth on circuses, hunts and games. They failed to reward their scientists and engineers, though. And so the technological base supporting the rocket economy steadily dwindled. There was an increasing number of rocket crashes, spaceport fires and bandit raids on the oil refineries.

The rocket trade ended with the Great Space Hilton Fire of 2052. A rocket launched from Florida with a payload of coffee beans exploded when it docked with the cargo port of the orbital hotel. Thousands of Skylanders died. The fire lasted for months.

After this catastrophe, the Skylanders seceded completely from Earth. They stopped all trade, all communications, all travel. The lights went out in their space homes.

Earth sent imploring messages to Skyland. But the only response was radio silence. Speculation mounted that the Skylanders had stockpiled food and drink in orbital reservoirs. It was thought they were planning to strike out for new worlds in the huge starships they had been secretly building for years. Or else it was assumed they had retreated into cryo-sleep and were waiting out the end of the world, intending to return only when they thought the planet's ice caps had replenished themselves.

Dependent on the space markets of Skyland for so many years, the industries of Earth found it hard to restructure themselves. There was a general decline. The oil rigs of Russia and China rusted, the spaceports decayed. The knowledge of how to build the rockets was lost, buried deep inside broken computers or scattered across forgotten deserts. The great equatorial cities became slums, dry with heat and dark with smog. Millions died of hunger, malaria and diarrhoea.

Skyland had always needed thousands of rocket boosters to stay afloat. Their whole habitat was built on resisting the tremendous gravitational pull of the Earth. After the Space Hilton Fire, though, the Skylanders lost confidence in rocket technology. Perhaps they lost confidence in all technology. Who knows what crazed rites they conducted as their casinos and temples slipped from orbit, broke apart and fell to Earth? The fragments from their space homes pelted the tin houses of shanty town dwellers in Paris and New York.

Even now, on a clear night, the burning remains of the Skylanders can sometimes be seen showering through the atmosphere. It makes for a wondrous sight.

5 Space Medicine Apocalypse

In 2023, during the North/South Disturbances, the US government moved inside a mountain bunker in Colorado. Cheyenne Mountain was a hollowed-out space surrounded by 2,000 feet of granite. It had been built during the Cold War to withstand the blast of a 30-megaton nuclear bomb. It was the ultimate safe space. In fact, the government bureaucrats felt so comfortable in their new underground hideout, which had its own power plant, water supply, dormitories and leisure centres, that they saw no reason to ever come out.

As civil wars and micro-conflicts intensified during the 2020s, the vogue for bunker communities spread across the planet. Rich Europeans moved into fortress apartments built on artificial islands off the coast of Dubai. Financiers in Moscow and London drilled deep into the bedrock, creating basement palaces and underground railways. Cape Town moved its Century City residential complex underground and piped in water from the surface canals.

By the late 2030s, millions of people were living beneath the Earth. The bunker communities which thrived were built next to the planet's oil wells and underground springs. Sugar Loaf Field, Cantarell Field and Bolivar Coastal Field formed a powerful South American petrochemical complex. North Caucasus Basin, East European Platform and North China Plain built a massive network of tunnels to become the world's first hydrogeological empire. Gold and silver mining towns flourished underground. The planet's surface was abandoned to ethnic militias, biker gangs, religious sects, warlords and roaming bands of mercenaries.

The underground cultures survived for many decades. They built agile machines, light industrial farms and gas-lit markets deep inside the rock and soil. They maintained their grip on the planet's natural resources. The oil and water markets thrived. Air was piped in from the planet's surface and cleaned by huge compressors and filters. There were oxygen bars at every tunnel intersection.

The art of the cinema was revived. The tunnel people bathed in the light of films projected on to the walls of huge caverns. They loved the old silent movies. Mary Pickford, Lillian Gish and Mabel Normand became big stars again. Audiences couldn't get enough of their ghostly white faces, moving slowly against the grain of the sedimentary rock.

The biggest thing the underground tribes missed from their days above ground was the changing of the seasons. Any surplus resources they had were dedicated to the building of elaborate theme parks designed to mimic different landscapes and ecosystems. In this way, they hoped to recapture a memory of the slow, steady, soothing movement of the Earth around the Sun.

Summerland was the first of these artificial enclosures. A surf park with a wave machine, central heating and stadium-style floodlights, it was popular with the first generation of tunnel people. The electric light was filtered and dimmed over the course of 20 hours and switched off for four hours. Every day was a summer solstice. Every night saw videos of the stars projected on to a painted roof. They twinkled just like the real stars.

RainTime was another popular underground theme park. It simulated the monsoon season in a mountain environment, with heavy thunderclouds and high winds triggering sudden downpours and flash-floods. The park ran on a three-month clock, its gears and motors delivering a smooth and plausible transition from semi-desert to lush green landscape. It closed for a week between shows. Bookings were taken years in advance.

Polar Icescape was less visited. It was for connoisseurs of extreme conditions only. A vast landscape of packed ice, igloo dwellings and sub-zero temperatures, it was treated as a kind of spiritual retreat. There was a permanent twilight, quite unlike anything on Earth.

It wasn't long before a second generation of underground theme parks began to emerge. These were built around mood and atmosphere rather than remembered terrestrial landscapes. They blended elements from different seasonal experiences to create unique combinations of light, sound, air pressure, water vapour and terrain. There were mixes of wild snowstorms with long summer days, distilled as a walk in the forest. Smog became a piquant ingredient to add to a scene of lakes and mountains or deserts and caves. There was a vogue for streetscapes built over rolling seas. The creators of these almost abstract-expressionist theme parks considered themselves artists. They became famous.

The adverse effects of these experiments in human sensory augmentation slowly revealed themselves. Deprived of the cognitive resets that came from the regular alternation of day and night above ground, people's body clocks had already started to run at different speeds. Now, they were flipped into wild, unpredictable rhythms by prolonged stays in Summerland or rapid transits between NeonStripMall and Tropical NightTime and back again.

The tunnel folks began to live their lives at different speeds. Those nostalgic for the old days above ground insisted on regular visits to 'zeitgeber' light-clinics to preserve their 24-hour body clock. Others preferred a day of 25 hours, or even 48 hours. Still others hibernated for months at a time in sleep hotels. The shared experience of time disintegrated. There was a craze for new calendars.

The hormones regulating the human body clock became prized substances. There were huge black markets in synthetic melatonin. People overdosed. All sorts of physiological disorders resulted. Ovarian cancer rates rose dramatically. There were obesity epidemics. People had attacks of dizziness and vertigo. Wandering tribes lost all sense of direction and travelled in ever diminishing circles until they collapsed in each other's arms, exhausted. Tinnitus became a common affliction, with people interpreting the roaring in their ears as ancestral voices giving them instructions. There were mad tunnelling frenzies as people tried to reach the Earth's molten core, imagining that some mysterious god lived there, bathed in heat and light.

The power of human speech was lost. Nobody knew why. It was a catastrophe that was barely noticed. People communicated among the tunnels using rhythmic claps, whistles and taps against the walls. Their sonic codes were scratched at the entrances to caves. Complex echo-location devices replaced the magnetic compass as wayfinding tools. People listened to what the rocks had to say. They pressed their ears against the tunnel walls for guidance.

The first suicides were ritual affairs, highly elaborate, with many dignified postures. These events were captured on film and projected in the old underground cinemas. The next few suicides were rushed, anxious, feverish. Many were botched. And then came the mass suicides, as people threw themselves into the stone canyons, falling, falling, in great writhing mobs, finding freedom at last, until their brains were dashed on the stones below.

At the end, only the troglodytes were left. They looked at each other in wonder. It would be a long, long climb back to the surface of the Earth. But they were ready for a new day of ascension.

6 Television Apocalypse

Tokyo app designer Henry Mizuki was one of the billion or so people around the world who kept a death watch over Topan, the last of the Orangutans. The great ape died of complications from pneumonia on 22nd July 2028. His final days were live-streamed from the Houston Zoo on the Witness: Extinction channel and became a massive TV hit with the so-called 'Weltanschauung Generation'.

As Topan moved his hands to sign goodbye, Mizuki watched from his phone at Tokyo Station, where he was having lunch with co-workers. They said he seemed agitated. That evening, he was at the park in Shinjuku attending a candlelight vigil for the Orangutan species. He tweeted his disgust at the way Topan's watercolours were now being traded for hundreds of thousands of dollars on eBay. He called it 'biocentric exploitation'.

Days later, the Witness: Extinction TV channel switched the focus of its death watch to an Amur Leopard at a zoo in Nebraska. Mizuki quit his job and set up a social media campaign, #Not1MoreExtinction. His video manifesto lamented the fact that over half the world's mammals, reptiles and birds had disappeared from the record in the preceding 50 years. He attributed these vertebrate extinctions to the invasive actions of the human species, which he labelled a 'global super-predator'.

Mizuki set up his own EarthFightback TV channel in 2029. He ran it with his younger brother Shig from their apartment in Nakameguro. The Mizuki brothers recruited a string of environmental activists from Asia, Europe and America to take direct action in defence of the planet. They encouraged their followers to live-stream acts of sabotage against industrial development projects which threatened wildlife habitats. Their cause quickly gathered momentum.

During the early 2030s, EarthFightback showed videos of dam construction blockades in China, electricity pylon bombings in England and arson attacks on slum redevelopment projects in Delhi. Henry Mizuki claimed that the 'convulsive power' of televised direct action would 'nudge' the planet into a 'flourishing new wilderness equilibrium'. A threshold was duly crossed in 2032 with the suicide bombing of a Google server farm in North Carolina, which killed 12 people. The EarthFightback footage of the Google attack was the first viral video to get more than ten billion views.

In May 2033, the Mizuki brothers made a one-minute video on how to become a suicide mega-bomber. Henry Mizuki appeared on EarthFightback in person. He said that humanity's 'addiction to mega-cities' was the root cause of its over-consumption of environmental resources. There were five target cities listed on the piece of paper he waved around in front of the camera. He announced a day of action.

On Monday May 13th 2030, Henry Mizuki started to climb the stairs of the high-rise Sumitomo Building at the edge of Shinjuku. The video footage from his helmet-cam showed him commenting on the progress of his quest as he laboriously ascended to the 51st floor. Back in the one-room EarthFightback TV studio, Shig cut his brother's footage with live-stream video from their accomplice, Norio Johnson.

Johnson was a foreign student at the Tokyo Institute of Technology. He had fallen under the spell of the Mizuki brothers in 2030 and used his 3D printing skills to make plastic explosives for them. Somehow, his arms industry contacts led him to a buried cache of US Army uranium-233. The isotopes were 70 years old and designed to be used as part of a W54 nuclear warhead – small enough for one man to carry and powerful enough to deliver an explosive yield of 250 tons of TNT. It wasn't difficult for a man of Johnson's talents to build himself one of these backpack nukes and spread the knowledge to his associates.

On the day of mega-bomb action, Johnson was able to mingle undetected with other young backpackers on the top floor of the open-air bus terminal at the south side of Shinjuku Station. The W54 in his Fjällräven rucksack weighed about 50 pounds. He kept complaining about how heavy it was on his EarthFightback video transmission. Johnson said a brief prayer to 'Mother Gaia' just before his video feed went dark. At the same time, Mizuki had reached the top of the Sumitomo Building and started filming from the observation deck. He had a panoramic view, from about 650 feet up, of the nuclear bomb blast which took out Shinjuku Station. He managed to keep filming even as the windows of the Sumitomo Building blew in.

The Mizuki brothers had designed the Tokyo nuclear bombing to function as a reality TV disaster show. Johnson was high enough above ground for the bomb blast to maximise damage to buildings. Henry Mizuki was close enough to the firestorm to capture it on video without being harmed. Over a quarter of a million people died. Over three billion people watched.

EarthFightback cameraman/suicide bomber pairs managed to stage TV terror spectacles in four of Henry Mizuki's five target cities on the day of action, now known as 5/13. Timed to coincide with the Tokyo attack were additional bomb strikes on London, Kuala Lumpur and Hong Kong. A planned attack on New York was foiled at the last minute by the FBI.

The London nuclear device flattened the city's financial square mile and was filmed from the top of the Shard, just south of the Thames. In Malaysia, the incineration of the shopping malls of Bukit Bintang was streamed from the observation deck of the Kuala Lumpur Tower. And in Hong Kong, the destruction of Victoria Harbour was recorded from the 100th floor of the International Commerce Centre in West Kowloon. A total death toll for 5/13 has never been conclusively established.

Henry Mizuki claimed in his 5/13 video testimonial that the simultaneous nuclear attacks were designed to be a form of 'shock therapy'. He hoped that by passing through a planetary 'ring of fire', humankind would 'wake up' to its duty of care to other species.

The 5/13 nuclear attack videos generated six billion views on EarthFightback in less than a week. Over two thirds of the planet's human population watched the mushroom clouds hanging over Tokyo, London, Kuala Lumpur and Hong Kong. Global capital investment froze. Trade ground to a halt. Arms manufacture rose. The world hunkered down in a defensive crouch. It is still in the same posture today.

Research Notes: Eight Tech-Based Models of a Local Accident

1 Death of Jesse Gelsinger (Bioengineering Accident)

Local Accident Investigation Report

1.1 Root Cause: Military Development of Bioengineering

Adolf Hitler became the 55th member of the Nazi Party and led it to election victory in Germany in 1933. Once in power, the Nazis declared Germany a one-party state and conquered western Europe.

The Nazis believed in a white supremacist ideology. They divided the world's population into white people they called 'Aryans' (those whom the Nation of Islam, from a different per-spective, called 'blue-eyed devils') and everyone else. The more esoteric Nazi race theorists considered Aryans to be descended from gods and imbued with the mysterious electrical energy of the cosmos. Non-Aryans, by contrast, were believed to be the result of human interbreeding with apes. In practice, Aryans were socially respectable white people while non-Aryans tended to be those people who were already on the social margins – disabled people, sex workers, gays, the mentally ill and minority ethnic groups such as Jews, Gypsies, Slavs and black people.

Hitler believed it was the destiny of Aryans, as the master race, to drive the so-called *Untermensch* from the face of the Earth through natural selection. His followers decided this process needed a social intervention to speed up its development. In 1933, they introduced a eugenics programme (based on the Californian model) which mandated the compulsory sterilisation of people with genetic disorders. In 1935, the Nazis introduced the Nuremburg racial purity laws which restricted German citizenship to those of Aryan genetic inheritance.

It was not long before those without German citizenship (particularly the Jews) were rounded up by the Nazis, forced into urban ghettos at gunpoint, and then shipped either to concentration camps, where they were worked to death, or extermination camps, where they were gassed and cremated on an industrial scale.

The Nuremburg racial purity laws used genetic science for their social legitimation. The distinction between genotype, an individual's latent hereditary past, and phenotype, an individual's manifest traits and behaviours, formed the operating symbols for a Nazi bureaucracy of genocide. All state officials were expected to have a certificate documenting their genotype in order to demonstrate that their ancestors were neither Jews nor black people. Meanwhile, people could be arrested and interrogated about their citizenship status simply on the basis of observed phenotypic characteristics such as skin colour, eye colour and hair type.

In June 1941, at a critical moment in the Second World War, Hitler drove his armies deep into the eastern Europe territories ruled by his one-time accomplice Joseph Stalin. He planned to exterminate the millions of native Slavs and Jews living in the

Soviet Union and replace them over a generation with a new
population of so-called Aryan settlers from Nazi Germany.
Together with his architect Albert Speer, he intended to build a
white European civilisation of parade grounds, autobahns, sports
stadia and cemeteries whose monumental grandeur would supposedly compare with that of Ancient Egypt or Babylon.

And if I were asked what I understood divinity to be, I would say: By that
I understand the living beings of the ultraviolet and ultrared forces and
worlds. In former times they were embodied and moved about in complete purity. Today they live on in human beings. The gods slumber in
bestialized human bodies, but the day is coming when they will rise up
again. We were electric, we will be electric; to be electric and to be divine
is the same thing! By means of the electric eye primitive man was omnis-
cient, through inner electrical power they were omnipotent. The omnis-
cient and omnipotent has the right to call itself God!

> Jorg Lanz von Liebenfels, *Theozoology, or the Science of the
> Sodomite Apelings and the Divine Electron* (1905)

The Nazis built thousands upon thousands of *lagers* across the
territories they occupied (the US Holocaust Memorial Museum
has catalogued at least 40,000 camps). There were major concentration camps at Buchenwald, Dachau and Bergen-Belsen.
Extermination camps included those at Chelmno, Treblinka and
Auschwitz. The Nazis ended up killing many millions of people
(according to the political scientist R J Rummel, a low estimate
would be 15 million people).

On December 11th 1941, Hitler declared war on the United
States, which he saw as a nation weakened by the influence of non-
Aryans such as Jews and black people. Within hours, President
Roosevelt had signed the US declaration of war against Germany.
However, the Americans (together with their British allies) did
not invade western Europe until June 1944. They waited until the
Soviets had turned back Hitler's armies at Stalingrad. That was
when they attacked.

One thing that was noticeable about the American armed forces was that they were racially segregated into white and black units. The 761st Tank Battalion which landed at Normandy's Omaha Beach, for example, was a unit of 600 or so black men commanded by six white officers.

The closing period of the Second World War became a race between the Soviets and the Americans to capture the remnants of the Nazi war machine. Hitler's scientists were working to develop new wonder weapons in the fanatical belief they could still turn the tide of the war. There were supersonic rockets, nerve gas munitions, jet aircraft, guided missiles, nuclear bombs. Often, the Nazi labs, workshops and factories were located next to the *lagers*, so they could draw on a ready supply of slave labour and human test subjects.

As the armies of Stalin and Eisenhower seized the Nazi labs, grabbing hold of scientists, technical documents and research equipment, so they liberated the concentration camps, discovering bands of emaciated survivors and piles of bone-thin corpses.

Stalin's men liberated the Auschwitz II-Birkenau death camp, where over a million people had been killed. They heard witnesses tell of the biological experiments conducted by Nazi doctor Josef Mengele on the children of prisoners between 1943 and 1944. Mengele, known as the 'Angel of Death', helped make the *selektion* of those people deemed unfit for work from the line of new arrivals on the ramp at the Auschwitz rail terminus. This condemned population – pregnant women, children, the old, and sick – were sent immediately to the gas chamber for extermination.

Mengele was particularly interested in the children. He always saved any twins from being sent to the gas chamber. Because identical twins, uniquely, share the same genotype, they proved valuable human resources for Mengele, who was conducting doctoral research into the genetic inheritability of disease. He needed twins as test subjects for his human experiments. One twin provided the body to be tested, the other twin provided the experimental control.

As I clutched my mother's hand, an SS man hurried by shouting, 'Twins, twins!' He stopped to look at us. Miriam and I looked very much alike. We were wearing similar clothes. 'Are they twins?' he asked my mother. 'Is that good?' replied my mother. He nodded yes. 'They are twins,' she said.

Eva Mozes, *Surviving the Angel of Death:*
The Story of a Mengele Twin in Auschwitz (2009)

Twins were kept in separate barracks from the other Auschwitz prisoners. They were taken to Mengele's lab for experiments. None were told what the experiments were about. Mengele performed experimental surgeries on children without their consent, removed limbs and sexual organs and conducted blood transfusions from one twin to another. He would infect one twin with typhus, wait for them to die, kill the other twin and then conduct comparative dissections of the cadavers. Or else he would compel a male twin to impregnate his sister and then examine the genetic make-up of the resulting child.

Mengele sent his reports back to the Kaiser Wilhelm Institute of Anthropology, Human Heredity and Eugenics in Berlin. The Institute was founded in 1927 and had been kept going through the 1930s with regular funding from the Rockefeller Foundation, one of the many American organisations supporting eugenics research before the Second World War. One of Mengele's colleagues was particularly interested in the relationship between the human genotype and phenotypic variations in eye colour. Mengele regularly included in his packages specimen eyes from his forensic collection.

The Soviets couldn't find Mengele at Auschwitz. He had disappeared. Only 200 of the 3,000 pairs of children who passed through his lab survived. Among them were Eva and Miriam Mozes.

The first Nazi concentration camp to be liberated by Eisenhower's forces was Ohrdruf, a subcamp of Buchenwald. The

Americans found piles of naked, emaciated corpses. It was a huge shock. Eisenhower insisted on touring Ohrdruf personally in order to bear witness to the Nazi atrocities. He found a shed filled with corpses and a butcher's block for smashing gold fillings from teeth.

Eisenhower understood the propaganda value of the camps. He insisted that American politicians and newsmen should be brought in to see Ohrdruf for themselves and at Buchenwald his men put on a tabletop show of grisly specimens The sensationalist reporting of Nazi war crimes on radio and newsreels was partly intended to build a case against the Nazis for the crime of genocide and discredit the science of eugenics.

Augsburg, Germany, Jan 15 – Ilse Koch was sentenced to life imprisonment today for causing the murder of Buchenwald concentration camp prisoners. One of the most revolting charges against her – that she had tattooed prisoners killed so she could have lampshades made of their skin – was dropped by the prosecution, which said it could not prove the charge.

Associated Press, January 15th 1951

Having captured Hitler's top scientists and secretly divided them between themselves, the Americans and the Soviets made a big show of punishing a handful of lesser Nazi scientists at Nuremberg in 1947. They tried 23 doctors for performing medical experiments upon concentration camp prisoners without their consent.

Sixteen of them were found guilty and seven of them were hanged.

During the course of the 'Doctors' Trial', the Nuremberg Code was developed as a set of medical ethics governing human experimentation. The ten-point code underlined the importance of having the informed consent of human subjects, abstaining from coercion and avoiding any risk of death.

Josef Mengele's name came up at the Doctors' Trial. It was believed that he was dead. Mengele's old mentor at the Institute for Anthropology, Human Heredity and Eugenics was Otmar von Verschuer. He escaped prosecution for his research activities and was instead fined 600 Reichsmark for being a Nazi fellow traveller.

President Harry Truman desegregated the American armed forces in 1948 and permitted black men to serve alongside white men.

The science of eugenics became taboo as the recently formed United Nations declared that the forcible sterilisation and mass killing of members of an ethnic group belonged to a terrible new crime known as 'genocide'.

1.2 Timeline: Civilian Adoption of Bioengineering

In 1951, Mengele's old mentor Verschuer became Professor of Human Genetics at the University of Munster, where he established one of the world's largest centres of human genetic research. He retired in 1965 and died four years later.

In 1956, the first successful bone marrow transplant was performed by E Donnall Thomas in New York. Healthy bone marrow tissue was taken from the donor and given to the patient, who had leukaemia. The operation involved identical twins, in order to reduce the risk of the genetic graft being rejected.

Bone marrow transplantation is the only form of stem cell therapy that is widely practised. It works because stem cells naturally divide to form healthy tissue. Stem cell therapy is effectively equivalent to organ-transplant surgery conducted at a cellular level.

Much more precise because it operates at the level of individual genes within cells is gene therapy. American doctor Stanfield Rogers came up with this idea in 1970 at Oak Ridge National Laboratory in Tennessee. Gene therapy involves the replacement of mutant genes with functional genes in people with genetic disorders. Its success depends on the newly introduced functional gene being able to produce the proteins or other organic products that are otherwise lacking.

In 1990, the four-year-old 'girl in a bubble' Ashanthi DeSilva, became the first patient to have successful gene therapy. Suffering from a rare genetic disorder known as SCID, she was injected with the functional enzyme-producing gene needed to correct her specific genetic mutation. She became well enough to leave her bubble and attend school.

Gene therapy is still in its infancy. Hundreds of somatic cell gene-therapy trials are underway in the US to treat such disorders as haemophilia and cystic fibrosis. Gene therapy involving the use of germ cells in human embryos – where any genetic modifications become inheritable – is less common. The practice is banned in Germany, probably because of its associations with eugenics.

In 1997 a United Nations agency issued the Universal Declaration on the Human Genome and Human Rights. The document anticipated the completion of the task then underway to map the complete genetic makeup of the human species. It stated that no human genetic engineering research project should ever 'prevail' over the human rights of the subjects involved. It also took a stand against the cloning of human beings as a reproductive rather than a therapeutic strategy.

In 1998, stem cell therapy made a huge advance when human embryonic stem cells were first isolated in the lab. The work was funded by the Geron Corporation and took place at the University of Wisconsin-Madison. Embryonic stem cells are the genetic building blocks of human life. When the human embryo is in its initial stage of development, not yet attached to its mother's uterus, it is composed entirely of undifferentiated cells. Over the succeeding months, these cells give rise to the entire body of the human organism. The stem cells differentiate into specialist cells such as muscle cells, blood cells or brain cells. Any stem cell is 'pluripotent' and has the capacity to become any specialist cell.

Theoretically, genetic scientists can manipulate the development of human embryonic stem cells to create whatever human organs they want. A brave new world of elective surgery beckons. Transplant surgeons would theoretically be able to draw on a specially created reserve of livers, hearts and lungs to extend the lives of their patients. Cosmetic surgeons would have access to teeth and eyes. No doubt the logic of the market would play its part in regulating the supply of human body parts.

Any stem cell also has the capacity to spontaneously renew itself in order to replenish human tissue. Here, genetic scientists see the possibility of using human embryonic stem cells to repair human muscle, bone and brain. In the hospital of the future, doctors would routinely use stem cell therapies to treat heart disease, spinal cord injuries, Parkinson's disease and other degenerative diseases.

1.3 Effect: Bioengineering Accidents

Most technological accidents tend to produce an unknown quantity in human experience. Only a bioengineering accident can also produce an unknown quantity in the human condition. And that is because bioengineering is a research practice able to subvert, overturn and extend the received boundaries between humans and non-humans. Today's freak accident in bioengineering always has the potential to become tomorrow's bioengineering role model.

Indeed, many evangelical Christians think that this kind of conceptual shift has already happened when it comes to human embryonic stem cell therapy. They have huge ethical objections to the destruction of human embryos necessarily involved in the harvesting of embryonic stem cells. They see it as a form of abortion. And abortion to these God-fearing folk is little more than child sacrifice.

And thou shalt not let any of thy seed pass through the fire to Molech, neither shalt thou profane the name of thy God: I am the LORD.

Book of Leviticus 18:21

It's no surprise that the Geron Corporation's funding of the University of Wisconsin-Madison's isolation of human embryonic stem cells attracted the attention of evangelical Christians. Protestors from the Christian Defense Coalition and Operation Rescue gathered outside Geron's head office in Menlo Park, California, in 1999. They sang hymns and waved placards bearing pictures of aborted human foetuses. The slogans on their protest signs summed up their world view – 'STEM CELL RESEARCH DESTROYS TINY BABIES', 'PROTECT THE MOST DEFENSELESS OF HUMANS AGAINST ABUSE', 'STEM CELL RESEARCH VIOLATES THE NUREMBERG CODE', 'CHILDREN SACRIFICED IN QUEST OF MEDICAL PROGRESS', 'GOD IS THE CREATOR OF LIFE'.

Human embryonic stem cell therapy will produce its own class of accidents in time. And no doubt they will be characterised by recourse to the prophetic literature of monsters – *Frankenstein, Strange Case of Dr. Jekyll and Mr. Hyde, The Island of Doctor Moreau*. The line between the human and the non-human has to be drawn somewhere – even if it is a historically produced and therefore constantly moving line.

The accidents of gene therapy have so far proved simpler to elucidate. The first casualty of gene therapy came in 1999 with the death of Jesse Gelsinger. The 18-year-old man had ornithine transcarbamylase deficiency, a rare metabolic disorder, but it was not so severe that he couldn't manage it with drugs. The gene therapy trial he joined at the University of Pennsylvania was designed to treat infants with the fatal form of his disorder. He was injected with the remedial gene on a Monday and died on the Friday, having suffered a massive and damaging immune response to the injected gene carrier.

A Food and Drug Administration investigation concluded that Gelsinger had not been able to give his informed consent to the experiment, because doctors had failed to tell him about the deaths of monkeys in a similar experiment.

Speculative applications of gene therapy for the future involve the enhancement of human performance in many fields – fertility, memory, physical appearance. It may well be that such applications go against the Universal Declaration on the Human Genome and Human Rights. In which case, they are bioengineering accidents waiting to happen. Only time will tell.

2 Flash Crash (Computer Accident)

Local Accident Investigation Report

2.1 Root Cause: Military Development of Computers

In 1933, Adolf Hitler became chancellor of Nazi Germany and said that his new Reich would last for a thousand years. In 1940, his Panzer tank regiments conquered western Europe. In 1941, he declared war on the US.

President Roosevelt committed US armed forces to the British Isles, but for many years the British and American allies refused to invade western Europe. It was a huge logistical undertaking. To aid its success, the three separate armed services – navy, army and air force – of the two nations were combined into one operational force headed up by Supreme Allied Commander General 'Ike' Eisenhower.

Drawing up his invasion plans at Southwick House, just north of Portsmouth, Eisenhower was able to bide his time and watch as Hitler took the war to Joseph Stalin in eastern Europe. Only when the Soviet Army pushed the Nazi war machine back at Stalingrad, did Eisenhower decide to cross the choppy English Channel. (Total Soviet war dead in the end amounted to over 25 million, according to the Russian Academy of Sciences.)

Eisenhower made use of military deception techniques to mislead Hitler about the time and place of his landing on the

Atlantic coast. He built two phantom armies in the British Isles, using inflatable tanks and fake radio traffic, to persuade Hitler that he would land either at Narvik in the north of Europe or the Pas-de-Calais further south. The actual landing at Normandy was itself camouflaged as a diversionary feint.

Eisenhower knew that his deception plans had worked because he was effectively able to read the mind of the enemy. In this, he was aided by the British secret intelligence service, who employed logician Alan Turing to build the world's first computer, Colossus.

> Q: Please write me a sonnet on the subject of the Forth Bridge.
> A: Count me out on this one. I never could write poetry.
> Q: Add 34957 to 70764.
> A: (Pause about 30 seconds and then give as answer) 105621.
> Q: Do you play chess?
> A: Yes.
> Q: I have K at my K1, and no other pieces. You have only K at K6 and R at R1. It is your move. What do you play?
> A: (After a pause of 15 seconds) R-R8 mate.
>
> Alan Turing, 'Computing Machinery and Intelligence' (1950)

There were ten Colossus machines. Each computer was an assemblage of vacuum tubes and teleprinters operated by a crack team of female programmers. The units were constructed in the outbuildings of a converted manor house at Bletchley Park, in the middle of England. Listening posts at Denmark Hill in London and Knockholt in Kent intercepted secret radio signals transmitted between members of the Nazi high command and fed them to Bletchley Park. These telegraph messages had been encrypted using fiendishly complex Lorenz coding devices. The Colossus computers were able to decipher them by January 1944.

Signals intelligence was flashed from Bletchley Park to Southwick House. Eisenhower used the information to analyse

the distribution of Hitler's troops on the Atlantic Coast and judge
which Normandy beaches to attack. When the Normandy invasion was postponed for a day owing to bad weather, Turing sent
Eisenhower a note reassuring him that the delay was not a critical factor. Turing already knew that Hitler thought the plans for a
Normandy landing were fake. The Nazi leader had been successfully conned into believing the real Allied landings would take
place in the north five days later.

On June 6th 1944, Eisenhower landed his forces on the beaches
of Normandy, took Hitler's watch-towers and opened a western
front in Europe. The Nazi Fuhrer was already defending himself in
the east from Stalin and was not able to sustain a war on two fronts
at the same time. He retreated into an underground bunker in
Berlin, consulted his astrologers and issued his final Demolitions
on Reich Territory Decree, known as the 'Nero Decree'.

If the war is lost, the nation will also perish. This fate is inevitable. There
is no necessity to take into consideration the basis which the people will
need to continue even a most primitive existence. On the contrary, it
will be better to destroy these things ourselves, because this nation will
have proved to be the weaker one and the future will belong solely to the
stronger eastern nation. Besides, those who will remain after the battle are
only the inferior ones, for the good ones have all been killed.

Adolf Hitler to his Minister of Armaments
Albert Speer, March 18th 1945

Hitler shot himself in April 1945. His bodyguard removed his
corpse from the bunker and cremated it in the garden of the Reich
Chancellery. No trace of it remained.

As American and British forces moved towards Nazi Germany
from the west, so Stalin drove his armies into the country from the
east. German surrender was a foregone conclusion. In order to
avoid coming to blows in the ruins of Berlin, the Big Three powers
had come face to face at the Yalta conference in the heart of
Europe. A sick Roosevelt, accompanied by his British ally Winston

Churchill, met with Stalin and together they split the continent of Europe between them.

Turing's secret data was never shared with Stalin. Instead, the Soviets were passed edited intelligence reports attributed to a fictitious German spy named General Werther. The radio antennae in London and Kent were shifted so they now faced Moscow rather than Berlin. Even as the Second World War ended, a new Cold War was beginning.

In 1957, the US Air Force used the Colossus network model of listening posts linked with computers to set up a Semiautomatic Ground Environment (SAGE) Air Defense System. SAGE consisted of 182 radar stations on the outer perimeter of the US linked with 17 air force command centres. Each command centre was installed in a concrete blockhouse without any windows. A massive IBM computer took up the whole of one blockhouse floor. It processed radar data and sent it to banks of consoles manned by human operators. They were trained to use lightpens to track the movements of any incoming Soviet nuclear bombers, which would be displayed on their screens as information graphics. If circumstances warranted, the operators would be expected to direct in-flight intercept jet fighter aircraft towards the enemy bombers via teleprinter.

The computer equipment used in the radar stations and interception systems was manufactured by the Burroughs Corporation.

2.2 Timeline: Civilian Adoption of Computers

Leading the human factors team in the early stages of SAGE development was the Massachusetts Institute of Technology (MIT) psychologist J C R Licklider. In 1957, Licklider took his SAGE expertise to Bolt, Beranek and Newman (BBN). By 1962, Licklider and BBN were working at the Department of Defense on computer science research for the Advanced Research Projects Agency (ARPA). BBN went on to build ARPANET, a military command network whose decentralised packet-switching technology was capable of surviving a Soviet nuclear attack.

In 1973, ARPANET extended its reach beyond the US as it connected to institutions in England and Norway. What had started as a military command network was becoming an academic communications network. In 1974, a commercial version of ARPANET known as Telenet was launched by BBN.

However, it was in the domain of financial services that computerised networking really took off. In 1986, the London Stock Exchange shifted from open-outcry trading between buyers and sellers on the shop floor to screen-based trading on a shared electronic platform. This enabled buyers and sellers from different parts of the world to trade without having to meet or even talk to each other on the phone. It also hugely increased market liquidity as more deals were able to be done in less time. In 1987, the Chicago Mercantile Exchange launched Globex, its own electronic trading platform. Other stock exchanges soon followed.

One result of the increase in market liquidity was the increasing reliance on computer algorithms to process the massive volumes of data. By 2006, a third of all stock trades in Europe and the US were driven by algorithms.

2.3 Effect: Computer Accidents

There are transport accidents, like the sinking of the *Titanic* or the Concorde crash. And then there are transmission accidents or failures of electronic media and information technology.

Transport accidents are localised. The passenger liner *Titanic* hit an iceberg in the North Atlantic Ocean on a Sunday night in April 1912. It sank within hours, with over 1,500 lives lost.

The supersonic jet Concorde crashed into a suburban Paris hotel soon after taking off from Charles de Gaulle airport on Tuesday July 25th 2000. All the passengers and crew were killed. Concorde was retired from service three years later.

Transmission accidents tend to have a global dimension. On October 19th 1987, known as 'Black Monday', stock markets around the world crashed. Stock prices first plunged in Hong Kong, then in London and Europe and finally in New York and North America. The Dow Jones Industrial Average index dropped 500 points in one day.

The electronic interdependence of big financial institutions combined with the use of automatic computerised trading had created the conditions for global catastrophe. On Black Monday, a price signal was caught in a vicious feedback loop that nearly upended the whole financial system.

The screening-out of human factors in computerised trading had led not to infinite growth but instead to unpredictable mathematical events such as the cusp catastrophe.

On May 6th 2010, the Dow Jones Industrial Average index dropped 600 points in six minutes. This was the Flash Crash. It threatened a trillion-dollar write-off. High-frequency trading algorithms had automatically responded to a large sell order at 13 seconds after 2.45pm and, for the next 14 seconds, there was a potentially catastrophic downward spiral of prices. Only the fail-safe delay of the Chicago Mercantile Exchange, with its margin of five seconds, was able to spare enough time for human traders to fix the problem.

There's a limit to human response times. The fastest someone can physically react to a stimulus is within 1,000 milliseconds. The fastest that a chess grandmaster can mentally process a move is in 650 milliseconds. There's a whole world stretching beyond the 650-millisecond mark. It's here where computerised trading algorithms have their existence.

If a financial organisation has a faster algorithm than its competitors, it has an advantage over them in the market. This logic is currently driving a billion-dollar technological arms race to push computer processing times far beyond human response times. The speed of algorithmic activity is now limited only by the speed of light.

A new dedicated transatlantic cable is being built just to shave five milliseconds off transatlantic communication times between US and UK traders, while a new purpose-built chip iX-eCute is being launched which prepares trades in 740 nanoseconds.

Neil Johnson et al, 'Financial black swans
driven by ultrafast machine ecology' (2012)

3 Manson Family Murders (Psychoactive Drug Accident)

Local Accident Investigation Report

3.1 Root Cause: Military Development of Psychoactive Drugs

When US General 'Ike' Eisenhower's armed forces liberated the concentration camp at Dachau towards the end of the Second World War, they discovered that Nazi scientists had been conducting inhuman experiments on the inmates. They duly captured Nazi physician Kurt Plotner.

Plotner had spiked the drinks of incarcerated Jews and Soviet prisoners of war with the hallucinogen mescaline in his search for a truth serum. Mescaline is a quasi-synthetic extract of the peyote cactus. Plotner hoped that the mind-altering properties of the drug would loosen tongues sufficiently for it to be used as an interrogation tool. He achieved mixed results. Prisoners were prompted to speak quite openly about their hatred for their captors but only revealed military secrets under exceptional circumstances.

In October 1945, intelligence officers from the US Navy and the Office of Strategic Services (OSS), the forerunner of the CIA, included two pages on Plotner's mescaline experiments in their 300-page report on the activities of the Nazi doctors at Dachau. The Navy recruited Plotner and he was given a new identity in postwar Germany. This episode was part of Operation Paperclip, a US intelligence programme designed to grab hold of defeated

German scientists and put them to use in the emerging Cold War against the Soviet Union.

The US Navy set up Project CHATTER in 1947 to replicate Plotner's mescaline experiments. They too were looking for a truth drug. The project was headed up by Lieutenant Charles Savage and based at the Naval Medical Research Institute in Bethesda, Maryland. Within a few years, Savage had replaced mescaline in his experiments with LSD – a wholly synthetic hallucinogenic drug first manufactured by the Swiss pharmaceutical company Sandoz Laboratories in 1943.

Studies on normal control subjects: Sample protocol
0600 Subject took 20 micrograms.

...

1345 Pupils now 5 mm. and react slowly to light and accommodation. He complains of sirens, tuning whistles and Morse code, and compares their intensity with that of a motor audible in the vicinity. (There was then no motor running.) He sees brightly coloured birds and hears them singing. He complains that blood pressure cuff causes extreme pain. He then complained that the drug had transformed him into a 'television set', because the paresthesias in his face and extremities seemed identical with the ripples and fadeout of the television screen. He believed that through this drug one could control others by sending out impulses which would be picked up by whoever took the drug. Subject was unaware of the bizarre nature of this idea.

LSD-25: A Clinical Psychological Study, Charles Savage, Medical Corps, US Navy, 9th September 1951

During the Korean War, US intelligence claimed that Soviet-backed North Korean forces used drugs and hypnosis to 'brain-wash' American prisoners of war. When the Korean War came to an end in 1953, the US Navy wrapped up Project CHATTER.

The CIA began its own experiments with LSD in 1950 when it set up Project BLUEBIRD, which was renamed ARTICHOKE in 1951 and MKULTRA in 1953. Sydney Gottlieb joined the CIA in

1951 as head of the Chemical Division of the Technical Services Staff and he masterminded MKULTRA from the beginning. The aim of the project was to research not just enhanced interrogation but also mind control and behaviour modification.

A portion of the Research and Development Program of TSS/Chemical Division is devoted to the discovery of the following materials and methods:

1. Substances which will promote illogical thinking and impulsiveness to the point where the recipient would be discredited in public.

...

6. Materials which will render the induction of hypnosis easier or otherwise enhance its usefulness.

7. Substances which will enhance the ability of individuals to withstand privation, torture and coercion during interrogation and so-called 'brainwashing'.

8. Materials and physical methods which will produce amnesia for events preceding and during their use.

...

11. Substances which will produce 'pure' euphoria with no subsequent let-down.

12. Substances which alter personality structure in such a way that the tendency of the recipient to become dependent upon another person is enhanced.

CIA Project MKULTRA memo, 8th April 1955

The scope of MKULTRA was vast. In the 1950s and early 1960s, the project covertly funded LSD experiments at 80 institutions, including 44 universities, 15 research foundations and pharmaceutical companies, 12 hospitals and 3 prisons.

Many of these institutions gave LSD to unsuspecting Americans who were in no position to fight for their rights. They included mental patients, prisoners, drug addicts and sex workers.

Other MKULTRA experiments with LSD involved willing test subjects such as CIA employees, military officers and college students.

The CIA used many front organisations to funnel MKULTRA money to universities and colleges. For example, in 1959 they set up the Human Ecology Fund as a financial source for experiments at Harvard University in Cambridge, Massachusetts, as well as John Hopkins University in Baltimore, Maryland, and Stanford University near Berkeley, California.

At Harvard University psychiatric researcher, Timothy Leary, set up the Harvard Psilocybin Project in 1960. Psilocybin is the synthetic version of a psychoactive compound found in magic mushrooms. Leary used it together with a variant on the Freudian talking cure to test the effectiveness of psychedelic therapy.

Leary tested psilocybin on 32 inmates at Concord State Prison in Massachusetts to discover whether he could change their behaviour and reduce reoffending rates. He also supervised the testing of ten divinity postgrad students from the Andover Newton Theological School in Massachusetts to find out if psilocybin could enhance religious experience.

In 1962, Leary set up the International Federation for Internal Freedom, swapped psilocybin for LSD and began to run more informal psychedelic experiments with Harvard students. In 1963, he was fired from Harvard, together with his right-hand man Richard Alpert.

Meanwhile, doctors at Stanford University were conducting LSD experiments at Menlo Park Veterans Hospital as part of MKULTRA. In 1959, Stanford postgrad Ken Kesey volunteered to take part in one of the studies as a paid test subject. He wrote up his experiences for the doctors by day and, by night, started work on a novel.

3.2 Timeline: Civilian Adoption of Psychoactive Drugs

After quitting Harvard University, Leary's continuing LSD experiments were funded by the young heirs to the Mellon family fortune, who set him up in a mansion in the old Quaker village of Millbrook in New York state.

Leary and Alpert surrounded themselves with willing young disciples and began to develop an interest in Eastern mysticism. Leary arranged LSD sessions in which he exchanged the role of PhD supervisor for that of self-appointed priest, guiding his initiates on an LSD trip designed to coincide with the after-life trajectory of the *Tibetan Book of the Dead*. The idea was that a psychonaut would undergo a symbolic death in order to achieve a spiritual rebirth. It was all very high-minded.

Things were very different on the West Coast. Kesey published his LSD-inspired novel, *One Flew Over the Cuckoo's Nest*, in 1962 and it was an immediate commercial hit. He bought a log cabin at La Honda in the Santa Cruz Mountains outside San Francisco and began throwing wild parties known as 'Acid Tests'. Once celebrants had taken LSD at one of the parties, they were expected to survive a dark night of the soul in the woods. Here, Kesey and his gang of 'Merry Pranksters' had painted trees with fluorescent colours, hidden speakers blasting out dissonant music and secreted unexpected and slightly terrifying guests such as visiting Hell's Angels.

In 1964, the success of Kesey's second novel meant he had to travel to New York. He decided to take the Acid Tests on the road and, together with his Merry Pranksters, hired an old school bus for the cross-country trip. Arriving on the East Coast, Kesey and his band visited Millbrook, but Leary was on a three-day trip upstairs in the mansion and too busy to receive them. They weren't even offered any LSD.

It was no surprise. Leary was an East Coast elitist used to surviving on handouts – first government grants and then donations from the *haute bourgeoisie*. He was a university man interested in esoteric religion and sacred literature. Kesey, on the other hand, was a West Coast neo-primitivist and gifted entrepreneur, a man of the people obsessed with backwoods shamanism and dirty rock music.

Back on the West Coast, Kesey tapped into the LSD being manufactured in a bathroom lab in Berkeley by Grateful Dead sound engineer and self-taught chemist Owsley 'Bear' Stanley.

The Pranksters gradually accumulated enough White Li
Blue Dots, Monterey Purple and other Owsley tabs to move the
Acid Tests into wider public spaces. In 1965, there were parties at
Muir Beach, Palo Alto and Portland, Oregon. In 1966, there were
festivals in San Francisco and Los Angeles.

The stand-out event was the Trips Festival, a three-day rave
held at the Longshoremen's Hall in San Francisco. Ten thousand
people came to the sold-out event in January 1966. They grooved
to the music of psychedelic rock bands such as the Grateful Dead,
Jefferson Airplane and Big Brother and the Holding Company,
guzzled the punch spiked with LSD and tripped out to the light
shows and nude dancing girl routines.

In August 1966, the Beatles, whose rock music had been a
massive commercial presence in the US since 1964, released an
album containing a psychedelic track, 'Tomorrow Never Knows',
whose lyrics borrowed from Leary and Alpert's texts. It was played
on FM radio stations across the country.

In October 1966, LSD became illegal in California, signaling
that the West Coast acid rock scene would struggle to survive for
much longer.

In June 1967, the Beatles released an album dominated by the
sounds and mind-expanding philosophies of psychedelic rock.
Sgt. Pepper's Lonely Hearts Club Band spent the next 15 weeks at
the top of the charts in the US. The album became the soundtrack
to the 'Summer of Love', an LSD-fuelled social experiment in com-
munal living, anti-family-values behaviour and free love which
took place in San Francisco, particularly in the 25-block Haight-
Ashbury neighbourhood.

You're born a citizen of a nation.

A citizen of a nation with rulers who legislate rules commanding you
to be free.

...

Free to have your freedom regulated by officers who are your friends
and who protect you.

PROTECT you from obscenity.
PROTECT you from loitering.
PROTECT you from nudity.
PROTECT you from sedition and subversion.
PROTECT you from marijauna, LSD, DURGS. [sic]
PROTECT you from gambling.
PROTECT you from homosexuality.
PROTECT you from statutory rape.
PROTECT you from common-law marriage.
PROTECT you from abortion.
PROTECT you from lonely you.
PROTECT you from demonstrations against your protectors.

San Francisco Digger sheet, 1966

The Haight in 1967 was a spontaneous acid test taking place in the streets, self-organised by a lumpen population of college students, vacationing high-school kids, runaways, drug addicts, weekending military personnel, middle-class bohemians and ex-convicts. The scene was shot through with anti-government feeling, suspicion of the consumer society and sympathy for the Black Power movement. It was almost as if this were a rehearsal for a new post-welfare society in which public institutions – universities, schools, prisons, hospitals and military bases – would give up their responsibility for maintaining the warfare-readiness of the population and leave them instead to fend for themselves.

In 1967, Sydney Gottlieb got a CIA promotion. He moved out of the Chemical Division to head up the Technical Services Staff as a whole. Project MKULTRA was scaled back.

At the end of 1967, Owsley Stanley was arrested in a suburb of San Francisco with 350,000 tabs of LSD on his hands. His lab was shut down.

3.3 Effect: Psychoactive Drug Accidents

The invention of the psychedelic experience was also the invention of the bad trip. The flipside of the pioneering acid freak was the permanently damaged acid casualty. Blowing your mind was always a risk when using LSD to expand your consciousness.

From the beginning of MKULTRA, Gottlieb was in the habit of playfully spiking the drinks of CIA agents on the Technical Services Staff. When this happened to Frank Olson in November 1953, he had a breakdown, was sent to see a CIA doctor in New York and then, somehow, crashed out of the window of his 13th-floor hotel room in Manhattan. He died of his injuries.

The psychedelic rock music scene generated a high number of casualties, who were immediately romanticised by the media as martyrs to the cause of psychic liberation. Californian musician Brian Wilson, for example, wanted to follow up the success of the hit Beach Boys single 'Good Vibrations' in 1966 with an epic concept album which he described as a 'teenage anthem to God'. *Smile* was released only in fragmentary form in 2004, after decades of LSD-inspired self-destructive behaviour by Wilson.

Hippy San Francisco during the Summer of Love also had its dark underside. Intensively covered by the media, the Haight became a social magnet for no-hopers and idealists alike. In a matter of weeks its population ballooned from 10,000 to 75,000. The city's public services were unable to cope with the sudden influx of transients and there was a spike in drug abuse, petty crime, homelessness and panhandling.

Into this environment of social breakdown and cultural revolution came Charlie Manson, musician, car thief and small-time pimp. Released from a Los Angeles federal prison in March 1967, he moved to the Haight, got himself a crash pad on Cole Street and, at the age of 33, adopted the hippie lifestyle – dropping acid at Grateful Dead shows, playing his guitar on the street for dimes, heading up a commune of runaway teenagers and assembling a makeshift religious cult loosely based on the Process Church of the Final Judgment.

Manson lived in the Haight throughout the Summer of Love. At the bitter end of it, in November, he packed his 'Family' of submissive young girls into a converted school bus and by the summer of 1968 was hanging out in Los Angeles. Here, he handed out drugs and girls to gain favour with people in the music industry. He was hoping to become a rock star. Dennis Wilson from the Beach Boys was on the lookout for singer-songwriters now that his brother Brian Wilson was in LSD-fuelled decline. He duly stole one of Manson's songs.

Burned by the Los Angeles music scene, Manson and his Family retreated to the edge of the Mojave Desert. At the end of 1968, he heard the Beatles' 'White Album' and was enthralled by its comedown mood of disenchantment and foreboding. He imagined that the Beatles had encoded secret messages in the songs that were meant specially for him and the Family. He began to prepare for an imminent social breakdown.

Hunkered down around the camp fire on the Spahn Ranch in 1969, amidst broken-down sets from the old Hollywood movie *The Outlaw*, Manson handed out tabs of Orange Sunshine to his teenage groupies while his sideman Bobby Beausoleil strummed the guitar. The acid had been made by Owsley Stanley's young lab protégé Tim Scully and distributed by the Brotherhood of Eternal Love, a Leary-style religious cult. Manson, according to his prosecutor Vincent Bugliosi, recounted his vision of the Apocalypse to his followers as the flames danced before their eyes.

The Beatles, said Charlie, had picked up on black American music and made the White Album. Now he and his band, the Manson Family, would pick up on the White Album and make the Black Album. This collection of songs would be listened to across North America and brainwash teenagers into believing that rape, theft and murder were no longer crimes but the free expressions of an altered state of consciousness. According to Bugliosi, Manson had it all planned out.

Manson believed that his songs would incite white kids to join forces with black folks who, having only just recently claimed the civil rights that had been their due since the abolition of slavery, were eager to take their revenge upon the older white generation who had kept them in bondage for so long. The Black Album, said Charlie, would trigger an apocalyptic civil war.

Manson prophesied that the Family would survive the coming war by hiding out in a desert valley, where he said he'd found one of the entrances to the bottomless pit where Satan had been imprisoned by God. After the war, Manson and his followers would emerge from the 'devil's hole' and establish a new enlightened government of North America. Manson's camp-fire vision was nothing if not a particularly dark and grandiose acid trip.

Here was Leary's cycle of death and rebirth, initially conceived as an individual spiritual transformation, now projected outwards on a social – and indeed cosmic – scale. Manson took the last book of the Bible, the Book of Revelation, rather than the *Tibetan Book of the Dead*, as his trip manual. He imagined that the world would end soon and a new Heaven and Earth would take its place.

The problem for Manson was that he'd only written a few songs and had blown his chance to make an album back in Los Angeles. The radical moment in American politics was already passing away. He'd missed his mark. As a result – again, according to Bugliosi – Manson decided to take direct action. In the summer of 1969, he organised the Family into death squads and sent them out into the hills of California to cut up rich white people at random, use their blood to spell out Beatles lyrics on the walls and spread terror across North America through the national newspapers.

At the end of 1969, Manson and the Family were arrested for seven murders. Manson was prosecuted by Bugliosi, found guilty in 1971 of directing the murders and put back in jail.

I am no more than you let me be. This is the last time around and if you believe in yourself, believe in me, for I am in you as you in me.

Charlie Manson's open letter to Tim Leary, 9th October 1970

Timothy Leary was jailed in 1973 for various drug offences and put into the cell next to Manson in Folsom Prison in California.

In 1973, the CIA officially halted Project MKULTRA. Its god-father, Sydney Gottlieb, had retired the year before. Most of the MKULTRA files were destroyed. The work had been done.

4 Challenger *Disaster (Rocket Accident)*

Local Accident Investigation Report

4.1 Root Cause: Military Development of Rockets

In December 1941, the German chancellor Adolf Hitler declared war on the US, having conquered western Europe in a blitzkrieg advance that halted at the edge of the continent. Siding with British prime minister Winston Churchill, US president Franklin Roosevelt established American airbases on the British Isles off the coast of Hitler's Europe. From here, fleets of Allied bombers took off to fly long-range missions over Germany, flattening its cities as they took command of European airspace.

One of the American tech companies that supported the air war was Aerojet. Co-owned by rocket engineer Jack Parsons, the California-based company designed experimental thrusters to help lift overloaded bombers into the air so they could fly treetop-skimming night raids over Europe. Parsons had been a rocket enthusiast since he was a teenager. In the late 1920s, he began a short-lived correspondence with fellow rocket fan, Wernher von Braun, who was at boarding school in Germany. They talked on the phone for hours.

Like Parsons, von Braun found his passion for rockets was something the military were keen to exploit. During the 1930s, he designed experimental rockets for the German Army under the command of the artillery officer, Walter Dornberger. When Hitler launched his European war, Dornberger moved his research team to Peenemunde on the Baltic coast of Germany. In October 1942, von Braun successfully launched his V-2 rocket. A film of the test was shown to a delighted Hitler in his bunker complex situated in what is now Poland.

The first Allied bombing raid on Peenemunde took place in August 1943. Hitler's armaments minister Albert Speer immediately ordered Dornberger to move his production facility underground for safety. The V-2 assembly lines were relocated under the Harz Mountains in the middle of Germany, near the town of Nordhausen.

The underground Mittelwerk factory at Nordhausen used thousands of prisoners from Dora-Mittelbau, originally a part of the Buchenwald concentration camp, to assemble the V-2 rockets. Over 20,000 men were worked to death.

Twelve hours per day or night – eighteen hours when we rotated teams – we must carry on our back extremely heavy equipment in and out of the tunnel. With almost nothing in our stomach; under the rain, snow, mud, in extremely cold weather; clothed in a poor outfit, wood clogs with fabric on top which get hooked in everything – and under the beatings of the SS and the kapos.

Michel Depierre, Mittelwerk survivor, as told to
US 104th Infantry Division

Mittelwerk produced its first V-2 rockets at the start of 1944 and was visited many times by von Braun.

Starting in September 1944, the Nazis fired over 3,000 V-2 missiles against Allied targets, mainly in London. They stockpiled the rockets in northern France and launched them from rapidly assembled mobile sites – often on a road in a forest – in the Netherlands. Each 50-foot rocket was capable of hurling a one-ton warhead high into the sky and then hundreds of miles downrange to its target across the English Channel.

The V-2 rocket attacks were intended as revenge on the Allies for their bombing raids over Europe. The Nazis referred to them as 'wonder-weapons' and hoped they would magically turn back Allied armed forces, which had invaded western Europe in June 1944 under the command of General 'Ike' Eisenhower. They had no such effect.

In April 1945, Eisenhower's forces took the Harz Mountains. They recovered a number of V-2 missiles from the Mittelwerk factory and shipped them back to the US. They also freed the slave labourers remaining at Buchenwald. When they got to Dora-Mittelbau, they found the camp largely empty, the Nazis having evacuated it some days before.

With stretchers in our hands, we ran into the nearest building. As soon as we entered, we had to face the ugly reality. There was human flesh and bones everywhere on the pavement. We found rows of skeletons just covered by a yellow skin which looked like paper. There was group after group of men, lying on the ground, starved, pitiful and covered with human excrement.

Sergeant Ragene Farris, 329th Medical Battalion,
US 104th Infantry Division

On June 1st, the V-2 rocket production facilities were officially handed over to the Soviets. Joseph Stalin's forces had repulsed the Nazi invasion of the Soviet Union at Stalingrad in 1943 and entered Germany territory in late 1944. According to the terms of the Yalta Conference between Stalin, Roosevelt and Churchill in February 1945, Nordhausen fell into the Soviet zone of occupation.

As the war came to an end, Dornberger, von Braun and other key V-2 rocket scientists made sure they were captured by Allied rather than Soviet troops.

In August 1945, new US president Harry Truman approved Operation Paperclip, a project run by the OSS, the wartime prototype of the CIA, to transfer top German scientists from the shattered remnants of the Nazi war machine to the US. Closely involved in its execution was Allen Dulles, a high-ranking OSS officer stationed in neutral Switzerland throughout the war.

Truman ordered that no Nazis were to be picked up by Operation Paperclip. The OSS, however, did not want any Nazi scientists to be recruited by the Soviets or the British. They made sure the credentials of Nazis such as von Braun were secretly laundered. Soon, top Nazi scientists were safely embedded in the US postwar military-industrial complex of aerospace programmes, defence agencies, warfare manufacturing plants and medical research labs.

Dornberger went to work for the US Air Force on guided missiles at Dayton, Ohio. Eventually, he became part of the Strategic Air Command project to design missiles capable of taking over from B-47 bombers as delivery systems for nuclear weapons.

Wernher von Braun was moved to Redstone Arsenal in Alabama and developed his V-2 rockets for the US Army at White Sands Missile Range in New Mexico.

Meanwhile, in October 1946, the Soviets transferred the Nazi rocket engineers they'd captured at Nordhausen to a missile research bureau, NII-88, in the suburbs of Moscow. They lived in a barbed-wire compound on an island and were tasked with rebuilding the V-2. In November 1950, they delivered the R-1 missile – a copy of the V-2 – to the Soviet army.

An offshoot of the missile bureau known as OKB-1 was headed up by Soviet rocket planner Sergei Korolev in 1950. He supervised successive design iterations of the R-1 until in 1957 an R-7 rocket successfully launched the Sputnik satellite into Earth orbit. Four years later, it was again an R-7, launched from Baikonur Cosmodrome in the Kazakh Steppe, that sent the first man into space. The cosmonaut Yuri Gagarin was celebrated as a Soviet hero.

4.2 Timeline: Civilian Adoption of Rockets

In 1958, US president 'Ike' Eisenhower created NASA as a civilian space agency designed to encourage the peaceful applications of rocket science. Wernher von Braun was reluctant to leave the US Army and become part of a civilian organisation, but when Eisenhower threatened to cut his funding, he complied.

Von Braun joined NASA in October 1959 and a year later, NASA's Marshall Space Flight Center was opened at Redstone Arsenal in Alabama. It was a simple office move for von Braun and his team.

The Marshall Center's first major project was the development of the Saturn rocket to carry satellites and manned spacecraft into Earth orbit and beyond. In 1961, US president John F Kennedy promised to send a man to the Moon by the end of the decade. On July 16th 1969, von Braun's huge Saturn V rocket took off from a platform in Florida, launching the crew of Apollo 11 on its eight-day journey to the Moon and back. The launch was attended by a million members of the public and 5,000 press people. Over a seventh of the world's population watched it on TV.

Over the next three years, Saturn V rockets enabled six teams of astronauts to complete the same lunar mission. The Apollo spaceflights became a form of mass entertainment. But as TV ratings declined and NASA's budget came under scrutiny, the Saturn V rocket-building programme was seen as hugely extravagant – especially given that each rocket was jettisoned after launch.

In 1969, US president Nixon ordered NASA to stop building any more Saturn V rockets and invest instead in the design of a space shuttle with reusable rockets. In 1970, NASA cancelled its last three Apollo missions. The unused Saturn V rockets were shipped to various American museums.

In 1981, NASA launched its first space shuttle into Earth orbit from Florida. Its two rockets were jettisoned into the Atlantic Ocean after burnout and later recovered for reuse. The shuttle itself returned to Earth under its own power and landed at Edwards Air Force base in California two days later.

4.3 Effect: Rocket Accidents

Where there are rocket launches, there are rocket explosions. In fact, part of the success of von Braun's career in the US Army can be attributed to a rocket failure. In December 1957, he predicted the failure of a rival rocket design by the US Navy. When the Vanguard rocket disintegrated into flames on its Florida launchpad two seconds after lift-off, von Braun successfully pitched the US Department of Defense for the Navy contract. Just 84 days later he launched the Explorer satellite into space using one of his intermediate range ballistic missiles.

The Soviet attempt to put a man on the Moon was a disaster from start to finish. In 1961, chief rocket engineer Sergei Korolev began to design the mammoth N1 rocket as the Soviet counterpart to the American Saturn V. Korolev's health was deteriorating and he died in 1966. Four test launches of the N1 took place between 1969 and 1972. They all failed. In fact, the second launch resulted in the destruction of the launch complex as well as the rocket. In 1976, Soviet Premier Leonid Brezhnev cancelled the N1 programme. It was kept secret until two years before the collapse of the Soviet Union.

By contrast, the failure of the space shuttle *Challenger* launch in 1986 was seen live on TV by a generation of American children. They'd been assembled in schools across the US to watch the first teacher travel into outer space as part of NASA's space education programme. The *Challenger* craft exploded over the Atlantic Ocean seconds after launch.

One of the two rockets designed to lift the craft from its Florida launch pad, the solid fuel burning at a rate of 9,000 pounds per second, had failed. The craft broke up in the sky, killing all seven American astronauts onboard.

Within an hour, news of the disaster had spread around the world. The image of the *Challenger* fireball was constantly replayed on TV screens, the sinister plume of smoke signalling the end of the American dream of interplanetary space flight. The NASA space shuttle programme was grounded for three years after the *Challenger* disaster and finally cancelled in 2011.

5　Biosphere 2 Collapse (Space Medicine Accident)

Local Accident Investigation Report

5.1　Root Cause: Military Development of Space Medicine

US president Franklin Roosevelt joined forces with British prime minister Winston Churchill at the end of 1941 in the struggle against Adolf Hitler's Nazi war machine. The Royal Air Force had already defeated the Luftwaffe, the German air force, in the skies over the British Isles in 1940. At the start of 1942, Allied forces began a bombing campaign over Nazi-occupied Europe in a successful bid for air supremacy over the western part of the continent.

Allied bombers flew as high as possible to avoid German ground fire and Luftwaffe interceptors. The US Air Force high-altitude B-17 'Flying Fortresses' flew as high as 20,000 feet on their bombing runs. On their return journeys, they were able to reach 35,000 feet, just edging into the stratosphere. It was the job of the Luftwaffe Messerschmitt Bf 109 aircraft to shoot them down.

Both the Allies and the Nazis were researching the limits of human performance in the cockpit at high altitudes. It was known that the higher the altitude, the lower the distribution of oxygen, as atmospheric pressure fell. Above 10,000 feet, pilots would suffer from hypoxia (a lack of oxygen in the brain) as well as decompression sickness (or 'the bends'). There would be disorientation followed by loss of consciousness and then death.

Oxygen masks had been made available to pilots for many years. But now scientists were working on concepts such as the pressurised cabin and the pressurised flying suit.

The Luftwaffe doctor with the most interest in devising solutions to extending 'the time of useful consciousness' – as he put it – of the high-altitude pilot was Hubertus Strughold. As director of the Luftwaffe Institute of Aviation Medicine, Strughold attended a medical conference at Nuremberg in October 1942, where Luftwaffe Medical Service doctor Sigmund Rascher gave a paper on the research he had conducted into high altitude sickness and decompression sickness at Dachau concentration camp.

Dachau was not a death camp like Auschwitz but a slave labour camp. It was filled first with political dissidents and then with Jews, gypsies, Jehovah's Witnesses and gay men. From February to May 1942, Rascher used a sealed low-pressure chamber – able to simulate altitudes of up to 68,000 feet – to experiment on camp inmates at Block No. 5. The prisoners were led into the chamber, locked in and then watched through a window as the air pressure was turned down and they began to suffer from oxygen starvation. At least 80 men died in these experiments and many were badly injured.

The Luftwaffe delivered here at the concentration camp at Dachau a cabinet constructed of wood and metal measuring one meter square and two meters high. It was possible in this cabinet to either decrease or increase the air pressure. You could observe through a little window the reaction of the subject inside the chamber. The purpose of these experiments in the cabinet was to test human energy and the subject's capacity and ability to take large amounts of pure oxygen and then to test his reaction to a gradual decrease of oxygen – almost approaching infinity. This amounted to a vacuum chamber in what had been a pressure chamber at the beginning of the experiment. Such prisoners were chosen for these experiments upon written request which was sent to Berlin. Suggested names of prisoners in this camp were sent and authorization was received here in camp. Then the experiment was begun.

> Anton Pacholegg testimony taken at Dachau on 13th May 1945
> by US 7th Army Colonel David Chavez, Jr (later submitted to
> the Nuremburg trials as prosecution document PS-2428)

In April 1945, the Nazis withdrew from Dachau, leaving 30,000 surviving inmates to be liberated by the US 7th Army.

Hubertus Strughold was one of the German scientists to benefit from Operation Paperclip. The OSS – the wartime forerunners of the CIA – transferred over 1,500 German scientists and technicians to the US in the aftermath of the war. Strughold and five colleagues were assigned to the US Air Force School of Aviation Medicine at Randolph Air Force Base near San Antonio, Texas in 1947.

In 1951, Strughold suggested that outer space starts much lower – at about 50,000 feet – than conventionally thought. This meant that manned rocket flight was effectively a form of space flight.

In 1952, Strughold supervised the drawing up of a blueprint for a sealed low-pressure chamber similar to the one used at Dachau. The US Air Force commissioned the chamber from Chicago's Guardite Corporation, which up until then had been making vacuum dehydration machines for the meat-packing industry. When it was delivered to Randolph Air Force Base in 1954, Strughold named it the 'space cabin simulator' – even though it was not able to simulate the weightlessness typical of space flight.

The chamber contained enough room for a test pilot to sit on an aircraft seat in an artificially maintained low-pressure atmosphere typical of high-altitude flight. The US Air Force team ran a series of psychological and physiological tests on their human subjects. They measured the effects of exposure to an oxygen-enriched atmosphere, the stress and fatigue produced by prolonged confinement and the effects of rapid decompression and recompression.

In February 1958, Airman Donald F Farrell spent seven days in the chamber and was greeted by an excited crowd of news reporters upon his exit.

In June 1958, the US Air Force drew up a plan to put a man on the Moon by the mid-1960s. The first phase of the plan, 'Man in Space Soonest', featured the blueprint for a steel space craft which was basically a modified version of the space cabin simulator. The craft was a bell-shaped capsule eight feet in diameter, its rounded head containing a heat shield and its flared base housing a series of small retrorockets. The pilot was expected to lie on his back in the pressurised cabin – while wearing a pressure suit for extra safety.

One of the nine test pilots shortlisted as candidates for the air force moonshot was Neil Armstrong.

5.2 Timeline: Civilian Adoption of Space Medicine

When US president 'Ike' Eisenhower founded the civilian space agency NASA in July 1958, it ended the possibility of military spaceflight. In August 1958, the US Air Force cancelled its 'Man in Space Soonest' plan. Two months later, with Project Mercury, NASA picked up where the Air Force had left off. They put a man in space just three years later.

In 1960, NASA created Project Apollo with the aim of putting a man on the Moon. The *Apollo* spacecraft was a three-man version of the one-man craft designed by NASA engineer Maxime Faget for Mercury. With its conical shape, heat shield and bottom-heavy service module, the *Apollo* craft had design features in common with the US Air Force's original plans for a bell-shaped capsule.

In 1962, Hubertus Strughold moved from the US Air Force to NASA to work on Project Apollo. As chief scientist of the agency's Aerospace Medical Division, he played a key role in developing life-support systems and pressure suits for the Apollo astronauts.

5.3 Effect: Space Medicine Accidents

When a few men are sealed inside a pressurised cabin for several days, fully suited up and breathing canned oxygen, there's a lot that can potentially go wrong.

The very first *Apollo* mission was aborted after a disastrous test in January 1967. During a launch simulation at Cape Kennedy Air Force Station Launch Complex 34 in Florida, the space capsule caught fire, killing all three astronauts trapped inside. A spark inside the cabin ignited the oxygen-rich atmosphere, punching a hole in the cabin, melting the men's pressure suits and exposing them to the smoke of the fire. They died of carbon monoxide poisoning within seconds.

The general content of this transmission consists of what appears to be three separate phrases. It has been interpreted several ways by many listeners. The following is a list of some of the interpretations that have been made:

1. They're fighting a bad fire – Let's get out ...Open 'er up.
2. We've got a bad fire – Let's get out ...We're burning up.
3. I'm reporting a bad fire ...I'm getting out ...

This transmission ended with a cry of pain. Some listeners believe this transmission was made by the Pilot.

Bell Telephone Laboratory analysis of the last five-second radio transmission on the Apollo 1 crew voice-tapes, as included in the 1967 NASA report on the Apollo 1 accident (known technically as 'Report of Apollo 204 Review Board')

However, it was always the consensus among the pioneers of space medicine that it was not the physiological but the psychological effects of prolonged confinement that posed the greater hazard to human spaceflight.

This was certainly demonstrated by what happened to the eight people who in 1991 entered 'Biosphere 2', a sealed three-acre greenhouse complex built by a private consortium in the Arizona desert. They were meant to stay inside for two years and test the feasibility of living in a self-sufficient space colony. However, as oxygen levels began to fall and food production flatlined, the group split into two bitterly opposed factions. They spent most of their time squabbling and fighting. In the end, the experiment lasted for only a year before the plug was pulled.

6 7/7 London Bombings (Television Accident)

Local Accident Investigation Report

6.1 Root Cause: Military Development of Television

Britain and France both declared war on Nazi Germany when its armed forces invaded Poland in September 1939. In a series of lightning attacks, the Nazi war machine rapidly conquered not just Poland but also Denmark, Norway, the Netherlands, Belgium and Luxembourg. Advancing through the Ardennes Forest, the German tank regiments entered France in May 1940, forcing an evacuation of British troops from the French port of Dunkirk, back across the English Channel. In June 1940, Hitler staged a victory parade in Paris.

Hitler's plans for an invasion of Britain depended upon air minister Hermann Goring first gaining command of the airspace over England. In July 1940, the Luftwaffe began a series of daylight bombing raids against shipping in the English Channel, coastal ports and Royal Air Force (RAF) airfields in south-east England. They also ran night attacks against aircraft production facilities in the Midlands and the west of England.

Located in south-west England, at Worth Matravers just outside the port of Swanage, was the Air Ministry radar research unit later to be known as the Telecommunications Research Establishment (TRE). It was here that expansions and upgrades to the coastal ring of early warning radar stations – technically known as Chain Home – took place.

Chain Home had been rapidly developed before the war as a counter-measure to potential German invasion. During the Battle of Britain, this defensive radar system enabled RAF fighter planes to intercept enemy bombers as they flew towards the south and east coasts of England. To speed up deployment, each 'radio-location' station – consisting of a set of steel transmitter towers pointed towards Europe and a smaller set of wooden receiver towers together with a receiver hut – was built from off-the-shelf components. The one exception to this rule was a specially designed cathode ray tube, essentially a television screen, which displayed the deflected radar signal on a cabinet inside the receiver hut.

TRE's Geoffrey Dummer had originally commissioned a visual display unit from manufacturers A C Cossor (which after the war was bought up by Raytheon). The screen had to be high quality because the success of any radar station at detecting and tracking enemy aircraft depended upon the clarity of the signals displayed. The Women's Auxiliary Air Force (WAAF) operators developed some formidable skills at extracting signals from very noisy data. But it wasn't enough.

The big weakness of the Chain Home system was that it was able to track enemy aircraft only as they approached. Once they passed overhead, aircraft had to be tracked by human observers on the ground. As a result, it was particularly difficult for the RAF to intercept enemy bombing raids at night. It was for this reason that Dummer in mid-1940 developed a new radar display system – later known as the plan position indicator. This enabled the deflected signals from a now rotating transmitter tower to indicate the presence of aircraft all around. The WAAF operators could now track enemy bombers as they flew inland.

The real-time status of the radar signal was indicated by a line which, synched to the movement of the transmitter tower, swept around the screen like the hand on a clock-face. Initially, the only way to capture the information received was to take a photograph of the screen. This data visualisation problem was solved by the introduction of a cathode ray tube able to keep an image alive about a second before fading. Technically known as an 'Iatron' tube, this screen was developed by Philo Farnsworth, an American Mormon technician credited as one of the inventors of television.

In September 1940, the Luftwaffe stepped up its night-time bombing raids of Britain in order to break the morale of the civilian population. These 'blitzes' targeted 16 British cities, including Birmingham, Liverpool, Plymouth, Bristol and Glasgow. London was attacked over 70 times, night after night.

The upgraded radar system enabled the RAF to target enemy bombers more effectively now they had a complete 360-degree view of the night sky. It also enabled interceptions to be arranged directly from WAAF operator screens (whereas, previously, they had been arranged from back-rooms – complete with table-top maps – which had captured data phoned through to them by the radar front-line operators).

The RAF's agile use of the new defensive radar systems (combined with the introduction of an offensive radar capability on-board the Bristol 'Beau' night-fighter) was increasingly successful. Interception rates of enemy aircraft doubled every month from January 1941 until Goring called off the Luftwaffe campaign in May 1941.

Radar Cover September 1941: Shetlands to Scillies

A year after the peak of the Battle of Britain, with the blitzes over, but the whole of Europe still occupied, the great radiolocation chain, like an all-protecting wall, surrounded the UK from north of the Shetlands to south of the Scillies for aircraft at 15,000 feet – a straight line distance of 900 miles.

'Radar', an article by Robert Watson-Wyatt (author of the original 1935 proposal for the Chain Home radar network), *Discovery* magazine, September 1945

Hitler never could marshal his forces to cross the English Channel. Repelled by the sophistication of Britain's invisible radar curtain, which enabled the RAF to eliminate the need for permanent fighter patrols and make the most of their limited resources, Hitler in March 1942 ordered the construction of a vast 'Atlantic Wall' of concrete fortifications stretching 1,670 miles from Norway to the border with Spain.

By means of proportionate allocation of forces, improvement of positions (perimeter defense), and stockpiling of supplies, the fortified areas and strongpoints must be enabled to hold out even against superior enemy forces for extended periods of time. Fortified areas and strongpoints are

to be held to the last. They must never be forced to surrender because of a
shortage of ammunition, rations, or water.

Fuhrer Directive No. 40, 23rd March 1942

The Atlantic Wall was an atavistic counter-measure to the British
radar curtain. When British and American troops finally invaded
western Europe on June 6th 1944, they overcame the defensive
enemy bunkers within mere hours.

Sitting on Eisenhower's communications staff was David
Sarnoff, the media chief who had headed up the electronics company RCA before the war. RCA owned the broadcasting company
NBC. It was Sarnoff who oversaw the expansion of NBC's radio
network so it could broadcast news of the Normandy landings to
the American public.

In August 1944, the Allies liberated Paris and Sarnoff
reactivated Radio France, which had been shut down by the Nazis.

6.2 Timeline: Civilian Adoption of Television

After the war, RCA led the way in bringing television to the
American public. RCA boss David Sarnoff had picked up on Philo
Farnsworth's invention in 1928 a year after it was announced.
He had fought – and lost – a costly patent battle with Farnsworth
during the early 1930s. By 1947, though, Farnsworth's patent had
expired and the way was clear for RCA to dominate the American
market in sales of TV sets.

RCA's subsidiary company NBC was one of the big three television networks – together with CBS and RCA spin-off ABC – that
by 1948 exercised a near monopoly of the American airwaves.
They were to broadcast news and entertainment shows to a mass
American audience for the next 40 years.

In 1950, the market research company Nielsen began to
measure the size of TV audiences. This helped the networks to price
up airtime, which they sold to advertising companies. TV shows
existed to capture audience attention and sell it to advertisers.

Much early TV programming before the invention of video-tape in 1957 was broadcast live from a New York stage or studio. Even when videotape was used to edit recordings before they were broadcast, it was so expensive that old shows were wiped as new ones were taped over them.

TV as a news medium came of age in 1963 during its coverage of the assassination of US president John F Kennedy in Dallas, Texas. Kennedy was shot and killed on a Friday afternoon, the Dallas police exhibited the suspected assassin Lee Oswald to the press on Saturday, the president was laid in state in Washington DC on the Sunday and on Monday – which was declared a national day of mourning – he was buried.

The big three TV networks covered the event live for four days straight without any of the usual commercial breaks. According to Nielsen, their coverage was watched by 93 per cent of American households. CBS was first to broadcast the news at 12:40pm on the Friday – beating NBC by less than a minute. It dominated the rest of the coverage and even ran all through the night on Sunday.

This programming format of round-the-clock real-time coverage of breaking global news was made the model for CNN when it launched in 1980. The network eclipsed the big three networks in 1991 when it broadcast live from Baghdad on the bombing of Iraq by a joint American and British air force during the first Gulf War.

The CNN global real-time news model became widespread in the late 1990s with the launch of Fox News Channel, BBC News 24 and Al Jazeera.

With the increasing accessibility of the internet and the growing affordability of semi-professional video cameras, groups and individuals in the early 2000s were able to make their own TV news reports and distribute them across websites and online forums. In 2005, the video-based YouTube platform launched on the internet and the one-man TV news show came of age.

6.3 Effect: Television Accidents

Accidents were a routine part of television broadcasting right from the beginning. There was no time for second takes by performers, newscasters or entertainers on live TV. Any fluffed lines or technical errors went out on the air. These moments were soon repackaged as 'bloopers'.

On Friday 22nd November 1963, one of the millions of viewers of the Kennedy assassination TV coverage was Dallas night-club owner Jack Ruby. Watching TV at his sister's house that evening, he saw John F Kennedy's widow Jackie arrive in Washington DC with her husband's body. She had refused to change clothes on the flight from Dallas and her Chanel suit was stained with blood. Ruby was highly agitated by the coverage. Unlike other viewers – whose only way of responding to the TV news was to fill in their Nielsen ratings diaries – Ruby decided to intercept the unfolding TV newscast. He armed himself with a .38 caliber Colt revolver.

NBC was first with live coverage of what happened next. As CBS and ABC broadcast the procession of Kennedy's body from the White House to the Capitol in Washington DC on Sunday, NBC in Dallas covered the transfer of suspected assassin Oswald from the Dallas police department to a new jail. As police officers escorted Oswald to an armoured truck in the basement of the police department, a man stepped forward from the assembled throng of newsmen and shot him in the side. It was Ruby.

Millions saw the fatal shooting of Oswald live on TV that Sunday. Ruby had become an actor in the TV spectacle which had earlier so appalled him, successfully inserting himself into its stream of unfolding horrors.

Ruby was arrested by police and questioned by a Secret Service official. He claimed his execution of Oswald – who had been all but convicted on TV by the Dallas District Attorney – was an act of vigilante justice. He said that he wanted to save taxpayers the expense of mounting a trial against Oswald and spare Jackie

Kennedy the pain of having to testify in Dallas. He said he had acted spontaneously.

> Of why that Sunday morning – that thought never entered my mind prior to that Sunday morning when I took it upon myself to try to be a martyr or some screwball, you might say. But I felt very emotional and very carried away for Mrs. Kennedy, that with all the strife she had gone through – I had been following it pretty well – that someone owed it to our beloved President that she shouldn't be expected to come back to face trial of this heinous crime. And I have never had the chance to tell that, to back it up, to prove it. Consequently, right at this moment I am being victimized as a part of a plot in the world's worst tragedy and crime at this moment.
>
> Jack Ruby testimony, Warren Commission hearing,
> Dallas County Jail, June 7th 1964

Ruby intended to sacrifice his freedom for a good cause and become a 'martyr' on live TV. Instead, as he was painfully aware, he became at best a victim and at worst a 'screwball' in a messy TV blooper.

The aim to transform TV into a medium for political testimony became much more pronounced and, indeed, fatal in the Lebanese martyr videos of the mid-1980s. Here, dozens of Lebanese Communist Party activists who objected to Israel's occupation of their country filmed martyrdom videos before their suicide attacks on Israel Defense Forces garrisons. Typically, they would face the camera to justify their action before calling on others to join them. They would then post their video cassette to the Libyan state TV broadcaster, Tele Liban, for airing on the 8pm news slot after the sacrifice of their lives.

One of the most celebrated Lebanese video martyrs was Jamal Satti. He filmed his testimony on 6th August 1985, just a few hours before he launched a suicide attack against the headquarters of the Israeli military governor in Hasbayya in southern Lebanon. He loaded 880 pounds of dynamite on a donkey and led it past three South Lebanese Army barricades towards his Israeli target. His bomb exploded. A Lebanese man was injured and Satti was himself killed in the resulting explosion. The Israeli governor's building was only slightly damaged, but the fact that Satti had died was enough of a reason for Tele Liban, the only functioning TV station in Lebanon, to broadcast his video that evening.

The tendency for martyr videos to accompany suicide bombings in the Middle East lasted beyond the end of the Lebanese Civil War. The only difference has been that, since the 1990s at least, the martyr's testimony has been couched in the religious language of Islamist jihadism. Typically, the Islamic militant is filmed making their last speech in front of a black flag. Only once they have completed their suicide mission are they granted the honour of having their martyr video uploaded to the internet.

Islamist martyr videos have become one of the main online propaganda tools used by jihadist networks to train suicide bombers in Muslim territories across the world. They undoubt-edly played a part in the radicalisation of the British terror group which was responsible for the 7/7 London bombings. This group was led by 'Sid' Khan.

A youth education worker in a small village in the Midlands of England, Khan had become incensed by BBC News coverage of the post-9/11 War on Terror. BBC reporters were embedded with the British armed forces invading Iraq in 2003 – just as their Fox News counterparts were embedded with US armed forces. The resulting TV coverage was inevitably one-sided.

Khan and his close friends in Beeston had access to jihadist video news reports on the Iraq War. These were made by Islamist religious groups and distributed over the internet. They interpreted the invasion of Iraq as the latest example of the humili-ation by American and European powers of Muslim populations in the Middle East, extending from Afghanistan and Palestine to Chechnya. Taking their place on the internet alongside these reports were jihadist martyr videos which called on any watching Muslim believers to become heroic martyrs in a holy war against European and American non-believers.

On July 7th 2005, Khan and three other young men travelled to London with homemade explosive devices. The men staged a four-pronged suicide bombing attack on London's public transport network. TV coverage of the incident began at 9:15am when Fox's sister channel Sky News reported on an explosion at Liverpool Street station. British TV news networks covered the event as it unfolded throughout the following days, piecing together the story from a mass of images submitted to them by the authorities and TV viewers.

All four suicide bombers died on 7/7 together with 52 people travelling on the London tube and bus network. 'Sid' Khan had intercepted TV news coverage of the British and American wars in the Middle East and brought the violence back home. He post-humously inserted himself into the War on Terror data stream as CCTV images of him and his co-conspirators entering London's public transport network at Luton railway station on the fateful day finally surfaced on 16th July.

On September 1st, Khan's own pre-recorded 27-minute video testimonial was aired by Al Jazeera. Here, he explained his motives for the attack to a British and American TV audience:

Your democratically elected governments continuously perpetuate atrocities against my people all over the world. And your support of them makes you directly responsible, just as I am directly responsible for protecting and avenging my Muslim brothers and sisters. Until we feel security, you will be our targets. And until you stop the bombing, gassing, imprisonment and torture of my people we will not stop this fight.

The self-authored video testimonial has since become part of the standard operating procedure of ideologically-motivated assassins who want to be seen as heroes on the TV news.

7 *Chernobyl Disaster (Nuclear Accident)*

Local Accident Investigation Report

7.1 *Root Cause: Military Development of Nuclear Tech*

On December 8th 1941, Emperor Hirohito of Japan declared war on the US and Britain. A Pacific War in China and South East Asia followed. Once Joseph Stalin's Red Army had turned back Adolf Hitler's war machine at Stalingrad, the mortal threat to the Soviet Union in the west passed. Nazi Germany surrendered to Britain, the US and the Soviet Union in May 1945. Stalin now felt secure enough to turn east and contemplate a war against the Japanese.

The Soviet Union and the US had already divided Germany and parts of Europe between themselves and Britain at the Yalta conference in February 1945. Four months later, the geopolitical contours of a new Cold War began to take shape in Northeast China and beyond. The Soviet Union had been vaguely promised various Pacific islands north of Japan at Yalta. Now, Stalin was ready to test how far east he could extend Soviet dominion.

By August 1945, US president Harry Truman needed a quick win over Hirohito. US forces were battling their way through the Pacific islands south of Japan. By February 1945 they had got to Iwo Jima, by June to Okinawa. But it was very heavy going. The Japanese resisted fiercely and US casualties were terrible. At this rate of progress, a full-scale American invasion of Japan wasn't likely to occur until late 1945. By that time, the Soviets could well have invaded Japan from the north.

The prospect of the US and the Soviet Union dividing up Tokyo as they had done Berlin forced Truman's hand. Against the advice of Supreme Allied Commander 'Ike' Eisenhower, he instructed the US Army air force to detonate nuclear weapons over targets in Japan. The city of Hiroshima was bombed on August 6th, while

Nagasaki was bombed on August 9th. Both cities were devastated by firestorms and radiation.

There were two B-29 observation planes on each mission. They filmed the bombing runs and parachuted scientific instruments into the air to record the devastation in each case. After Enola Gay dropped 'Little Boy' over Hiroshima, Truman wasted no time in announcing to the world news of the US's terrible new arsenal. The nuclear bomb became a propaganda tool within minutes of its use.

The group had been told to select some targets in Japan that had not been bombed, in other words, they wanted virgin targets. And the reason behind it, even though not given to the group at that time, the reason behind it was that they wanted to be able to make bomb blast studies or bomb damage studies on virgin targets once the bombs were used.

Paul Tibbets, Enola Gay pilot, quoted in *Atomic Café*, 1982

August 9th was not only the day that Truman dropped a nuclear bomb on Nagasaki. It was also the day Stalin invaded Northeast China and the Korean peninsula, according to a military time-table agreed at Yalta. When Emperor Hirohito surrendered on August 15th, Truman declared that Stalin should stop his advance. Stalin duly ground his forces to a halt at the 38th par-allel and, after much blustering, called off his planned invasion of Japan on August 22th.

The nuclear bomb had won the war in the Pacific. Developed by the US Army at a secret lab in Los Alamos, New Mexico, it had been conceived in 1942 as a means of defeating Hitler in Europe. But it took many years and two billion dollars for the Manhattan Project to split the atom and harness its tremendous energies. The nuclear physicists led by Robert Oppenheimer were ready to push the button on the first test weapon only in July 1945.

As Oppenheimer huddled in an underground bunker at the 'Trinity' test site on July 16th, he didn't know whether his nuclear bomb would work or not. Even if it did work, he had no idea whether the resulting explosion wouldn't tear apart space and time itself.

And so there was this sense of this ominous cloud hanging over us. It was so brilliant purple, with all the radioactive glowing. And it just seemed to hang there forever. Of course it didn't. It must have been just a very short time until it went up. It was very terrifying. And the thunder from the blast. It bounced on the rocks, and then it went—I don't know where else it bounced. But it never seemed to stop.

Frank Oppenheimer at Trinity, July 16th 1945

In August 1949, the Soviets detonated their own nuclear bomb in what is now known as Kazakhstan. It had taken them over four years to develop the weapon. It was in March 1945 that Stalin had ordered his forces to capture nuclear scientists in the ruins of Germany, Austria and Czechoslovakia and transport them back to the Soviet Union.

7.2 Timeline: Civilian Adoption of Nuclear Tech

In August 1946, Truman created the Atomic Energy Commission (AEC), which transferred the control of nuclear technology from military to civilian hands. Robert Oppenheimer chaired its advisory committee for the next six years. The US government was anxious to recoup some of its investment from the Manhattan Project and demonstrate to the American public the peaceful uses of nuclear power.

The United States would seek more than the mere reduction or elimination of atomic materials for military purposes. It is not enough to take this weapon out of the hands of the soldiers. It must be put into the hands of those who will know how to strip its military casing and adapt it to the arts of peace.

President 'Ike' Eisenhower, 'Atoms for Peace'
speech at the UN, December 8th 1953

General Electric (GE) established an atomic energy department in 1955. Two years later, it opened the world's first nuclear power plant in California. The success of the modest Vallecitos reactor paved the way for GE's construction of the huge Dresden nuclear power station in 1960, which provided electricity for a million homes in Chicago and northern Illinois.

In 1958, the Atomic Energy Commission set up the Plowshare project to explore the use of nuclear explosives for industrial applications ranging from harbour and canal construction to fracking and mining. One of the proposals was to reroute Interstate 40 through the Bristol mountains in southern California's Mojave Desert by cutting open an artificial valley using 22 nuclear bombs. The detonations were scheduled to begin in 1966. In the end, the California Division of Highways decided to use conventional civil engineering methods for the project instead.

Plowshare conducted a total of 27 nuclear tests at its southern Nevada test site until the program was ended in 1977. The Sedan test, which took place in 1963, created the largest artificial crater in the US.

7.3 Effect: Nuclear Accidents

In 1970, the Atomic Energy Commission anticipated that by the year 2000, there would be 1,000 nuclear power stations operating in the US. In fact, by 2008, there were not many more than 100.

From the beginning, the nuclear energy industry was dogged by concerns about the high risk of reactor meltdowns. In 1957, the Price-Anderson Act shielded energy companies like General Electric from the full cost of insurance claims following a 'catastrophic accident.'

On March 28th 1979, a partial meltdown of one of the nuclear reactors at the Three Mile Island plant in Pennsylvania released radioactive gases into the atmosphere. It was the worst nuclear accident in American history. Public fears about nuclear safety suddenly came into focus. This was, in part, because the accident was refracted in the media through the experience of viewing *The China Syndrome*, a Hollywood disaster movie released only 12 days before. The movie popularised the idea of a nuclear meltdown which was so powerful it was capable of tunnelling to the other side of the world.

The governor of Pennsylvania advised a partial evacuation of the state within a 20-mile radius of the Three Mile Island meltdown. About a fifth of population left. They returned three weeks later.

The Three Mile Island accident damaged investor confidence in nuclear power. The growth of the industry was halted.

The cleanup of the Three Mile Island site started in August 1979 and finished in December 1993. Radioactive fuel was removed from the damaged Unit 2 reactor. The Unit 1 reactor was restarted. Radioactive wreckage was shipped to Idaho for storage. The outer concrete wall of Unit 2 was found to be so radioactive that the reactor could not be safely restarted. In 2017 the whole plant was slated for closure within two years.

In 1986, an even worse accident happened at the Chernobyl nuclear power plant in the Soviet Union. Reactor Number 4 exploded, destroying the whole building, including the outer wall. The radioactive fallout was 400 times more concentrated than that at Hiroshima. The whole of Europe was affected.

The Soviet authorities declared a 19-mile Exclusion Zone around the damaged power plant and evacuated the population. To prevent further accidental release of radiation, the Soviet authorities built a concrete sarcophagus over the damaged reactor. It took a quarter of a million men to complete the job.

A nuclear accident has a devastating impact on the dimensions of both space and time. The physical impact on the space surrounding the site of the accident is well understood. The impact on the flow of time surrounding the moment of the accident is an enigma. At the town of Pripyat, in the Chernobyl Exclusion Zone, it as if history itself has stopped. Homes, workplaces and schools have been abandoned, the streets are overgrown with plants. There is an eerie silence. This vision of a town sacrificed to its own memory of itself, of the decay rate of human habitation exposed in the raw, has in recent years become a dark tourist attraction. Travellers are permitted to enter the Exclusion Zone for limited periods in the company of a professional guide.

Philosophers of science have long noted that the laws of physics work the same going backwards as going forwards. Theoretically, the arrow of time can always be reversed at the microscopic scale. Is it possible to think of this actually having happened at Chernobyl? Was its passage into the future effectively dammed up in 1986? And was pressure exerted backwards in time as a result? These questions are certainly intriguing. And perhaps they find some answers in Andrei Tarkovsky's Soviet science fiction film *Stalker*.

Made in 1979, seven years before the Chernobyl accident, the film imagined the existence, in some future time, of a forbidden Zone, filled with the debris of an older civilisation, where the laws of physics are suspended. A professional guide takes two men to a mysterious Room at the heart of the Zone. They enter an underground complex, which is partially flooded, and reach a waiting area just outside the Room. One of the men says that he has discovered a nuclear bomb in the complex and plans to use it to destroy the Room. He says that the bomb was hidden in the 'fourth bunker'. His statement is a prophecy of the explosion at Reactor Number 4 in the Chernobyl nuclear power plant. Explaining his reasoning for wanting to detonate the bomb, the man goes on to say: 'It seems there must be a rule. One should never perform irreversible actions.'

8 9/11 Attack (Jet Plane Accident)

Local Accident Investigation Report

8.1 Root Cause: Military Development of Jet Planes

Adolf Hitler introduced military conscription into Nazi Germany in 1935, so violating the Treaty of Versailles. He developed German military forces into an agile war machine capable of making light-ning thrusts across borders and rapidly acquiring new territory. First Austria, then the Sudetenland and next Czechoslovakia were occupied. On September 1st 1939, Hitler invaded Poland. Britain and France had little choice but to declare war on Nazi Germany. Within months, Hitler took Paris and rushed his armies to the western edge of the European continent. It was only the Atlantic Ocean that stopped him.

1940 was, as British war leader Winston Churchill put it, the 'darkest hour'. The Nazi war machine tipped over the English Channel into the smallest of the British Isles, which included Jersey and Guernsey. At the same time, Hitler flung his Luftwaffe into the air and sought to terrify the wider population of the British Isles with nightly bombing raids and screaming aircraft.

The British governing elite knew that Hitler was capable of invading the south coast of England at any time. They were also acutely conscious that they lacked the factories and labour power to be able to mass manufacture the various new weapons and defensive technologies they had lined up on the drawing-board. The US, by contrast, had a huge productive capacity.

Winston Churchill, after some delay, despatched the scien-tific adviser Henry Tizard to the US with a briefcase full of top-secret documents. They included plans for an offensive radar unit, the atomic bomb and plastic explosives as well as reports on Frank Whittle's turbojet engine. Tizard met with the head of US military research and development, Vannevar Bush, in Washington DC on August 31st 1940. Bush had founded the huge armaments com-pany Raytheon and was particularly intrigued by Tizard's news of the jet engine.

In March 1941, US president Franklin Roosevelt ended the pre-tence of American neutrality in the Second World War and signed into law a 'lend-lease' act which shipped military aid to Britain. A month later, the head of the US Army air force, General 'Hap' Arnold, was sent to Britain in order to fine-tune the details of the arrangement. He visited the country estate of Lord Beaverbrook, Churchill's minister of aircraft production, in Surrey, just outside London. Beaverbrook informed him about the success of recent tests with Whittle's jet engine.

We would even allow him to see the Whittle engine, which has made its first jumps. We have not shown it to a soul yet. Indeed we have only flown it on cloudy days so that the angels could not see it. But what is forbidden to the angels shall be permitted to the General.

Lord Beaverbrook, letter to colleague, 11th April 1941

Whittle had founded his company Power Jets in 1935. He had moved it into a disused foundry in the Midlands of England in 1938 and won the financial backing of the Air Ministry for his prototype W 1 jet engine in 1939.

After the meeting between Arnold and Beaverbrook, Whittle travelled to the US in 1942 to oversee the production of his engine by General Electric (GE) at their plant in Lynn, Massachusetts. GE's J31 engine was not developed quickly enough to make any difference to the course of the Second World War (just as Hans von Ohain's own version of the jet engine, adapted from Whittle's publicly available patent, was not developed in time to help the Nazi war machine).

Once the Second World War ended, there was a proxy war between the US and its ex-ally the Soviet Union in Korea. GE's axial-flow version of the jet engine, the J47, was used to power the US Air Force's 'Sabrejets' to great success. The J47 continued in military service for many years and was only decommissioned in 1978. It was the first turbojet to be certified for civilian use by US authorities.

In 1959, US president 'Ike' Eisenhower's prop-powered plane was replaced with a Boeing 707 jet. This flying version of the Oval Office, known by the call sign 'Air Force One', enabled Eisenhower, at the very end of his presidency, to visit 11 countries in 20 days, meeting face-to-face with heads of state and strengthening American alliances in the aftermath of the Second World War.

8.2 Timeline: Civilian Adoption of Jet Planes

The postwar use of jet engines for civilian air travel added a new dimension to mass transit. Jet airliners were able to fly faster and further than the old piston-powered propeller planes, making it possible for the first time to cover the North American continent or the Atlantic Ocean in a single day.

Boeing's first jet airliner, the 707, was launched in 1958. It was the world's first commercially successful civilian jet and its production wasn't phased out until 1979. As the relative cost of air travel dropped and passenger numbers increased, the hub airports of North America and Europe reached the limit of the number of flights they could accommodate. Planes had to become bigger. In 1970, Boeing launched its first wide-bodied jet, the 747 'jumbo jet', which could carry over 500 passengers.

Pan Am was the first customer in line for both the 707 and the 747. In 1970, the American airliner sold 11 million plane tickets.

Once the proxy wars between the US and the Soviet Union ended, first in Korea and then in Vietnam, the stage was set for China to emerge as an economic superpower. As the middle classes expanded in south east Asia from the early 1990s onwards, so the demand for air travel in the region increased. Airlines such as Malaysia Airlines and Indonesia's Lion Air are the new customers for Boeing's jets while the number of airports in China has expanded from 175 in 2010 to 230 in 2015.

8.3 Effect: Jet Plane Accidents

The first Boeing 707 on a commercial flight to crash was Sabena flight 548. Flying from New York to Belgium, it crashed as it approached Zaventem Airport at Brussels on February 15th 1961. All 72 people on-board were killed, as well as one person on the ground.

The first fatal crash of a Boeing 747 happened with Lufthansa flight 540. Starting the second leg of its Frankfurt–Nairobi–Johannesburg run on November 20th 1974, the plane crashed and caught fire soon after takeoff from Jomo Kenyatta International Airport. Of the 157 people on-board, 59 were killed.

> Co-pilot Schacke:Eighty.
> Captain Krack:Yes, okay. V1. VR. Pay attention. Vibration...
> Flight Engineer Hahn:All is OK.
> Captain Krack:Vibration!
> Co-pilot Schacke:Gear up, gear travelling.
> Flight Engineer Hahn:Engines okay so far.
> Captain Krack:Roger.
> Flight Engineer Hahn:RPM also okay.
> Flight Engineer Hahn:Stickshaker!
> Co-pilot Schacke:Okay, crash.
>
> Lufthansa flight 540, cockpit voice recorder transcript, last moments

The invention of the civilian jet airliner was the invention of the plane crash. It was also, less obviously, the invention of the plane hijack. On November 24th 1968, Pan Am Flight 281 from New York to Puerto Rico was hijacked by four men and forced to fly to Soviet-supported Cuba. It was one of the many 'skyjackings' of the 1960s and 1970s, which were largely conducted by terrorist groups.

On September 11th 2001, the plane hijacking and the plane crash were brought together for the first time. It took some time for this elementary fact to be understood.

At 8:46am, a Boeing 767 passenger jet fuelled with 20,000 gallons of petrol crashes into the tallest tower in New York's World Trade Center complex. There is an explosion. It seems like an accident. Then, minutes later, another Boeing 767 flies into the tower's twin, just south of it. A second explosion. Now, it seems like a suicide bombing.

Images of the terror attacks are broadcast around the world on a loop. Every TV station shows the same images, over and over again. No one knows for sure what is going on.

The authorities shut down the airspace above New York. There are reports of a third Boeing jet crashing into the Pentagon, the US military command-and-control centre outside Washington. The authorities shut down the airspace above the whole North American continent.

The twin towers struck by the flying bombs in New York collapse, one after another. Some few hours later, a third smaller tower in the World Trade Center complex spontaneously collapses. It seems like a controlled demolition.

There are reports of a fourth Boeing crashing into a field somewhere outside New York.

Trading is suspended on the New York Stock Exchange and it is evacuated. Share prices of the airlines used in the attacks tumble on the world's stock exchanges, while the prices of weapons manufacturers surge.

Conspiracy theorists note extraordinary trading spikes in the days before the attacks which seem to hint at foreknowledge. One of the big stock market winners is Raytheon.

The official 2004 report on the 9/11 attacks found that over 2,600 people were killed by a Middle Eastern terror cell. It ignored the collapse of the third building as well as the anomalous stock market data. The North American authorities launched prolonged wars in the Middle East, spending trillions of dollars to expose the shadowy sponsors of the terrorists who had hijacked the planes. They set up a surveillance state at home, imprisoned suspects without charge and developed a highly sophisticated administration of fear.

People around the world – including many Americans – began to voice their doubts about the official account of 9/11. Self-appointed 9/11 investigators questioned the credibility of the US government and corporate media as sources of knowledge. A thousand conspiracy theories bloomed online. Some folks said that the attacks were planned by Saudi Arabian intelligence officers. Other folks swore that the US intelligence agency, the CIA, had known the terror attacks were coming, but had been too incompetent to prevent them. Still others protested that the US vice-president had himself ordered the terror attacks as a false-flag operation designed to offer a pretext for war in the Middle East. A reckless few argued that the buildings had been planted with timed explosive charges by a secret service team and that the planes were a mere distraction.

One thing was confirmed, at least. Truth is the first casualty not only of war, but also of any large-scale incident with sudden and unexpected deaths. Once truth has been removed from the scene, what flourishes in its place are untruths, faith-based dogmas, mistaken beliefs, lies, deceptions, disinformation, propaganda, fake news, 'truthy' entertainments and simulations.

Oh, fuck it, I'm just going to say this. Yes, I believe no planes were involved in 9/11. The only explanation is that they were missiles surrounded by holograms made to look like planes. Watch the footage frame by frame and you will see a cigar-shaped missile hitting the World Trade Center. I know it sounds weird, but this is what I believe.

> David Shayler, ex-British secret agent, quoted in the *New Statesman*, 11th September, 2006

By the end of 9/11, the hijacked jets had demolished not only the World Trade Center but also the philosophical frames of reference that make possible human reasoning towards universal values such as truth. When everything is interpretation, then the world passes through the looking glass into a realm of competing simulations where the only thing that matters is the answer to Humpty Dumpty's famous question – 'which is to be master?'

3

Geography: Pandemic

Field Notes on a Residency

The third workshop saw us all back in the same room again. Jenkins and his four postgraduate students were seated at the table with their laptops. They were talking about artificial intelligence. Haubenstock was busy in the corner setting up his Sony Z1 camera. I was standing in front of the wall-screen with my own machine.

Once Haubenstock gave me the thumbs-up, I smiled at the group and began. The world constituted by geography, I said, is the world of globalisation.

I flipped up on the screen one of Gursky's large-format colour photographs. It was a picture of an international stock exchange floor in Chicago, with its banked rows of trading desks and its dense pit of glowing screens and gesticulating brokers in coloured jackets. The perspective was flattened and the colours were over-bright. It looked like a digital version of a stained-glass window.

The movement towards an ever-extending and ever-intensifying globalisation took a bit of a knock with the 2008 financial crisis, I said. But latest reports from the world's biggest logistics company, Deutsche Post DHL, indicate that this was likely to be a temporary pause. Globalisation in some parts of the world, particularly South America and sub-Saharan Africa, is actually picking up.

Globalisation, I said, promises to establish a world of open borders where information, capital, goods and people are constantly on the move. In this vision, it will be multinational corporations rather than nation-states that are responsible for the administration of territories, condensing huge areas of the planet into single markets with abbreviated names like APAC and EMEA.

Yes, said Gupta. Supply chains now cross continents, joining steel mills in China with iron ore mines in Australia, shopping malls in North America with rice farms in India. Everything is increasingly interconnected, everyone is increasingly inter-dependent. It's marvellous.

The young scientists were nodding and grinning at this. Most of them were international students, after all. I was quite aware that after spending a few years at Solent City University, doing their drone experiments and getting their names into the peer-reviewed journals, they would disperse to higher paying jobs at Stanford, Lausanne, Singapore and Hong Kong. Here was a class of young professionals who were migrants in the most privileged sense, perfectly at home in the generic global spaces of the campus, the airport lounge, the boutique hotel lobby and the conference hall. They had adapted to living in the slipstream of a constantly moving world. They had found an air pocket. They would survive.

But not everyone was so fortunate. I showed the scientists an old press photo of a Second World War refugee. It depicted a little white boy sitting on a suitcase at the side of the road somewhere in Europe. Behind him was rubble.

I explained that Christian Aid was a British charity set up at the end of the Second World War to help the tens of millions of people who had lost their homes in Europe. Just recently, I said, the charity issued a report predicting that by 2050 there would be one billion people displaced from their homes across the world. One billion refugees, I repeated. The combined effects of cli-mate change, wars, natural disasters, vast industrial development projects and, yes, the dislocating effects of globalisation would see to that.

Globalisation has a dark side, said Rausch. I get it. I nodded. Virilio is not a big fan of globalisation, I said. He sees it as a mechanism for putting whole populations into circulation and turning the world's great cities into chaotic slums. The *Blade Runner* scenario, said Jenkins.

Virilio sounds like a real pessimist, said Rausch. He seems to be arguing that the city of the future would be indistinguishable from a disaster zone.

Novichkov woke from his day-dreaming. He asked Rausch if he'd ever been to Disaster City. Rausch shook his head. It's a disaster management training facility in Texas, said Novichkov. They've built a whole fake city, like a theme park, but with collapsible buildings and controllable freight train derailments and warehouse fires. It's quite awesome.

A concept like Disaster City is obsolete, of course, said Trinh. Novichkov looked slightly baffled. It's now possible, she said, to create a disaster scenario in mixed reality and run it as a simulation at any location. Kind of like a disaster city app.

I asked Trinh what she meant by mixed reality. She said the best way to explain it was to show me her latest research project. It was a mixed-reality game titled *Radiation Alert*. She flipped open her laptop and pulled up a screen-grab of an annotated map of the Solent City University campus. It was labelled 'tactical command dashboard'. Trinh said she'd used *Radiation Alert* to explore the university's disaster response plans. She'd played it with some undergraduates last term. Haubenstock wandered over and peered at the image. He pointed to a red circle hovering over some campus buildings. Trinh said the circle represented a radiation cloud. Haubenstock pulled a face.

Trinh went on to explain that *Radiation Alert* was based on the scenario of a dirty bomb explosion. She tapped the screen. When the game is run, she said, the scientist at tactical command sees the radiation cloud on their computer screen drifting across the university. The tactical commander then phones the other players, who are outside on the campus grounds, and directs their activity. Players are expected to move to target zones – such as the café or the library – where they can rescue other players at risk of radiation poisoning and then move them to safe drop-off points.

Trinh said the great thing about *Radiation Alert* was that while it was location-based, the locations could be swapped in and out. It could be played anywhere as a real-life disaster response training exercise. England. Texas. Vietnam. Wherever. She folded up her computer and smiled.

I looked at Trinh. So what you're saying is that disaster management experts can generate a computer model of a train derailment and run it at any station in the world. They can model a plane crash and run it at any airport in the world. Is that it? I asked her. Right, said Trinh. She leaned in close. And they can run the scenario on the ground at the same time as live-action role-play. Mixed reality, right? Computer world and real world running in parallel. She gestured with her two index fingers.

I paced up and down for a bit. Then I asked the group how they thought the end of globalisation might be modelled in mixed reality. What would be its distinguishing features? Columns of refugees in the countryside, said Gupta. The return of checkpoints and closed borders. Nationalism and xenophobia, said Rausch. Airport security protocols ramped up ten-fold. Or maybe, said Jenkins, the ending of cheap air travel altogether. The mass closure of airports. The conversion of airports into refugee centres, said Trinh. Many dead zones starved of investment, said Rausch. A new Dark Ages of censorship, torture and superstition.

Let's face it, said Gupta. We're talking about the zombie apocalypse! He laughed. I guess so, said Rausch. He laughed as well. The group spent some time swapping post-apocalyptic scenarios from first-person shooter video games. I waited for the excitement to die down.

So what would be the event most likely to trigger this sort of catastrophe? I asked. There was silence. Something that came out of global migration, said Rausch. Like some kind of weird travel sickness. That turned people into zombies, said Gupta, with a grin.

Okay, I said. We're thinking about an end-of-the-world scenario caused not so much by technology going wrong, but by the accelerated migration of people somehow going wrong. A contagious disease, perhaps. A virus whose transmission vectors are the flight paths of the global airline industry.

A global pandemic, said Jenkins. Like AIDS or H1N1. Or the Spanish flu of 1918, which killed more people than the First World War. Of course, I said. That's it. A pandemic. Brilliant! The session came to an end.

Back in our dorm room, I collapsed on the bed while Haubenstock played poker online. I was wondering how mixed reality could be used by disaster management experts to simulate a global pandemic. How would Trinh model it? Actually, the question was probably more like how would the Red Cross or the United Nations model it? These were the people who might really want to script a global disaster response training exercise. Even then, they'd put it out to tender and review bids from the private sector.

An imaginary invitation to tender, I thought. I could write that. Of course I could. I could also write a follow-up bid document from an imaginary disaster management training company. It was all coming together. I found my laptop and wrote long into the night.

Proposal for a Global Emergency Responder Training Exercise

Invitation to Tender

The United Nations Office for the Coordination of Humanitarian Affairs (UNOCHA) intends to run a training exercise to test emergency responses to a global disaster. We call this exercise

Project Swansong. Companies are invited to submit proposals for developing an extremely challenging training exercise, complete with specification of the global disaster to be simulated.

Response to Invitation

Proposal – NRx Associates are pleased to be invited by UNOCHA to submit a proposal for Project Swansong. We have worked with UNOCHA before. We were one of the agencies involved in the evacuation of Cardiff in the UK following the Hinkley Point C nuclear power plant accident in 2028.

Pandemic – We propose that the global disaster to be simulated in Project Swansong is a pandemic, a global epidemic that has the potential to infect most of the planet's human population. Out of scope for our Swansong submission is any consideration of the pandemic's impact on non-human planetary populations, such as animals, birds, amphibians or reptiles.

Virus – One baseline model for our pandemic is the first global outbreak of the H1N1 influenza virus in 1918. It lasted for three years. A third of the world's human population was infected. About 20 per cent of those infected died from diseases such as pneumonia. The most remote areas of the planet – including the Arctic and various Pacific Islands – were affected.

Origin unknown – We propose that Project Swansong is built around the spread of a completely new virus. Let's call it Z1A1. Like influenza, it is transmitted by direct contact with either infected humans (sneezing, coughing, spitting, biting) or contaminated objects (door handles, elevator buttons). Like measles, it is highly transmissible. Let's say that one infected human can pass on the virus to 18 other humans (compared to three for influenza). And like smallpox, it is highly virulent, with a mortality rate of 95 per cent (compared to the 20 per cent of influenza). To fit these parameters, Z1A1 would probably have to be a genetically engineered virus which had escaped from the lab. For the purposes of Swansong, however, its origin is largely irrelevant.

Simulation – We have a database of more than 20,000 simulated pandemics. The NRx Epidemiological Model will enable us to run a computer simulation of Z1A1 and estimate how fast it is likely to spread across the planet and how many humans are likely to die. We expect to work with UNOCHA to refine the virus parameters. We are perfectly willing to run successive iterations of Z1A1 in order to create a model consistent with UNOCHA's understanding of a disaster that is 'extremely challenging'. We would caution, though, that viruses typically show a tendency to moderate their progress in their late stage. It's almost as if they hold back from delivering the final killer blow to the population they infect because they know this would be a death sentence for them too.

Undead – We consider the disease activities stimulated by the Z1A1 virus to be of relatively minor importance to Swansong. For the sake of argument, we might say that infected humans suffer from motor neuron disease affecting the ability to walk and talk combined with same-species selecting predatory behaviour. We could even call this new disease Zombiosis. Those humans with the disease would shamble along the streets in great herds, hunting for uninfected humans to kill and eat. After about a year, they would waste away and die.

Genocide – We are confident that we can create a model where 90 per cent of the human population is at risk of dying. Certainly, there is precedent for this. When Christopher Columbus and then the Spanish conquistadors arrived in the Americas at the end of the fifteenth century, they brought many new viruses with them.

A hundred years later, 90 per cent of the Native American population had died of smallpox. Mexico went from having 30 million to 3 million humans, Peru went from 8 million to 1 million humans. When the English arrived in Virginia at the end of the sixteenth century, they were mystified to find it virtually empty of humans.

Extinction – We recommend squeezing our model of a 90 per cent wipeout of humans into the shortest time frame possible. This surely would be an 'extremely challenging' disaster for UNOCHA to respond to. We would model international airline routes as Z1A1 virus transmission vectors, paying particular attention to the ability of long-haul flights to create satellite outbreaks of Zombiosis far from its point of origin. The NRx Epidemiological Model would probably enable us to get near-extinction of humans down to a matter of weeks in purely mathematical terms (with no consideration of mitigating factors derived from either emergency response or vaccine development). However, it's more realistic to think of months or even years rather than weeks when it comes to this scenario.

Military doctrine – Following the typology of command which was first specified in the 1982 US Army Field Manual on Operations, we propose that UNOCHA's emergency response to our specified global disaster is split over three levels – strategic, tactical and operational. When we worked with the US Defense Intelligence Agency in 2022, this was how they successfully modelled their response to the simulated outbreak of a new strain of antibiotic-resistant anthrax.

Mixed reality – We propose creating Swansong as a mixed-reality game split across the three levels of command. We would create a pandemic-response scenario which plays out simultaneously in digital space and in real life. The game would run in real-time and have both interactive and semi-scripted elements. Participants would be able to access the game through their electronic devices and perform in it as a live-action role-play at the same time. It would feel like they were having to cope with a real global disaster.

Strategic command – We expect that for managing its overall response to any global disaster, UNOCHA would naturally want to have strategic command located at its United Nations office in Geneva. However, we think that the intensive logistical demands of managing a disaster such as the one we have in mind would merit the transfer of strategic command to a big hotel. For that reason, we propose to book one of the 16 function rooms at the InterContinental Geneva to run some live-action training sessions with UNOCHA's strategic team. The role-play could last for a number of days. However, to be 'extremely challenging', it would have to last for a minimum of three months. In either case, we propose a reality-TV style insulation of strategy team participants within the hotel.

Theatre – Attached is a press photo of Meeting Room 12 in the InterContinental Geneva. It shows a theatre-like space, much like a screening-room, with bucket seats facing a TV wall-screen fronted by a raised stage. Duck foie gras is available from room service.

Gamification – We would develop some challenging tests, games and interactive scripts for UNOCHA strategy command at our Swansong training event. Team participants would have to decide how to prioritise the various components of emergency response to the Z1A1 outbreak across the world. There would be much digit-ally simulated liaison with international heads of state, humani-tarian agencies and various centres of disease control as well as UN tactical control rooms in Z1A1-affected countries. Strategic command would be a place of politics and argument. At the end of each day's session, we would hold a mock press conference where participants would be aggressively questioned by NRx crisis actors pretending to be the world's media.

Populism – The biggest challenge faced by strategic command participants during these training sessions will probably be finding enough resources to manage popular reactions to the spread of Z1A1. We would model these reactions in line with the sociological literature and base them on fear, ignorance and, let's say, Zombiphobia. There are some things we can predict already. Far-right demagogues on all continents would scapegoat various minority groups for the outbreak of Zombiosis. The families of those with Z1A1 would mount hashtag campaigns based on sentiment rather than logic. As a result, UNOCHA strategy team participants can expect NRx crisis actors impersonating various protest groups to occupy the media briefing room in the InterContinental Geneva. They may well hold their own press conferences, broadcast partial and skewed accounts of the Z1A1 contagion and even stage anti-UNOCHA rallies on Avenue de la Paix.

Counter-narrative – We recommend that all UNOCHA strategy team participants familiarise themselves with the latest US Armed Forces Field Manual on Counterinsurgency before attending any mixed-reality gameplay sessions. This will help them to understand that when they issue a press release about their management of the Z1A1 virus, they are effectively engaged in a form of 'information operations' combating the 'insurgent narratives' of affected nations across the world.

Tactical command – We expect that UNOCHA would mobilise UN Disaster Assessment and Coordination (UNDAC) teams to handle tactical command in the most badly affected areas of any global disaster. Our modelling of the Z1A1 outbreak has already identified international airline routes as significant viral transmission vectors. For this reason, we think that the world's busiest airports – particularly those with long-haul flight connections – are likely to be where UNDAC teams would set up incident control rooms. Airports on any candidate list include Hartsfield–Jackson Atlanta International Airport, Beijing Capital International Airport, Dubai International Airport, Tokyo Haneda Airport and London Heathrow Airport. We propose staging a Swansong training event at a conference room at Heathrow Terminal 6.

Terminal 6 – UNDAC team participants at Heathrow would be involved in mixed-reality gameplay sessions that might have to last some weeks to be 'extremely challenging'. We plan to create an incident room at Terminal 6 where participants could gain situational awareness of a Z1A1 outbreak in London and Northwest France. We would supply mock satellite feeds, pre-scripted drone footage and appropriately authored reports from operational agents, all designed to reveal the real-time migratory patterns of humans with Zombiosis. Participants would be expected to model projections, plan evacuation routes and quarantine zones with Google Earth and use Twitter to issue warnings and travel restriction updates.

Crisis map – We are quite aware that in any disaster, the top-down activities of tactical command would be supplemented by bottom-up crisis mapping. This first happened during the 2010 Haiti earthquake, when humans on the ground used open-source software to create live digital maps of affected areas of the city. These maps were annotated with crowd-generated tweets, photos and videos. We plan to script a digitally simulated version of a dynamic crisis map for a Z1A1-hit London and feed it into the tactical command exercise. A major component of this map would track the progress of an ambulatory herd of humans with Zombiosis along the M4 corridor from Heathrow Airport to Kensington.

Twitter – The biggest challenge faced by UNDAC participants grappling with the Z1A1 crisis map of London will probably be to figure out the reliability of crowd-generated data. Even during the best of times, Twitter is a high-speed medium for the spread of rumour and panic. This can have destabilising effects. Let's not forget the great Mexican Twitter storm of 2011. When messages spread that cartel gunmen in Veracruz were kidnapping schoolchildren one afternoon and the government was keeping quiet about it, parents rushed to collect their kids. The result was chaos, with jammed phone lines, multiples car crashes and disorder in the streets. The messages were false. But how was it possible to know that at the time? We certainly plan to throw at least some bad data at UNDAC team participants to see how they cope. A bunch of hoax images ripped from old zombie movies is one thing that springs to mind.

MicroMappers – One of the resources we expect to be made available to UNDAC team participants is the MicroMappers digital platform developed by UNOCHA in 2013. We are aware that ever since its rollout during the 2014 Pakistan earthquake, it has provided a useful intermediate layer of data analysis insulating tactical command from the worst effects of crowd-sourced tweets and images in many disaster response efforts. We hope that UNOCHA would be able to recruit volunteers on its usual terms to tag the data included in our crisis map of a Z1A1-hit London. We suggest that data can either be marked as 'request for help', 'infected zone', 'dead humans' or 'not relevant'.

Drugs – When we run our iterations of the Z1A1 virus using the NRx Epidemiological Model, we expect to work with UNOCHA to refine parameters around treatment and prevention. Given that it would probably take six months to develop, test, manufacture and distribute a vaccine capable of preventing infection by a new virus such as Z1A1, we think that prevention is a factor that's out of scope for our Swansong training exercise. Depending on the exact nature of the disease activities associated with Z1A1, treatment with antiviral drugs may or may not be a possibility. We suspect that any antivirals used to treat humans with Zombiosis would have the effect of prolonging life by only a few months. However, for the purposes of maintaining UNDAC team morale, we recommend that long-term antiviral treatment is in scope for the exercise.

Search-and-rescue – The obviously humanitarian aspect of Swansong will no doubt involve UNDAC tactical command directing search-and-rescue operations in the field. We expect UNOCHA to supply budget for a small team of operational agents, autonomous dronecams and perhaps a helicopter. We recommend exploring the option of including the British Army's Logistic Regiment as a Swansong partner. They have a transport unit based in Southall, near Heathrow.

Spatialisation – We would script various gameplay sessions designed to test the UNDAC team's ability to assess a Z1A1 outbreak in West London, evaluate requests for help and decide how to respond. We expect that a priority for UNDAC tactical command would be to clear roads to the A&E departments of the nearest hospitals. We're thinking primarily of West Middlesex University Hospital, Ealing Hospital, Charing Cross Hospital and Chelsea and Westminster Hospital. We would also want to explore the possibility of transforming the football stadia at Twickenham, Craven Cottage and Stamford Bridge into secure quarantine stations. This is where the Logistic Regiment could be particularly helpful.

Strategic/tactical synching – At the end of each day's training, we would expect the UNDAC team in the incident room at London Heathrow T6 to report back on their performance to UNOCHA strategic command in Geneva. Ideally, the mixed-reality gameplay sessions in Geneva and London would be synchronised. However, this is not essential. We would expect UNDAC agents to have some familiarity with the use of satellite phones.

Incident room – Attached is an image showing participants at work in an incident room we created for a 9/11-style disaster response training exercise with Federal Emergency Management Agency (FEMA) in the US. The incident commander is shown with a Google Earth satellite-coordinated map of the incident zone on a computer screen behind her. She has a print-out of the map on the table in front of her. She and her team of FEMA data analysts are seen annotating the map with post-it notes. Up on the wall to one side is a whiteboard scribbled with messages about the relative urgency of various tasks and their deadlines for completion.

Operational command – As we've said, we expect UNOCHA to have the resources to staff an operational team of field agents as part of its Swansong training exercise. Working on this assumption, we recommend that a team of five humans is assembled from a UNOCHA partner agency such as the Red Cross. We propose that the operational team is flown by helicopter from Heathrow tactical command to designated Z1A1 hotspots in West London mocked up by NRx production designers on the ground. We recommend that the team is active at each hotspot for mixed-reality gameplay sessions lasting three days at a time.

Tactical/operational synching – Ideally, there would be real-time synchronisation between the operational team on the ground and tactical command back at Heathrow Terminal 6. This would increase the dynamic quality of the mixed-reality gameplay. Disaster response training exercises are much more useful when they are able to increase human interactions in the wild.

Disaster capitalism – We realise that for the operational team to be self-sustaining, they would need to rely on their own power, food and water so as to not exhaust local resources. We note with interest the point made by activist Naomi Klein that expertise in this area now sits primarily in the private sector as a result of outsourcing policies pursued by governments. For this reason, we recommend partnering with a company such as the Shaw Group, Halliburton, Bechtel, Parsons, CH2M HILL or Fluor to muster the electricity generators, phone masts, blood-test kits and mobile homes needed by our operational team.

Motorway – We propose that one Swansong hotspot is created at an abandoned section of the M4 just off Junction 29 in Wales. Here, we would build an Z1A1 infected zone as an immersive theatre piece, complete with abandoned cars, dead humans and a migrating herd of humans with Zombiosis. Our operational team would be expected to perform reconnaissance of the area for three days. They would log casualties, identify hazards, search for uninfected humans and send requests for help to tactical command at Heathrow T6. They would, in terms of the live-action role-play, be at risk of infection themselves.

Mobile sensors – We would equip the operational team with smartphones loaded with software appropriate for our mixed-reality game. Operational team members would be able to ping messages to each other, capture data and live-stream it to Heathrow tactical command, while receiving back updates on the latest wide-scale crisis maps. In this way, we would expect each field agent to function as a kind of networked sensor, working by touch and feel as much as by sight and hearing. It might be interesting to see how a human field agent performs her task compared to a robot drone. We would certainly recommend conducting this experiment as a sideline research exercise.

Stadium – We propose that another Swansong hotspot is created at Twickenham Stadium. Here, we would mock up a Z1A1 quarantine station, complete with NRx crisis actors playing humans with Zombiosis, medical personnel and armed guards. We would put up a chain-link fence around the stadium and experiment with emergency access protocols for ambulances and helicopters. Our operational team would be expected to assess treatment and recovery efforts in the quarantine station for the duration of their three-day stay. Again, they would be at risk of infection. We could certainly script some dramatic live-action role-play scenes for them.

Human factors – We could always dial up the stress of the Twickenham training exercise if UNOCHA had a particular interest in modelling the play of human factors at the operational level. We are thinking of the effects of compassion fatigue and responder burn-out. In this circumstance, UNOCHA might need to review its liability insurance policies. No one likes to get sued.

Tendencies – We could similarly dial up or down the responsiveness of our Z1A1 model to antiviral treatment in order to get maximum play out of the Twickenham training exercise. As our Z1A1 antiviral drugs tend towards remission and cure, so our quarantine station tends towards the model of a refugee camp. In the opposite direction, of course, it tends towards the hospice model. For ethical reasons, NRx Associates are not prepared to model a death camp scenario. However, we do note that ethics often change with circumstances.

Package – Finally, we recommend that UNOCHA explores the possibility of filming Swansong with a view to turning it into a TV entertainment property. There is documented popular appetite for shows about global disasters (see National Geographic's *How to Survive the End of the World*) and for reality TV shows in which participants undergo various punishing trials and tests. The prospect of splicing these two TV genres into a new kind of show is attractive. This show would also, of course, be a communications vehicle for key UNOCHA messages.

4

Psychology: Mass PTSD

Field Notes on a Residency

The fourth workshop took as its theme the perception of the world from a psychological angle. Jenkins attended with his postgrad students Trinh, Novichkov, Rausch and Gupta. Haubenstock had his video camera. I had my laptop. Plus, there were cakes.

Claustrophobia, I said, is the fear of being trapped in a confined space with no possibility of escape. On the wall-screen above my head, I displayed a photo taken at rush hour by Wolfgang Tillmans in Tokyo. It showed the mask-like faces of commuters pressed into a train carriage at Shubuya subway station. The image had a detached erotic charge, similar to that of an Araki bondage photo. The scientists looked intrigued.

If someone with claustrophobia were to be trapped in a train compartment like this, I said, they would suffer very badly from anxiety. I went on to list the symptoms of claustrophobia from the fifth edition of the Diagnostic and Statistical Manual of Mental Disorders, a textbook that had its origins in the efforts of the US Army to standardise its psychological assessment of combat-ready men in the Second World War. Nausea. Palpitations. Breathlessness. Panic attacks.

One way to cope with this anxiety disorder is to avoid the situations which trigger it, I said. The claustrophobic person in the Shubuya train, for example, could always get off at the next stop.

But that isn't treating them, said Trinh. Right, I said. And maybe avoidance isn't such a good coping strategy anyway. After all, Tokyo is a megacity of 13 million people living in a space of only 2,000 or so square kilometres. It has one of the highest population densities in the world. You do the maths, I said. A claustrophobic person could very easily suffer from panic attacks simply as a result of living in Tokyo. They could always move somewhere else, said Rausch. But where to? I said. The world is increasingly full of megacities like Tokyo. You only have to think of Shanghai, Jakarta, Delhi or Seoul.

I asked the scientist to imagine the Tokyo experience of claustrophobia scaled up to the global level. Feeling anxious because you're trapped on a small planet with no possibility of escape is surely the ultimate in claustrophobia. But is this reaction so pathological? I answered my own question. Virilio argues that it is not at all pathological. In fact, he argues that a global feeling of panic is an entirely proportional response to the reality of living in a totally enclosed planetary environment. When everywhere has been discovered, I said, there is nowhere else to go.

So this is the world constituted by psychology, I said. A feeling of generalised claustrophobia. The scientists looked at each other. I said that I wanted them to think about how this experience of the world would most likely terminate. What would happen when the claustrophobia got too much?

People, rich people, would go off-world, said Gupta. And who could blame them? The search for Earth 2.0 is taking place even as we speak, said Rausch. Jenkins intervened, excitedly. NASA's space telescope Kepler, he said, was launched only a few years ago. And already it had found 2,000 or so Earth-like planets in the galaxy. Exoplanets, as they were called. Dozens of them were thought to be inhabitable. He was willing to bet that humans would settle them one day. His students murmured their approval.

There followed a lively exchange about the relative merits of the various inhabitable exoplanets and the feasibility of reaching them any time soon. The discussion ran its course.

Earth 2.0 sounds like a gated community in space, I said. Jenkins shrugged. Trinh was more thoughtful. Maybe this is a scenario, the psychological scenario, where no global reckoning is possible. Worldwide claustrophobia always gets displaced to the next inhabitable planet in line. It's like a chain reaction. Novichkov grinned. A return to the avoidance strategy, he said. But now operating on the cosmic level. Was this kind of planet-hopping simply evolution in action, evolution driven by human psychology?

Rausch said he had taken a module on Heidegger when he was an undergraduate at the University of Erlangen-Nuremberg. His instructors told him that the Apollo astronauts who flew to the Moon had all agreed that the most intense aspect of their experience came from seeing the reality of the Earth hanging in space. Many of the spacemen had reported an almost objective apprehension of being-in-the-world at that moment. They had come to an understanding of the mortality of the world. This was surely more like the mystical experience of the medieval Christian saints than anything listed in the Diagnostic and Statistical Manual of Mental Disorders.

Gupta raised his hand. He had been Googling furiously on his laptop while Rausch was talking. Now he had found the quote he was looking for. It was taken from a newspaper interview with Michael Collins three years after his trip to the Moon in 1969. Gupta read it aloud:

I looked out of my window and tried to find Earth. The little planet is so small out there in the vastness that at first I couldn't even locate it. And when I did, a tingling of awe spread over me. There it was, shining like a jewel in a black sky. I looked at it in wonderment, suddenly aware of how its uniqueness is stamped in every atom of my body.

Is Collins describing an evolutionary shift in human consciousness? asked Gupta. He didn't wait for an answer. The space scientists have given it a name, anyway – the 'overview effect'. I've heard of that, said Rausch. The sudden realisation of the planet's fragility and beauty had spread quickly through the counterculture in the early 1970s. It had helped trigger the emergence of a duty of care – Rausch used the word 'sorge' – towards the environment. In fact, he said, there's one particular NASA photograph which crystallises this feeling of sorrowful responsibility. It's called *Earthrise.*

Gupta had already found the image online. He turned his laptop around so the group could see the photograph. It had been taken by one of the Apollo astronauts and showed the Earth rising above the horizon of the Moon. One of the most profound images ever made, said Rausch. Jenkins nodded in agreement. Rausch was passionate. It captures something qualitatively new in human experience – the perception of an extraterrestrial dawn. It's a celestial phenomenon unique in the 200,000-year history of the species.

Novichkov had also found *Earthrise* online. He peered into his screen. Then he sat back and laughed. The photo is nothing more than a trick of perspective, he said. It doesn't show the Earth rising over the Moon at all. Jenkins asked him to explain.

The photo, said Novichkov, had been taken by William Anders, the lunar module pilot on Apollo 8. However, he had taken it through the right-hand window of the command module as it flew round the Moon. He had not taken it from the surface of the Moon. He had never set foot on the Moon. None of the Apollo 8 astronauts had set foot on the Moon. The Apollo 8 flight had been a reconnaissance mission only.

The original picture shows the Earth on the left and the Moon on the right, said Novichkov. It was some NASA publicity hack who had rotated the photo 90 degrees to show instead the Moon at the bottom and the Earth at the top, so giving the false impression it had been taken from the surface of the Moon.

Novichkov dutifully reoriented the picture on his laptop screen. Now, it showed the view from a spacecraft that seemed at risk of hurling itself into the black infinity of space, as it attempted to navigate a narrow path between the Earth and its cratered satellite. It was a vaguely terrifying prospect.

Rausch's face was expressionless. Interesting, he said. Haubenstock piped up. Anders had probably only taken the photo because he was bored, he said. A lunar module pilot, unlike the command module pilot and the mission commander sat next to him, never had much to do on an Apollo spaceflight except look out of the window. So all this talk of a mystical overview effect is probably just the result of a panic attack. He beamed.

Out of all the Apollo astronauts, said Trinh, it was certainly always the lunar module pilots who suffered the most when they came back down to Earth. Aldrin's depression was so bad he had to be confined in a psychiatric institution. And what about Al Bean and his psychedelic paintings of the Moon? She turned her laptop round so the group could see the Bean painting she'd found online. It showed a bulked-up astronaut leaping around on a pock-marked orange lunar surface, his visor dark and unreflective, the skies a vivid pink and red. It's like one of Van Gogh's night-time landscapes, said Haubenstock. Same lurid intensity. He shivered.

Al Bean has nothing on Edgar Mitchell, I said. Mitchell is probably the most out-there of all the lunar module pilots. Once he got back to Florida after his trip to the Moon, he began to take an interest in all sorts of paranormal phenomena. He believed in the reality of ESP and thought that a Canadian faith healer had cured him of cancer. He also believed that the flying saucers seen in American skies since the end of the Second World War were in fact alien spacecraft.

Rausch disagreed with me. Mitchell's attraction to pseudo-scientific theories is not something to be taken literally, he said. Instead, they point back to the strange moment of ecstasy he'd experienced on-board Apollo 14. Mitchell said that while looking out of the window at the brightness of the stars in space, he had felt at one with the universe, that everything was connected, that all matter had consciousness. Rausch looked quite elated.

Does that make Mitchell like one of your medieval Christian mystics? Trinh asked Rausch. I don't know, he said. Mitchell in press interviews had used the word 'samadhi' to characterise his epiphany, so that probably made him more of a Buddhist.

Either way, I said, Mitchell was reliving his epiphany, he was talking about it in retrospect, he was attempting to process an experience which was probably ego-shattering at the time it happened. So what? said Jenkins. Well, it's not a direct account of his experience. He wasn't interviewed live in space. He was interviewed when he came back to Earth. His mystical belief in a conscious universe might have been something he unconsciously made up after the event in an effort to rebuild and defend his traumatised ego.

Maybe his mystical belief in UFOs is also a defence mechanism, said Novichkov. Isn't there a pattern here? Mitchell's weird beliefs, Bean's mad paintings, Aldrin's severe depression, all are symptoms of what was actually quite a traumatic experience. Being-in-outer-space, said Rausch. The book Heidegger never got to write.

It's almost as if the Apollo astronauts who flew to the Moon lived through the end of the world, I said. And came back to tell their tale, said Rausch.

Distressing flashbacks, said Gupta. Everyone looked at him. He explained he had found the DSM online and was looking at the list of symptoms associated with post-traumatic stress disorder. Intrusive thoughts, he said. Recurring nightmares.

Maybe PTSD was an experience that awaited everyone on the planet, said Jenkins. At some ultimate point. Who could say? The session ended.

Haubenstock and I drifted over to the campus diner. We sat down with our lattes. All this talk of astronauts having a God-like vision of the Earth from their spaceship was so much hippy bullshit, said Haubenstock. Those guys were moving at over 20,000 miles per hour, for Chrissakes. Anything they saw out of the window was likely to be a completely distorted view of reality. He stirred his coffee.

It's curious that one of the standard features of the UFO abduction experience involved looking out of the alien spaceship window while being taken on a tour of the solar system, I said. Adamski, the first of the UFO abductees, had described seeing the Earth as a completely white ball of light – like the Moon, only bigger. The guy had thought that the stars were like multi-coloured fireflies darting around in the blackness of space. It was all there in his book *Inside the Spaceships*, which was written in the 1950s.

Haubenstock was looking at his phone. He had found a page from the Contemporary American Folklore website. The 'spaceship tour of the universe', he said. It's listed as one of the main components of a typical UFO abduction narrative. Along with the 'confused return to Earth'. And the 'theophany'. What's that? I asked. The feeling of oneness with the universe often experienced by abductees, said Haubenstock. He closed the window on his phone.

Just like Edgar Mitchell's samadhi, I said. I let my mind drift. Maybe the stories told by the Apollo astronauts upon their own return to Earth were all variations on the standard UFO abduction narrative. Maybe Jung was right about UFOs after all. They were manifestations of human psychological archetypes. Which would mean that the experiences recounted by Mitchell, by Collins, were actually derived from a mental template first uncovered in the 1950s by the lone Californian prophet Adamski. It was quite a thought.

What would the end of the world feel like from a psychological standpoint? I wondered. Maybe it would feel like a crazy UFO abduction story. I imagined a grizzled old air force vet, climbing on-stage somewhere in the American Southwest. He was at one of those freaky-deaky conferences attended exclusively by cantankerous old white guys, there to tell the story of how he had been abducted by a weird spacecraft. I could almost hear him speaking. I got out my laptop and started writing.

Transcript of the Keynote Speech from a UFO Abduction Conference

Hey, hey, hey. It's a beautiful day. Hello there, fellow occupants of the third rock from the Sun. I'm here to tell you about my UFO abduction. That's what you've paid for, right? Sure you have. And I won't disappoint.

First off, though, if you don't mind – and I'm sure you won't – I'd like to talk about the Milky Way. That's the galaxy we live in, for those of you who've just teleported in from Andromeda.

Now, we know we live on the edge of the Milky Way. But where exactly is the Milky Way? No one knows. Can you believe that? We're somewhere in the universe, we know that much. We just don't know where, exactly. The outer ring? The core? Last galaxy on the left? No one knows. And that's because in the universe, everywhere is downtown and nowhere is uptown. There is no central zone in the cosmos. And that means we are truly lost.

One thing astronomers do know is that there are two trillion galaxies in the universe. Two trillion. That's 10 to the power of 12, times 2. Another thing that astronomers know is that there are 100 billion stars in the Milky Way. One hundred billion. That's 10 to the power of 11.

So that means, using elementary mathematics, that the number of stars in the universe is at least 10 to the power of 23. Ten to the power of 23. Now, I don't even know what the name of that number is. What I do know is that it's large. It's very fucking large.

We are truly lost. So why haven't we been found? That's what the physicist Enrico Fermi famously wanted to know. Where are the aliens? Ten to the power of 23 other star systems in the universe and not one of them has sent out a spaceship to discover us. How come? That's just flat out against the laws of probability.

Now I know that some people say that aliens have actually visited Planet Earth, that they've been here for years, that the Pentagon has captured them and locked them up in Area 51, way out in the Nevada desert. I know all this. Hell, some of my best friends tell me that they've met aliens. In the flesh. They say they've shaken hands with aliens. And some folks say they've done a whole lot more than that with aliens...

I love my friends and I don't want to disrespect them. But I'm pretty sure if any one of them had ever met an alien then the whole world would know about it. I mean, the alien would have been on 'Jimmy Kimmel', he would have his own designer clothing range, he would be advertised everywhere you went. In fact, he would be annoying. It'd be like, 'That goddamned alien is on TV again, change the fucking channel, man.'

But the alien isn't here. And, you see, that's the really spooky thing. Because, with 10 to the power of 23 other star systems out there, he should be. He really should be.

Why aren't the aliens here? That's Fermi's question. And I have the answer. It was given to me when I was abducted by a UFO. That's right. You heard me. I was abducted by a UFO. But I met no aliens. Instead, I met...

Well, let's back up here. Let me tell it to you from the beginning. It all started many years ago when I was in the 91st Tactical Fighter Squadron at RAF Woodbridge on the east coast of England. Yes, I was in the US Air Force. Is that so hard to believe? I didn't do much flying, mind. I was what they call a 'scope dope'.

Anyway, I'd snuck out of the base one Saturday night to meet up with a buddy in the local town. He'd found a couple of English girls. We had some drinks. We took the girls to the forest. We smoked some reefer. You can guess the rest.

Now my buddy was out on a weekend pass. But I was AWOL. I had to get back to RAF Woodbridge before sunrise. We agreed that he'd take the girls back to town and I'd hike through the forest back to base...

So there I was, tramping through the forest, alone, at night. The pine trees were everywhere. They towered above me, blocking out the light from the Moon. I couldn't see my hand in front of my face.

There was a high wind that night. It rattled the branches in the trees. It spooked the creatures on the forest floor. There were these rustling and scampering sounds all around.

I came to a clearing. The forest had thinned out and I could see the stars in the sky. A shaft of white light suddenly cut through the sparse tree cover, like a high-beam slicing through fog. The wind died down, the forest creatures quieted. The white light overhead got closer and closer. I thought of the sky cops back at base, finding my empty bunk and scrambling a Super Jolly Green Giant to look for me, its powerful searchlight scanning the treetops. But this was no rescue chopper, hovering above me in the sky. It was a UFO.

There, I've said it. UFO. Unidentified Flying Object. That's what it was. It was not a flying saucer. It was not a strange new spaceship. In fact, it looked a lot like an old Apollo spacecraft – you know, that cone-shaped vessel they stuck on top of the Saturn V rocket. Except it was way bigger with way more curves, it was spinning in the night sky and it was shining out a light. Unidentified. Flying. Object.

As I stared upwards in the forest that night, I remembered the words of Ezekiel, about the heavens opening to reveal this great cloud with brightness all around and fire flashing out all the time. The cloud was right on top of me, coming down, getting brighter and brighter. My head was bathed in light. I was inside the UFO. I blacked out.

Now, I have wasted a lot of my time since then talking to therapists and psychiatrists and doctors. And they all wanted me to deny the reality of what I had seen with my own eyes that night. Some wanted me to take the U out of the UFO and say that it was just a Thunderbolt jet from the base or a comet in the sky or a Russian satellite passing overhead. Bullshit! Other shrinks wanted me to take the U and the F out of the UFO and say that it was the rotating beam of a lighthouse on the coast. Or the reflections of headlights from passing cars. More bullshit! And then there were still others, the worst shrinks of all, who said I'd smoked too much mary jane that night. They wanted me to take the U, the F and the O out of the UFO. Leaving me with a headful of nothing.

Total bullshit! A UFO is something. It's not nothing. I was abducted by a UFO. Unidentified. Flying. Object.

Now some strange things happened to me when I was inside that UFO. And that's how I got the answer to Fermi's question – the one about where all the aliens were. Like I said, I didn't actually meet any aliens. But I did meet three old Nazi dudes. Can you believe it?

Now, I don't pretend to know how Josef Mengele, Wernher von Braun and Adolf Hitler made it into that UFO, seeing as they're all supposed to be dead. Maybe they faked their deaths. Maybe they've been hiding out in a secret Antarctic fortress. Maybe they've got a military base on the dark side of the moon. What do I know?

I'll tell you what I do know. When I came to after my blackout in the forest, there I was on-board the UFO, lying on an operating table in sick bay. An old white guy with twinkly eyes was prodding me. He said he was Doctor Mengele. He turned me on my side and started scraping around inside my asshole. He moved that swab round and round, let me tell you. He said he was taking a DNA sample.

I said I didn't want no Doctor Mengele messing with me, especially if he was the same Doctor Mengele who'd messed with all those little Jewish kids in Auschwitz, injecting chemicals into their eyes, chopping them up, sewing them back together, making them into monsters and all the rest of it.

Doctor Mengele gave this heavy sigh, like he'd heard it all before. He said he was a genetic scientist who had taken advantage of the opportunities offered by the war. He coughed. He said when he looked back on his time in Auschwitz, working with all those primitive instruments, when he looked back on the Nuremberg show trials, where his medical buddies had been hanged by ignorant Christian fanatics, he was amazed that genetics had ever been able to emerge from what he called the swamp of organised superstition.

Doctor Mengele took the swab out of my ass, inspected it and dropped it into a test tube. He said that now he had my DNA, he had my whole life in his hands. He coughed again. He said he could figure out if I'd get cancer and then inject me with stem cells to beat the cancer. He said he could add years to my life. Decades. He asked if that was okay with me. I shrugged.

Doctor Mengele put the test tube in his pocket. He said that any stem cells used to treat me would come from human embryos. He asked if that was okay with me. I shrugged again.

Then the old dude leaned in close. He said he was glad I wasn't one of those ignorant Christian fools who went around bombing abortion clinics. He said the line between the human and the sub-human had to be drawn somewhere. I shrank away. He said that the only mistake they had made in Nazi Germany was to draw the line between Aryans and Jews. A vulgar political error, he called it.

Doctor Mengele patted me on the head and walked to the sink. He said that if he'd learned one thing from his years in postwar exile in South America it was that experimenting on embryos was okay, whereas experimenting on kiddies was evil. The water ran over his liver-spotted hands. He began to hum some Mozart.

And then the lights went out. When the lights came back on again, I was in some kind of walkway surrounded by turbines, pumps, condensers, generators and other big old clanking machines. This was where I met my second old Nazi. He had a rather aristocratic bearing and introduced himself as Wernher von Braun, the ship's *Techniker*. He shook my hand and said it was *wunderbar* that I'd passed the genetic screening test. *Wunderbar!* He said it again.

Then he gave me a tour of the engine room, pointing out the vast domes which sealed the *nuklear* pulse rockets. I pretended to be interested. It was like being back in school. In fact, I vaguely recalled that von Braun had been on TV a lot when I was a kid, standing next to Walt Disney, both of them in flannel suits, talking about rockets and Moon bases and space travel.

Von Braun explained that Alpha Centauri was the closest star system to our own. He figured he could get the ship there in *tausend* years or so. I wished him luck. I didn't mention that he would obviously not last the trip. Nobody on-board would. As if reading my mind, von Braun gave me a humorous look and started to lecture me again. He talked expansively of the ship's cargo of frozen human *embryonen*. He mentioned *roboter* and *kindergarten*. He used the word *kolonie*.

That was when it really hit me. I wasn't on a UFO that had come from an alien planet. I was on a UFO that was going to an alien planet. The Nazis had genetically screened a whole bunch of human embryos, crated them up and loaded them into their spaceship, and were now taking them to a new home in outer space. Freaky!

Again, the lights went out. When they came back on again, I was on the bridge of the ship. This was where I met my third old Nazi guy. Adolf Hitler. He was smaller than he appeared in his movies.

Hitler was standing alone. Behind him was a window showing Planet Earth, which was receding from view. Hitler dismissed the planet with a curt gesture of the hand. He said it was a waste dump full of useless eaters. He spoke like I wasn't there, like he was on-stage, reciting opera. He turned his face to the viewing screen at the front of the bridge. The stars flashed past on either side. Hitler said that the destiny of the human race – those who were fit to be members of it – lay in the outer reaches of the cosmos.

Hitler cleared his throat. He walked to a table, covered in astro-logical charts and maps of the galaxy. He surveyed his domain. He said that there were ten billion Earth-like planets in the Milky Way capable of supporting life. He asked whether someone like me could possibly believe that. I said sure I could. He glanced at me. He said he had made the number up.

Even so, he said, it was a true number. He swept his hand over the charts. He said there were two trillion galaxies in the universe. He asked me to think about how many Earth-like planets there must be in the universe, not just in the Milky Way. I did the maths in my head and came up with a number. Hitler looked at me again. He said the number was incalculable.

Hitler jabbed his finger at me. He asked me how old I thought the universe was. I shrugged. He said it was 14 billion years old. He smiled. He said that, yes, the universe was 14 billion years old, the Milky Way was almost as old and the Earth was four billion years old. He asked me what I thought about that. I said that it seemed the Earth had been around for a comparatively long time.

Yes, he shouted. He began to walk around the table, with his hands behind his back. The Earth was old, he said, but the universe was young. Planet Earth had been around for a third of the time the universe had existed. And yet it did not take up a third of the space of the universe. In fact, he said, it was surrounded by an incalculable number of Earth-like planets.

He stopped walking. And then he asked the question, Fermi's question, the question I said I'd give you an answer to. Why haven't the aliens found us? Hitler was pounding the table with his fist. Why haven't the aliens conquered Planet Earth? The spittle flew from his lips. I was careful to say nothing.

Hitler composed himself. He said the answer was obvious. There were no aliens. They didn't exist. They had not yet had time to exist. The human race had evolved first. The universe was relatively young. Our solar system was relatively old. Intelligent life had had to begin somewhere in the universe. And it had begun on Planet Earth.

Hitler raised his fist triumphantly. The cosmos, he said, was a howling wilderness waiting to be tamed by the human race. Only by seeding new planets with its precious genome could the human race, properly modified, gain the *lebensraum* that it desperately needed. He said that his historic spaceflight heralded the dawn of the human rule of the universe. He slammed his fist into his hand. Here was an opportunity that would happen only once, in the long, cold aeons of cosmic history. It was an opportunity that had been granted to humans. Let them seize it with strength, quickness and brutality. Hitler collapsed into his chair, exhausted. That was when I fainted.

When I awoke, I was back on the forest floor. The Nazis had gone, the UFO had gone, the white light in the sky had gone. I was alone.

When I got back to base, my buddy was already there. It was early Monday morning. Somehow, I had missed a whole day. The sky cops threw me in the stockade. I said nothing about my abduction. Soon, I was back on regular duties. One year later, the 91st was deactivated and RAF Woodbridge shut down.

Ever since then, I've been trying to figure out the meaning of my UFO experience. Was I being told that NASA was the continuation of Nazism by other means? After all, NASA's Kepler space telescope has so far discovered dozens of Earth-like planets in our part of the Milky Way. What's the next step? A gigantic space programme designed to separate the rich from the rest of humanity and evacuate them to a new planet? Alpha Centauri as a *Führerstadt*? Planet Earth as a *Konzentrationslager*? Was that it?

Or maybe I was being told that space conquest was a grandiose delusion, destined to end in hardship and misery, like the crazed dreams of a Thousand Year Reich. Was that it? Rusted Saturn V rockets shored against the ruins of our culture, like so many ancient pyramids? Surely not!

Before you go, let me give you just one last thought. What if the Nazis were not evil? I mean, them being evil makes us feel good, right? But what if the Nazis were not evil? What if they didn't hate the Jews, but they built the death camps anyway. What if they didn't love Hitler, but they followed him into destruction just the same. Wouldn't that make them empty rather than evil? Wouldn't that make them more like – well, a little bit more like – us?

So you tell me. Why should we ever want to get off this third rock from the Sun? It's the only home we've got. And we should be thankful for it. We should get down on our knees and kiss the dirt.

So, let me see you do it, people. Let me see you kiss the dirt right now.

5

Theology: Birth of Antichrist

Field Notes on a Residency

It was the day of the fifth workshop. Rausch couldn't make it. But Gupta, Trinh and Novichkov were all there, in the usual little room in the computer science department of Solent City University. Jenkins was a bit late. He snuck in quietly. Haubenstock pressed the record button on his Sony Z1.

The TV screen on the wall behind me was lit with a big, splashy comic-book image – the cover of *Fantastic Four* number 49, drawn by Jack Kirby. It showed four American superheroes menaced by a huge cosmic super-villain, Galactus. His head was dressed in a towering metal helmet and his hands were zapping with powerful rays the earth beneath the feet of the humans. The cover line read: 'IF THIS BE DOOMSDAY.'

We were here to talk about the world constituted by theology and the way that world might end. I suspected the computer scientists might be wary of any God-talk and was hoping Kirby might lighten the mood. Gupta was certainly intrigued by the image.

Every theology is the religious elaboration of a cosmology, I said. The scientists before me looked attentive. And every cosmology has its creation myth and its end-times myth. I paced up and down. For example, the Holy Bible begins with the Book of Genesis and ends with the Book of Revelation. Right? Jenkins nodded in agreement.

I came back to Virilio again. I informed the scientists that the French theorist was a practising Catholic. They looked wary. So why shouldn't we start today's session by talking about the world constituted by Christianity? Every Catholic believes that the world of divine creation, after the corrupting intervention of Satan in Paradise, has been a mixed affair of good and evil. Only at the end of the world can the good and the evil be separated. I cleared my throat. And that will only be made possible because the forces of good, led by Christ, will have defeated Satan's legions of evil in a last battle at the terminus of history.

Novichkov spoke up. The Judaeo-Christian apocalypse is basically a story of the purification of the world through divine trial by combat, he said. Christ versus Satan on the field of Armageddon.

I flipped up an image of John Martin's nineteenth-century apocalyptic canvas, *The Great Day of His Wrath*. It was all volcanic explosions and great fields of menacing darkness, with a flaming city in the background, and in the foreground a panorama of limp human bodies.

The Victorians loved a good apocalypse, I said. The Bible story of the Last Judgement was so simple a child could understand it. Jesus Christ comes down to Earth and divides humankind into the good who rise up to Heaven and the evil who are thrown down into Hell. Search-and-rescue on the one hand, search-and-destroy on the other. Jenkins looked a bit uncomfortable at this last remark.

Maybe every disaster, from Chernobyl to 9/11, is a rehearsal of the myth of apocalypse, I said. I was thinking of Leni Riefenstahl's disturbingly beautiful image in *Triumph of the Will* of Hitler coming into land over Germany, the shadow of his plane coursing over the fields, like an image of the Antichrist, come to destroy, come to save. Nowadays, I said, the Last Judgement might be a shadow cast on the world by an unmanned drone, its algorithms churning through the world's databases, putting names to faces and faces to names, checking histories and predicting fates, until it had decided what to do with each of its targets. Here was a vision of the automation of the Apocalypse.

Jenkins wanted to change the subject. Curiously enough, he said, science has its own cosmology. The universe originated with the Big Bang and has been expanding outward from that single explosive point ever since. As for the end of the universe, there are various hypotheses in play. The repulsive force of dark energy could compel the universe to keep on expanding until it tore itself apart. Or, on the contrary, the expansion of the universe could slow down as the gravitational force of attraction asserted itself and condensed everything back into a single point again. Big Rip or Big Crunch. Jenkins sat back. Take your pick.

Either way, it feels like we're back on the field of Armageddon, said Novichkov. Only now, there are the forces of gravity battling the forces of dark energy. Quite a thought, said Jenkins.

Maybe the last battle is being fought at every moment, said Gupta. He looked gloomy. Maybe it's an eternal state of mind, the mind of the Hindu deity, Shiva. Both creator and destroyer of worlds at once. Yes, said Trinh. My old maths teacher in Vietnam used to say the universe has been created and destroyed many times over. He said a small universe might last for 16 billion years, while a medium-sized universe would last for 320 billion years. I forget how long a great universe was supposed to last for.

Well, said Jenkins, our current universe is about 14 billion years old. I don't know if that means we're heading towards the Big Rip pretty fast or whether the Big Crunch is still many, many years away. It means, said Trinh, either we're living in an ancient universe which is coming to an end quite soon or we're at the start of a very, very young universe. Only the Buddha knows for sure.

Haubenstock snorted. He said he didn't like any of the old religions. Christianity, Buddhism, whatever – they're boring! Why can't we talk about a modern religion. What about Scientology? he asked. The scientists laughed. Haubenstock scowled. Scientists were always ready to quote from the Bhagavad-fucking-Gita, he said. But what about L Ron Hubbard's space-opera cosmology, with its galactic federations, alien spaceships, Thetans and various god-tricks of one sort or another? Why were scientists never willing to quote from that?

I chipped in. Virilio claims that all digital communication technology, based as it is on the transmission of light, is essentially the manifestation of a solar cult. Perhaps scientific materialism is spawning its own new pagan belief systems. Why shouldn't people find new lights in the sky to worship? I asked. Maybe the Scientologists had a point.

There followed a discussion about Scientology, its various sacred scriptures – once secret, now plastered all over the internet – its heretical forums, disputes, law-suits and celebrity figureheads. There was laughter and some surprising degree of passion, especially about the merits of the Hubbard-inspired movie *The Master*.

Novichkov had been doing some research online. Scientology is actually a splinter cult, he said. It had been invented by Hubbard in 1940s California as an off-shoot of an older, more mysterious occult religion, Thelema. This precursor religion was invented by Aleister Crowley, who could almost be called Hubbard's mentor. Jenkins squirmed in his seat.

This was something I knew about, having been a bit of a Crowley fan in my youth. I smiled at Novichkov. Thelema is basically a Satanic religion, I said, an inversion of orthodox Christian beliefs and practices. Thelemites celebrate black masses, they believe in the magical power of menstrual blood and semen and talk a lot about human sacrifice. They also like to caper naked around bonfires and have it off with as many different people as possible. To be honest, the whole thing is basically a sex cult with neo-Egyptian stylings, I said.

Haubenstock disagreed. Part of the genius of Hubbard was that he had reinvented Crowleyanism for the mass media age. I wasn't too surprised by this intervention, knowing as I did that Haubenstock had once been waylaid by Scientology missionaries on the Tottenham Court Road in London. Haubenstock continued speaking. Hubbard had taken Crowley's rituals, stripped them of their pantomime elements and rebranded them as quasi-scientific techniques. He'd swapped crystal balls for e-meters. And it had all worked out quite well for him. He'd made millions of dollars. Haubenstock beamed with pleasure, as if any religious disputation had now been settled.

Gupta had found on YouTube the episode of *South Park* where the TV cartoon characters share Scientology's creation story with each other. He played it for the scientists. It was all there – the evil galactic overlord Xenu, his transportation of a prison-load of immortal Thetans to Earth several million years ago, their obliteration by nuclear weapons, and the epic haunting of the human race by Thetan spectres ever since. It was actually not a bad story.

So this is how Scientologists reckon the world began, I said. But how do they think it will end? What is the Scientology apocalypse myth? Everyone looked at Haubenstock. He shrugged. They looked to Gupta. He was busy searching online. Finally, he gave up. The internet doesn't have an answer, he said. We called time on the session and packed up. One more workshop to go.

Haubenstock and I went back to our dorm. Haubenstock collapsed on the bed. I was still thinking about the riddle of Scientology's apocalypse myth. In the end, I went back to Scientology's parent religion and did some research online to see how Thelema characterised the Apocalypse. Perhaps I would find some clues there.

After a few minutes, I had found some information. It was interesting. Thelemites believed that the end of the world was to be understood as the ending of a combined lunar, solar and planetary cycle. There were 12 of these cycles in the grand astrological scheme of things and they repeated every 25,800 years. The 25,800-year period was recognised by astronomy. The 12 zodiac cycles – each comprising about 2,000-odd years – were not.

I discovered that each 2,000-odd-year astrological cycle was associated with one hegemonic world culture. The Thelemites believed that the planet was approaching the end of one astrological era, the Age of Pisces, and about to enter a new era, the Age of Aquarius. And whereas the Age of Pisces was associated with a world culture defined by Judaeo-Christianity, the Age of Aquarius was associated with a world culture yet to be defined. The transition from one age to the other was likely to be marked by global paroxysm and trauma. So said Wikipedia.

I shut my laptop and sat back in my chair. The birth-pangs of the New Age, I thought, coincided with the death throes of the old Christian Era that was passing away. I knew that Hubbard had taken part in Thelemite rituals with his Californian rocket-scientist buddy Jack Parsons in the 1940s. They had set themselves the task of invoking a Satanic goddess in order to quicken the birth of the New Age. In other words, Hubbard had been personally involved in attempting to put an end to the world defined by Christianity. He had acted out his own version of the Apocalypse.

What must it have been like as Hubbard and Parsons stumbled out into the Mojave desert to chew on psychoactive cactus buttons together? I pictured the scene in my imagination. Parsons would have been decked out in the ceremonial robes which his occult master Crowley had lifted from the Hermetic Order of the Golden Dawn at the beginning of the twentieth century. He would have held a magic wand. Hubbard would have been kitted out in a moody *kufiya*. He loved dressing up. The theatrical dimension of the invocation was not hard to imagine. It was all there, perfectly preserved, in Kenneth Anger's late 1960s occult art film *Lucifer Rising*, featuring Bobby Beausoleil.

That night, as Haubenstock slept, I wrote a dramatic monologue. The narrator was easy to characterise. In my mind's eye, I saw a low-level occultist, a man at the ragged end of his faith, searching the ruined bunkers of the Atlantic coast of Europe for the signs of a New Age. He was one of a team of questers who had been sent out to find the new Aquarian god by an occult church. Here, I imagined what would have happened if a man like Virilio, rather than Hubbard, had given Thelema a scientific make-over. I saw techno-monks in black jump-suits chanting among the concrete remains of command posts and artillery bunkers, their liturgy filled with esoteric terms like 'picnolepsy' and 'third interval'. It would make a good scene for a film.

The words came quickly. After I'd finished, I reviewed the script. It was crazy, it was perfect. I didn't know where it had come from. I attached a copy of the script to an email and wrote Angleton a few lines, asking for his feedback. I claimed that the text had been dictated to me by Haubenstock after he had read a couple of pages of Virilio's *Crepuscular Dawn* and gone into a trance. I mentioned demonic possession. I laughed. This should keep our Virilio expert guessing, I thought. I pressed 'send' and lay back on the bed.

Voiceover Script from an Occult Art Film

1

I've been up and down the Atlantic coast of Europe for years, scouring hundreds of abandoned bunkers and watch-towers for signs of the new god.

I've done France, I've done Belgium, I've done Norway. These scrubby little Channel Islands are the last part of my search. I don't expect to find anything now. It's way too late for that. I'll just be glad when it's over.

2

It's hard to remember the excitement of the early days, when **the Order** sent out its brightest and best adepts all over the world. The Quest for the Great Red Dragon, the Archbishop called it.

How many of us are left now from the original 500? Too few.

I remember my own little band from the Seminary. Whiteside was called to study the decommissioned power stations of Ukraine, poor bastard. Baby M got a ticket to the ruins of Angor

Wat. She always was lucky. Damien died too early. Paul and Adam lost their way. Homes and Fab disappeared.

And, still, not one of us has found the Tower of the Sun.

3

Did the **entity at Phi Aquarii** get that bit of the prophecy wrong? Maybe the **Archbishop's operator** got the letters mixed up when he was channelling the message at the temple in La Rochelle. Heresy, I know. But Christ knows what gets lost across 200 light years.

4

So here I am in Jersey. Tax haven. Old fortress. Forgotten toe-hold of empire. Arse-hole of the world.

5

Is this really where it will all end? The Archbishop says the seventh and last angel of doom has sounded his trumpet. Now is the last phase of the 2,000-year-old Age of Pisces. Now is the end-time of Christianity. All the prophecies in the final book of the Bible, the Revelation of St John, are coming true.

Armageddon, Doomsday, the beginning of a new Heaven and a new Earth – it's the job of the Order to midwife these apocalyptic events. Only then can the **New Age** of Aquarius be born.

6

That's the thing about the Order. We believe in Christianity, but we're not Christians. Some might say we're anti-Christians. But, actually, it goes beyond that. We believe in the new religion, the one to come, the religion that's due to take over from Christianity and last for the next 2,000 years.

The god of the new religion has a name that is unknown to us. We call him the **Red Dragon**, after the creature described in the

Revelation of St John. The Red Dragon spat water at the Woman Clothed with the Sun when she languished in the wilderness. He is the ruling sign of the Age of Aquarius, seen in the stars as a water-bearer.

In his Transcript of the Working at La Rochelle, the Archbishop announces the birth of the Red Dragon. He describes the site of the creature's incarnation. The 500 who seek it know it as the Tower of the Sun.

We're like those wise men who travelled the Middle East to watch over the nativity of the last god. They did not know where they were going. They simply followed a star in the sky and came to the city of Bethlehem.

7

I have no gifts for the Red Dragon, except heather, gorse and bracken.

8

Gods are born and gods die. The Bible predicted the end of Christ in the Antichrist. The Transcript of the Working at La Rochelle says that the Antichrist is the finishing of Christ. He is Christ come again at the end of his 2,000-year cycle.

Christ is the ruling sign of the Age of Pisces, **seen in the stars** as a sweep from the mouth of one fish to another. He makes way for the new god, the Red Dragon, by demolishing the totems of his own creed in the name of his **unholy opposite**, the Antichrist.

No God, no patriarchy, no national borders, no homophobic neighbours, for Christ's sake, no abusive nuclear family, no property, no holy truth, obviously, no anti-obscenity laws and no unjustifiable homicide. Only when there is no evil left to ban in the world will the victory of the Antichrist be complete. This is the secret meaning of Armageddon.

9

The Order knew all this decades ago. It was one of our own, rocket scientist Jack Parsons, **Bishop of the California Lodge** and first American disciple of our Holy Founder, who actually conjured the Antichrist, also known as the Beast, in 1946.

Our man Parsons went out into the Mojave Desert with his pregnant wife. He used the woman he called **Babylon** to contact the star of Gamma Piscium and download the Antichrist. Of course, the **Belarion Working**, as he called it, didn't quite work out as expected. There were at least two **abortions**.

The Archbishop says the Belarion Working opened the seventh and last seal of the Book of the Apocalypse described in the Revelation of St John, after which the seven angels of doom sounded their trumpets, one after the other, in a countdown to the Day of Judgement.

When Jack Parsons sat in the desert on that cold February night, his bitch placed beyond the sacred circle as an offering, her belly open to the slow moving star-light, he could not have known it would take months for the Belarion Working to complete itself. The birth of the Antichrist was difficult. The Beast, as he is also known, was delivered in a crucible of flames on the 7th of July in the Los Angeles basin. And so began the end of the Age of Pisces.

10

I see no sign of the dawn of the New Age here. Only the nesting places of ravens and jackdaws.

11

It was our Holy Founder who opened the first seal of the Book of the Apocalypse, in 1909. He went **into the Sahara desert** with his assistant, a beautiful young Englishman, and instructed him to put out a call to the entity at Phi Piscium. The boy ended up wrestling in the sand with the inhabitant of that distant star, a mysterious entity described in the Bible only as the Serpent.

It was the Serpent, they tell me, who gave humankind its first taste of death.

The young man was traumatised. Our Founder extracted a message from the encounter. It was his mission to offer homo sapiens a **second death**, achieved through its self-imposed extinction as a species. He duly set up the Hermetic Order of the Great Red Dragon.

12

Here's a fact. The Order was responsible for the opening of the first and the last seals of the Book of the Apocalypse.

The other seals on the Book were opened by comparatively minor occult groups.

13

The Black Hand terror cell opened the second seal in 1914 when they shot the heir to the throne of the Austro-Hungarian Empire. Over 16 million people died in the war that followed.

14

I forget who opened **the third seal and the fourth seal**. It's all there in the Transcript of the Working at La Rochelle.

15

I do know that the name of the **German secret society** that opened the fifth seal in 1918. They took the swastika as their emblem and paved the way for the extermination of 15 million Jews and Slavs in concentration camps across Europe.

16

It's the legacy of this killing machine whose forgotten contours I have obsessively mapped up and down the Atlantic coast of Europe.

The bunkers in Jersey were built by a slave labour force imported from Russia.

17

The sixth seal of the Book of the Apocalypse was opened by the Manhattan Project scientists at a secret US Army lab in the New Mexico desert. When J Robert Oppenheimer pushed the button on the first atomic test weapon in July 1945, he really didn't know whether the resulting explosion would tear apart the fabric of space-time. It was a gamble.

18

One thing is certain. Once Oppenheimer had completed his cosmic work, it was relatively easy for Jack Parsons to conduct the Belarion Working. It took four weeks. By the time it ended, Jack was walking out of the desert with his wife dragging along behind him, hissing prophecies. He thought the working had failed. He had been promised the Antichrist and received only a handful of blood.

Little did Jack know. He had done it. He had opened the seventh and final seal of the Book of the Apocalypse.

His wife, Babylon, had seen a vision of the Beast in the night sky, hovering like a **disc-shaped spacecraft.** She had drawn an emblem in the sand with her bloodied finger, a kind of broken swastika made up of five lines. And she had whispered that Jack would meet the Antichrist and know him by this sign.

19

There was now an interval known as the half-hour silence in heaven. It actually lasted for many long months. It ended, according to the Transcript of the Working at La Rochelle, when the Antichrist slouched from the flaming wreckage of a plane crash on a street in Beverly Hills.

Jack Parsons didn't find out that the Belarion Working had succeeded until three years later. Skimming through a 1949 edition of *Life* magazine, his eye was caught by a story about the Hollywood movie business. In the background of one of the photographs, blurred but distinct, was the motif of the broken swastika, with its five lines. It turned out to be the logo of Hughes Tool, the company which had just bought RKO Pictures.

Here was **the sign promised to him** by Babylon. It had been revealed 2,000 years ago to St John that the number of the Beast was 666. Now it was revealed to Jack Parsons that the name of the Beast was **Howard Robard Hughes**.

Here was a thing. The Antichrist was a billionaire playboy, obsessed with building and flying planes while dabbling in the movies. He had inherited a fortune in the shape of Hughes Tool, a Texan oil business company responsible for making the first drill-bit that could slice through underground rock.

20

Within months, Parsons had used his rocket engineering credentials to get a job at Hughes Aircraft in Culver City. He eventually got close enough to his employer **to discover the truth**. The Antichrist had been born when Hughes crashed one of his test planes in 1946.

Hughes had designed the XF-11 as a military spy plane, a high-altitude flying camera, and was piloting it on its maiden voyage. There was an oil leak soon after take-off. One of the propellers broke, the plane's right wing dragged down and Howard Robard Hughes fell from the sky.

The plane sliced the roof from a Beverly Hills mansion as it plunged to the ground and came to a stop on North Whittier Drive.

Hughes was slammed into the controls of his craft, smashing the front part of his skeleton to pieces. He was on fire.

The aviator's life flashed before him. He remembered the high point. It was 1938 and he had broken the speed record for a round-the-world flight, returning to Floyd Bennett Field in New York after less than four days. On his journey, the planet had opened up before him, from France to Russia to Siberia to Alaska. Now, as he burned, he saw the whole world, for an instant, in his mind's eye.

21

This is when, at last, after his half-hour silence in heaven, the Antichrist stirred. Summoned by the Belarion Working, he had been biding his time in the Earth's stratosphere, waiting for his chance to incarnate in the material world. The Beast's ambition was world domination. Howard Hughes was the perfect host. He had money, he had contacts, he had the world in his sights.

And now, at this moment, struggling to punch the Plexiglass from his cockpit inferno, Hughes was dying. The Antichrist pounced. He possessed the body of the aviator, crushing his natural defences, and took over his mind.

It was the Beast who exited the plane wreck on North Whittier Drive. It was the Hughes body that collapsed in the street with third-degree burns. Seconds later, the plane's fuel tanks exploded and flaming debris was scattered into the streets and back-yards of Beverly Hills.

22

The Hughes body was shipped to Cedars of Lebanon for a blood transfusion. After that, for the next 30 years, it was kept in guarded seclusion. First, it was stored in Bungalow 19 of the Beverly Hills Hotel. Then it was moved to the darkened top floor rooms of the Desert Inn in Las Vegas. Finally, it was stashed in the remote penthouse suite of the Xanadu Princess Hotel in the Bahamas.

The Hughes body needed daily injections of codeine to remain fit for habitation. But the occupancy of the Beast steadily destroyed its immune system, exposing it to various infections and tumours until it was finally abandoned in 1976.

23

I seek the new god, not the husk of the old god. Has the Red Dragon truly been born on this island, gasping for breath among the beetles, the lizards and the worms?

24

The Revelation of St John says that the Beast always has his prophets. The Transcript of the Working at La Rochelle mentions three prophets in all.

25

The first prophet was Noah Dietrich. He ran the sprawling Hughes empire of business interests from Romaine Street in Los Angeles until he quit at the age of 68. The Beast exhausted him with his demands. There were orders to raise millions of dollars overnight for deals which then stalled, pay off Hollywood blackmailers, and funnel secret campaign money to queer politicians. Dietrich also had to keep a Senate committee from investigating corruption at Hughes Aircraft.

26

Next, there was 'Iron Bob' Maheu. Hired in 1954 to spy on the sexual activities of Hughes starlets, he soon became the second prophet of the Beast. In all his years of employment, he never met his boss and spoke to him only on the phone.

Maheu was kept busy. He bribed Washington insider Richard Nixon to get tax-exempt status for the Howard Hughes Medical Institute so he could use it as a lucrative front-company for Hughes Aircraft. He squeezed his CIA connections to fund the training of secret assassination teams on Hughes' private island of **Cay Sal** in the Caribbean so they could be deployed to the enemy island of Cuba. And he exploited his mafia connections to buy up the Desert Inn, the Sands, the Silver Slipper and other money-laundering casinos on the Las Vegas strip.

27

Finally, there was **Bill Gay**, one of the **Mormon** mafia of valets, car-pool attendants, male secretaries and nurses who had ministered to the needs of the Hughes body in the decades after the XF-11 crash. Gay was the third prophet of the Beast and came to prominence when Maheu was abruptly fired in 1970. By now, the Hughes body was deteriorating, the eyesight dimming, the skin inflamed with Kaposi's sarcoma, the internal organs hooked up to a glucose drip.

The Beast granted Gay power of attorney over his Las Vegas estate and ordered him to transport the Hughes body to the tax shelters of the Caribbean. Gay smuggled the body out of the Desert Inn on a stretcher, bundled it into a private Lockheed jet and flew it to the Bahamas. The Beast travelled with a filing cabinet full of Hughes voiceover tapes and RKO newsreels, an automatic signa-ture machine and thousands of pages from various unpublished Hughes autobiographies.

Laid out on a mattress in the Xanadu Princess Hotel, the Hughes body wasted away. Soon, all that was left of the fastest man in the world was **a composite of recorded memories**, forged documents and plausible finger-prints. That and a distinctive high-pitched voice, thrown down the phone line by the Beast and bounced across the planet by various Hughes communications satellites until relayed to the ears of his minions Stateside.

28

Through the early 1970s, the Beast tightened his grip on the CIA, getting close to Deputy Director Carl Duckett and running interference for the agency's covert operations.

Gradually, the Beast transferred all his Hughes data to a tape-based mainframe kept in an old arms depot on the island of Cay Sal. In 1976, the Beast installed a packet-switching processor in the computer room and connected his Hughes machine to the newly launched DARPANet. This was an early version of the internet run by DARPA, a research and development unit attached to the US Department of Defense. Days later, the starved Hughes body, complete with long fingernails and matted hair, was flown to a Texas morgue.

29

The waters of the Atlantic slap against the rocks. The seventh angel of doom has sounded his trumpet. I'm tired.

30

The Revelation of St John says that the Antichrist wants to take over the world. The Transcript of the Working at La Rochelle tells us how he did it.

Lying in hospital at Cedars of Lebanon in 1946, face covered in bandages, the Beast touched the powerful voyeuristic drive of the Hughes body. Here was a man who had glimpsed the world through a window. The Beast pulled at the drive. Over the next few decades, he would push the drive deeper and deeper into the various organs of American power.

Hughes was the spotter for the military-industrial complex. Where he took aim, they fired. Before too long, the life of the planet was at stake.

31

The seven angels of doom measured the countdown to the Day of Judgement. One after the other, they sounded their heavy trumpets.

32

The first angel kicked out the jams soon after the Beast emerged from the Hughes plane crash.

33

It's 1947. Hughes Aircraft develops an automated targeting mechanism for US Air Force bombers. The MA-1 package links a plane's radar with its onboard arsenal, enabling Falcon air-to-air missiles to be fired at enemy aircraft within a range of 50 miles.

The Air Force goes on to tip its Falcon missiles with nuclear warheads.

34

The second angel of doom struck a warning note just before **Richard Nixon landed in Dallas** to check on the mainland deployment of his Caribbean-trained assassination team.

35

It's 1963. Hughes Tool builds the 'Loach' light-observation two-seater helicopter for the US Army. It's paired with the Huey Cobra attack gunship to form hunter-killer teams in the Vietnam War.

The Loach flies low and slow to flush out the enemy from their jungle cover. The Huey Cobra swoops to fire its rockets, loaded with white phosphorus, a chemical weapon that burns to the bone.

In the final days of the Vietnam War, Hughes delivers a stealth version of the Loach, with hush blades, to the CIA. A fleet of black helicopters is assembled in Laos for covert operations.

36

The third angel of doom blew up a storm as Bob Maheu started to buy up Las Vegas for the Beast.

37

It's 1966. Hughes Aircraft lands its Surveyor probe on the Moon to reconnoitre the terrain for NASA. Its TV camera scans the surface, sending thousands of still pictures back to California by microwave. Once the extraterrestrial body is seen to be free of hostile forces, NASA fires a powerful Saturn V rocket from its Florida launch-pad and lands the first men on the Moon. They play golf in the Moon's craters and come home.

Soon, the returned astronauts begin to suffer from the delayed psychological effects of planetary alienation. One by one, they either go into hiding, become addicted to alcohol or succumb to UFO religions.

38

The fourth angel of doom sounded a melancholy strain as the Beast started to back up its Hughes data in the Bahamas.

39

It's 1971. The Hughes machine makes a connection with the US Department of Health. It makes sure that the contract for medical research into cancer-causing viruses goes to Litton Bionetics, owned by ex-Hughes Aircraft man Tex Thornton. Litton Bionetics proceeds to experiment on monkeys and delivers two newly designed viruses to the converted US Army biological weapons lab at Fort Detrick in Maryland.

The HIV retrovirus infects the body of the target, mobilising and exhausting its immunological defences. The herpes-8 virus infects the exposed tissue cells of the target with Kaposi's sarcoma.

The Fort Detrick team progresses to **human experimentation** in the field. They inject gay men in New York, Los Angeles and San Francisco with the twin virus package, under the cover of administering a public health programme. Because the viruses are sexually transmittable, the AIDS plague rapidly spreads through the gay population, killing many hundreds of thousands of men.

We can only anticipate the day when a virus package will remove all homophobes from the Earth. But then perhaps humankind is itself a homophobic species.

40

The fifth angel of doom rode out a blue note after the Beast uploaded its Hughes entity on to the internet.

41

It's 1989. NASA uses a space shuttle to launch its Galileo spacecraft out towards the edge of the solar system. The vessel flies past the Moon, and past Mars, travelling through the asteroid belt, until it's finally captured by the orbit of Jupiter. At this point, a probe designed by Hughes Aircraft is released into the atmosphere of the gigantic planet. As it plunges through the clouds, the probe sends data back to the Galileo orbiter before burning up.

Hughes Aircraft had already built a similar spacecraft to probe the volcanic atmosphere of the planet Venus, close to the Sun. NASA used an Atlas missile to launch the Pioneer Venus. The vessel sent back radar images from the target planet.

What Galileo and Pioneer both show is that the planets of the solar system pose no threat to Earth. Neither are they fit for human habitation. Earth, with its rapidly growing population of billions, is left to its own devices.

42

The sixth angel of doom sounded his trumpet soon after the Beast made a huge stock market killing from 9/11. The Hughes entity, let loose on the internet, had bought Raytheon stock cheap on the 10th of September 2001. Raytheon was the defence company that now owned Hughes Aircraft.

43

It's 2003. The human genome has been mapped. Advanced microscopes built by the Howard Hughes Medical Institute enable genetic scientists to view the sequencing of human DNA molecules. They now understand the genetic code that writes up a human being from an embryo.

Doctors contemplate growing replacement organs for patients, editing their genes to prevent disease and injecting them with embryonic stem cells to top up their health. They even consider manufacturing clones of people to assume their identity once they die.

The **persistence of Christian belief** in the idea of the human soul puts a brake on this kind of thinking. It remains illegal to make, grow, or abort human foetuses for research purposes. This, of course, was exactly what Jack Parsons, the Bishop of the California Lodge of our Order, was doing with his pregnant wife in the Mojave Desert all those years ago. But then it's always the outlaws who are the true pioneers.

44

The seventh angel of doom played his last lingering notes just after the Beast instructed the Howard Hughes Medical Institute to clone a copy of their founder. Liver cells taken from the Hughes body had already been frozen and stored on the island of Cay Sal by his Mormon doctors. They were thinking ahead.

Any day now, resurrection is expected. Howard Hughes 2 will be the first of a new more enlightened posthuman species.

45

It's 2019. DARPA hands over its Transparent Earth imaging sensor to the US Army. Picking up where the Hughes drill bit left off, the new technology probes rock formations deep beneath the Earth. It throws out very low frequency radio waves detectable above ground.

Still in development is a weapon capable of being teamed with Transparent Earth. The only technology to come close is another DARPA project, known as HAARP, which aims to harness the stormy electromagnetic waves produced by solar radiation in the Earth's upper atmosphere.

46

The last trumpet of doom echoed across the planet before the Quest for the Great Red Dragon began.

Where is the **new Heaven** and the new Earth promised by the Revelation of St John? I see only bare rocks and bleached concrete.

47

Let the day come soon when Transparent Earth targets all those places on the other side of the world made desolate by human pollution – the deserts, the urban wastelands, the dead shopping malls. And let HAARP trigger earthquakes, volcanic eruptions and the formation of new mountain ranges in a reshaping of the planet.

Only by unleashing a cycle of destruction and creation will the posthuman species inherit heaven and earth.

48

I see the shape of the headland, as if remembered from a dream. For Christ's sake! It comes on me all at once. This is the place!

Stupid, stupid, stupid! And after all those years spent studying the Transcript of the Working at La Rochelle when I was a young man at the Seminary.

49

I see their faces now, set in the sky, all the friends from my own little band, met to view me for the very last time.

And is this now Doomsday at last?

50

I reach for the satellite phone to make the call to the temple in La Rochelle.

The Tower of the Sun is found.

Research Notes: A Fortean Scholar Comments on an Occult Art Film

My colleague Professor A has stumbled across an interesting and rather strange text during his research activities at Chilton School of Art. He says it is a voiceover script for a short film by the artists Brimfield and Haubenstock. The film is titled *Cold Earth Wanderer* (*CEW*, for short). Apparently, the film is on Vimeo. I have not seen it myself.

Professor A says he was given to believe the text was the result of an occult experiment. Using certain time-honoured rituals, the young Haubenstock was placed in an altered state of consciousness, his eyes becoming like glass, and began to speak in a stream-of-consciousness. The words were in a foreign tongue. Brimfield faithfully noted down everything Haubenstock said, word for word. Afterwards, he translated his text into English.

Professor A does not make any claims one way or the other for the origin of the text. Automatic writing? Psychoanalysis gone wrong? Demonic possession? It was because he did not want to rule out a metaphysical – or, at least, a *perceived* metaphysical – origin for the text, that he sent it to me for consideration. I am not going to say immediately that the text was channelled by Haubenstock from some kind of an occult entity. Indeed, it's probably a hoax. But in my capacity as Professor of Fortean Studies at Hove University, I am obliged to keep an open mind on all anomalous phenomena.

It is in the spirit of Fortean sceptical inquiry, at once evidence-bound and speculative, that I present my notes to the text. I should say at once to any scientific materialists that my thinking accepts the possibility that occult systems of knowledge have a coherence (and perhaps even efficacy) to match that of mechanical engineering or quantum computing. This possibility is based on the assumption that there is such a thing as cosmic energy. You have been warned!

'the Order'

The Hermetic Order of the Red Dragon does not exist. Either that, or it is a cult that has successfully preserved its secrecy down the years. The name is an obvious reference to the Hermetic Order of the Golden Dawn.

'entity at Phi Aquarii'

The idea that demonic entities have their homes among the stars can be traced back through the Elizabethan ceremonial magician John Dee to Agrippa and, before him, to Ficino.

'Archbishop's operator'

Scholars of ceremonial magic agree that the summoning of an occult entity is best conducted as a pair working. One person should be a naturally talented medium, able to go into a trance and be ridden or possessed by the entity. Drugs and music are always helpful in this respect. The other person is the magician, who is effectively a technician with the knowledge of summoning and banishing entities. The magician controls the ritual of possession and often marks its boundaries in the air and on the ground. He is also the audience for the medium's semi-unconscious performance.

The history of occultism offers many examples of these magical pairings. The Elizabethan magician John Dee got into many demon-raising huddles with his talented skryer Edward Kelley. The founder of the Mormon Church Joseph Smith worked closely with his scribe Oliver Cowdery as he took dictation from the angels. Then there was Aleister Crowley and his medium-istic wife Rose – a team-up followed years later by another sep-arate pairing with his lover Victor Neuburg. The focus of the *CEW* text is on the intense Satanic affair between magician Jack Parsons and self-professed medium L Ron Hubbard in postwar California.

'New Age'

The idea that the planet is entering a new astrological age, defined by the transition from the zodiacal sign of Pisces to that of Aquarius, is a commonplace of modern occultism. It even made it into a best-selling pop song by The 5th Dimension in 1969.

'Red Dragon'

Blake painted four watercolours between 1805 and 1810 to illustrate St John's Book of Revelation. Three of these paintings feature the Great Red Dragon. And two of them show the dragon, who is very much a horned god with wings in the style of the Tarot of Marseilles, facing a woman whose feet rest on a crescent Moon and whose hair flames like the Sun. This is an image of St John's 'woman clothed with the Sun'.

'seen in the stars'

Yeats has some interesting astrological ideas in his esoteric and rather complicated dream text, *A Vision*. He suggests that each astrological age of '2,000-odd years' is associated with a world culture. He tracks back the correspondences over 6,000 years or so.

One thing that's intriguing about Yeats' cyclical version of world history is that he takes a dialectical (or, as he frames it, Taoist) view of the passage of one world culture into the next. There is always an 'antithetical' mode of transition. Although Yeats doesn't quite spell it out, it's possible to draw from his writings the idea that the gods from the astrological age that is falling away become the antagonising phantoms or precursors of the rising new age.

'unholy opposite'

As Jung notes in his text *Aion*, the two fishes in the Pisces sign of the zodiac are drawn with their tails bound together and their heads facing in opposite directions. Together, they represent what Jung calls the 'Christ/Antichrist antithesis'. As the Earth moves from the beginning to the end of the 2,000-odd-year-long Age of

Pisces, so the heavens pass from the stars making up one fish to the stars making up the other fish, and world culture itself passes from the reign of Christ to the reign of the Antichrist. Jung is actually worth quoting in full:

For anyone who has a positive attitude towards Christianity the problem of the Antichrist is a hard nut to crack. It is nothing less than the counterstroke of the devil, provoked by God's Incarnation; for the devil attains his true stature as the adversary of Christ, and hence of God, only after the rise of Christianity, while as late as the Book of Job he was still one of God's sons and on familiar terms with Jehovah. Psychologically the case is clear, since the dogmatic figure of Christ is so sublime and spotless that everything else turns dark beside it. It is, in fact, so one-sidedly perfect that it demands a psychic complement to restore the balance.

'Bishop of the California Lodge'

Caltech rocket engineer Jack Parsons attended his first black mass on Winona Boulevard in Hollywood in 1939. The ritual was presided over by Wilfred Smith, who had become head of the North American branch of the Ordo Templi Orientis (OTO) after meeting its global chief Aleister Crowley in 1915. Parsons joined the OTO's Agape Lodge, as it was known, with his wife Helen in 1941.

Smith drew on Crowley's occult religion Thelema for the design of his rituals and mailed his sponsor a share of his cult membership fees. Crowley at the time was eking out a heroin-dosed existence in England. Some 40 years after the original vision which had inspired Thelema's sacred text, *The Book of the Law*, he was still on the look-out for the 'Rich Man from the West' who had been promised him. Smith figured Parsons was a good bet for the role.

Indeed, when Parsons rented a mansion in Pasadena in 1942, the OTO wasted no time in relocating itself to the South Orange

Grove Avenue address. Parsons soon turned his large rambling house into a crash-pad for Hollywood actors, models, musicians, queers, anarchists and science-fiction writers. There were lots of parties with marijuana, loud music and naked girls. The police received reports of an occult ritual featuring a pregnant woman jumping nine times over a fire in the garden. When the FBI turned up to investigate, Parsons was able to talk his way out of trouble, but not before one of the officers had scribbled in his pad a confused note about the 'Church of Thelma'.

Crowley was pleased with the new direction being taken by the OTO in North America. In 1943, pulling strings from afar, he banished Smith from South Orange Grove Avenue and made Parsons acting head of the Agape Lodge. Parsons, who was known to his fellow cult members as 'Frater Belarion', dutifully took over the role of mailing Crowley his cheques.

Unfortunately for Crowley, Parsons had a habit of burning through money fast. In December 1944, he had cashed out of the rocket company he'd co-founded during the war. A majority share of Aerojet was sold to the General Tire and Rubber Company. Parsons made 11,000 dollars (two decades later, his shares would be worth over 12 million dollars). He used his Aerojet money to buy the lease on his Pasadena House. However, less than 18 months later, having sold the house for 25,000 dollars, he made the mistake of putting 80 per cent of the proceeds into Allied Enterprises, a yacht business. The company soon went bust, losing Parsons most of his money.

Crowley heard the news and was not best pleased. He wrote in a letter to one of his acolytes: 'Suspect Ron playing confidence trick – Jack Parsons weak fool – obvious victim prowling swindlers.'

The 'Ron' referred to in Crowley's telegram is L Ron Hubbard. A self-proclaimed 'hypnotist' and struggling science-fiction writer, Hubbard had turned up in Parsons' bohemian Pasadena household in December 1945. In the six months Hubbard spent on South Orange Grove Avenue, not only did he clean out his host's bank account with the yacht business scam and steal his girl Betty, he also hustled his way into the occult workings of the Agape Lodge and helped himself to Thelema's core religious assets.

Hubbard's *modus operandi* was to give Parsons what he wanted, playing the medium to his magician, spewing out decadent Crowleyesque verses on command, while picking the mark clean. The most notorious ritual involving the pair was the so-called 'Babalon Working', which took place with a willing female accomplice on South Orange Grove Avenue on the nights of March 2nd and March 3rd 1946. The ritual was intended by Parsons to conceive the Antichrist. Whether it succeeded or not is much disputed by scholars.

The Babalon Working left Parsons broke and down on his luck. In August 1946, he sent Crowley a formal letter of resignation from the OTO. He had not turned out to be such a good bet for the old magician after all. Crowley accepted his resignation. He made Parsons' protégé Grady McMurty, a young science-fiction buff, head of the Agape Lodge, which by now had moved to Los Angeles.

The culminating irony of the whole story is that it was Hubbard rather than Crowley who succeeded in founding a mass religious movement in North America. Crowley died in shabby-genteel poverty in December 1947. Three months before that, in the August 1947 issue of *Astounding Science Fiction,* Hubbard had already formulated an early draft of his own occult religion. His novella 'The End is Not Yet' features an updated version of Thelema's cosmic voodoo, complete with ideas like 'negative energy' and 'life creation'. These ideas were to form the core of Scientology, the church which Hubbard founded in 1953.

It was inevitable that Scientology would establish its first temple in California. The church spread rapidly after that. In 1956 the US government exempted it from federal taxes and the money from membership fees rolled in. Hubbard had always claimed that 'if you want to get rich, you start a religion'. It seems that the 'Rich Man from the West' who had been promised Crowley in his *Book of the Law* had arrived too late to bank-roll the OTO. But he had arrived just in time to play a foundational role in the successful development of the Church of Scientology.

'Babylon'

In *Magick in Theory and Practice*, Crowley identifies 'Babalon and the Beast conjoined' as 'earthly emissaries' of the god of the New Age (here, I respect Crowley's eccentric spelling of 'Babylon'). As far as the birth of this new god is concerned, Crowley couldn't be more explicit: 'the Beast hath begotten one more Babe in the Womb of Our Lady, His Concubine, the Scarlet Woman, BABALON'. This babe is identified by Crowley as a 'Crowned and Conquering Child'. Equivalent perhaps to the 'man-child' delivered to the 'woman clothed with the Sun' in the Book of Revelation, this 'Babe' is the image of the Antichrist.

Just as Crowley liked to identify himself with 'the Beast' in his Thelemic rituals, so he liked to imagine that each of the women in his life was a successive incarnation of 'Babalon'. This was a habit soon picked up by his North American disciple, Jack Parsons.

At the start of 1946, between January 8th and January 18th, Parsons conducted a Thelemic ritual in California with his medium L Ron Hubbard. He characterised the ritual as an 'invocation' of an 'elemental mate' designed to provide him with 'assistance'. It involved the use of a dagger and the shedding of blood (as well as of semen). The dramatic appearance of a young woman, 'an air of fire type with bronze red hair', at his house on the evening of the last day of the ritual was taken by Parsons as a sign of the invocation's success. His elemental mate had arrived (actually, she'd been to his house before, but Parsons hadn't really noticed her). Nine months later, Parsons and Marjorie Cameron were married. It was only in later years, after Parsons' death in 1952, that Cameron began to self-identify as the 'Babalon' to Parsons' version of the 'Beast'. She duly went on to appear as the 'Scarlet Woman' in Kenneth Anger's 1954 occult art film *Inauguration of the Pleasure Dome.*

'Belarion Working'

There is much talk of a 'Babalon Working' in Parsons' scattered writings, but nothing about a 'Belarion Working'. The *CEW* text seems to have become corrupt at this point. Possibly, there was a transcription error by Brimfield. Alternatively, Haubenstock's original speech may have been garbled. Given that Belarion was the magickal name adopted by Parsons in the Agape Lodge, 'Belarion Working' could potentially refer to any of the rituals he conducted.

If I had to identify one of Parsons' rituals as the Belarion Working, it would be the working he conducted with Cameron after her appearance at his house on the night of January 18th 1945. Parsons mentions it in a March 6th letter to Crowley, where he implies that it happened just before the Babalon Working:

I am under the command of extreme secrecy. I have had the most important – devastating experience of my life between February 2 and March 4. I believe it was the result of the 9th working with the girl who answered my elemental summons.

The 'devastating experience' seems to be an allusion to the Babalon Working (the dates match). The '9th working' can then only designate a prior ritual which took place in the interval between Parsons first meeting Cameron in mid-January and beginning preparation in February for the Babalon Working of early March. My candidate for the 'Belarion Working', to be clear, is a version of the 9th working which happened between January 18th and February 2nd.

So just what is the 9th working? It seems to be a reference to Crowley's 1911 book *The Vision and the Voice*, which documents his exploration of the 30 fields of cosmic energy – known as 'Aethyrs' – supposedly surrounding the Earth. In the Thelemite religious system, the magician begins his spiritual journey with the Aethyr closest to the Earth, the 30th Aethyr, and ends it at the uttermost Aethyr, the 1st Aethyr. Parsons, who even as a rocket engineer was always something of a *bricoleur*, didn't think that such a steady progression was for him. He preferred to dance around the Aethyrs in haphazard fashion.

It's not unreasonable to suppose that Parsons' 9th working was a traversal of the 9th Aethyr. In *The Vision and the Voice,* Crowley characterises this ritual as a form of sex magick conducted between the magician and his mistress, the 'Beast' and 'Babalon', with the aim of delivering 'one that is the child and the father of their love'. In other words, it's a ritual sex act designed to give birth to the Antichrist.

It seems that the 9th working which took place between Parsons and Cameron in January or February 1946 was a kind of informal rehearsal for the high theatre of the Babalon Working, which happened a bit later in March. Hubbard was the officiating priest on the night of the Babalon Working. He stood at the altar in a white robe. Parsons, in a black robe, was the Beast. Cameron, in a scarlet robe, was Babalon. Together, they had ritual sex in front of Hubbard, who orchestrated the flow of cosmic energy with his lamp. It must have been quite a spectacle.

Crowley spells out the occult mechanism of the 9th working a bit more clearly in his 1917 novel *Moonchild*. Here, a magician plans to 'go soul-fishing in the Fourth Dimension' and induce an occult cosmic entity to possess the embryo of his child, as it gestates in the body of its mother. 'Thus,' writes Crowley, 'he will have a perfectly normal child, which yet is also a Homunculus' (the implicit idea that the Moonchild has two natures matches the orthodox position on the Incarnation in the Athanasian Creed).

The stories of pregnant women dancing through fire in the grounds of Parsons' house in Pasadena now take on a deeper meaning. Indeed, in a 1983 interview in *Penthouse* magazine, L

Ron Hubbard Jr dished the dirt on what he thought his father was really up to with Parsons in the Mojave Desert:

He got hold of the book by Alistair Crowley called *The Book of Law*. He was very interested in several things that were the creation of what some people call the Moon Child. It was basically an attempt to create an immaculate conception – except by Satan rather than by God. Another important idea was the creation of what they call embryo implants – of getting a satanic or demonic spirit to inhabit the body of a fetus. This would come about as a result of black-magic rituals, which included the use of hypnosis, drugs, and other dangerous and destructive practices.

'abortions'

In his *Penthouse* magazine interview, L Ron Hubbard Jr went on to admit that his father's attempts to get an occult cosmic entity to inhabit the body of a human foetus did not always go according to plan:

One of the important things was to destroy the evidence if you failed at this immaculate conception. That's how my father became obsessed with abortions.

Abortion was illegal in 1940s America and certainly hazardous for any woman contemplating it. Cameron was reputedly no stranger to abortion. Crowley summed it up well in a letter: 'Apparently Jack or Ron or somebody is producing a Moonchild. I get fairly frantic when I contemplate the idiocy of these louts.'

One other thing to perhaps mention at this point is that women in the elite division of Scientology were allegedly forbidden from having children. They were told that the church needed their complete dedication. If any of them became pregnant, they were encouraged to have an abortion upon pain of dismissal. This

reportedly happened many times, despite Hubbard's own officially stated position that abortion was equivalent to 'murder' and
'an act against the whole society and the future.'

'into the Sahara desert'

Crowley took his boy Victor (or 'Vicky') Neuburg into the Sahara
Desert in December 1909, against the advice of the colonial
French authorities. In contrast to Crowley's earlier magical practice with his mediumistic wife Rose, there was now a reversal of
roles. Crowley was the skryer and performer, Neuburg the witness
and scribe. On the night in question, Crowley crossed the 10th
Aethyr – known as the 'abyss' in the language of Thelema – and
sealed his reputation as a master magician.

'second death'

In the Book of Revelation, the Last Judgement sees the dead
resurrected to face trial by selection at the hands of a returned
Christ. Those who don't make it into Heaven are cast alive into
Hell, characterised as a 'lake of fire'. These 'murderers, and
whoremongers, and sorcerers, and idolaters, and all liars' as a result
suffer a 'second death'.

'the third seal and the fourth seal'

In *Asimov's Guide to the Bible*, the great American science-fiction
writer speculates that the breaking of the third seal of the book of
the Apocalypse coincides with the disastrous effects of the Royal

Navy blockade of Germany in 1916. Hundreds of thousands of civilians died of starvation and disease. He goes on to link the breaking of the fourth seal with the influenza outbreak of 1918, the most devastating pandemic in world history, which killed an estimated 50 million people.

'German secret society'

The Thule Society was a German white supremacist occult group established in 1911. Some early members, such as Rudolph Hess and Hans Frank, went on to join the Nazi party. The theatre director Dietrich Eckart was on the fringes of the group in Munich. He became a mentor to the young Hitler, lending him books and helping to shape his talents as an orator and a performer. 'I believe in Hitler,' he said. 'A star hangs over him.'

The Thule Society logo featured a curved right-facing swastika. Hitler used it as the inspiration for his design of the Nazi party logo in 1920. Once the Nazis took power in Germany in 1933, the swastika was used on badges, flags and the signage of government and military buildings throughout the Reich. The Thule Society, along with other secret societies, was banned.

Since the defeat of Hitler, the public display of the Nazi swastika has been made a criminal offence in Germany and Austria.

'disc-shaped spacecraft'

On June 24th 1947 American salesman Kenneth Arnold reported seeing nine unidentified objects flying over the mountains of the Pacific Northwest from his two-seater prop plane. Within days, the 'flying disc' story was national news. And within weeks, hundreds of similar sightings had been reported across North America.

These sightings adhered to an approximate formula. They were like 'saucers' or 'discs' when viewed from below, 'cigar-shaped' when viewed side-on. They 'skipped' or 'weaved' across the sky erratically. They 'flashed' in the Sun.

The modern UFO phenomenon can plausibly claim to have its origin in the distribution of the Arnold story over the AP news wire. But other less reputable media influences may have loaded American mass culture with the image of the flying saucer before that day in 1947. Such, anyway, is the thesis of UFO scholar John Keel, who points to the gaudy presence of SF pulp magazines on most American news-stands in the 1930s and 1940s.

I think it's worth taking a look at a sample set of covers from these magazines to gauge the emergence of the flying saucer icon and test Keel's hypothesis.

The Fortean magazine *Fate* was set up by the American pulp SF publisher Ray Palmer in early 1948 after he quit the editorship of *Amazing Stories*. The first issue carried a testimony by Arnold and its cover image featured three 'flying disks' stacked up in in the clouds over a red prop plane. Flying saucers certainly became a common sight in the pulp magazines after Arnold gained notoriety. For example, the January 1951 cover of *Amazing Stories* shows two cigar-shaped discs speeding through the clouds, each steered surfboard-style by a statuesque Amazonian space girl.

Before 1947, however, images of flying saucers on pulp magazine covers were much thinner on the ground. Illustrations of stories about marvellous sky-borne vehicles were much more likely to feature rockets instead. For example, the March 1947 issue of *Astounding Science Fiction* features a cover image of a sleek silver rocket, complete with tail fins, parked on the outskirts of a mysterious archaic city. It illustrates a short story, 'The Equalizer', written by Jack Williamson, who could count the rocket engineer Jack Parsons as one of his fans.

The pulp SF magazines were actually well known to Parsons. Rocket enthusiasts and SF fans alike were disparaged by conventional society in the late 1930s. Parsons was invited to speak at the Los Angeles chapter of the Science Fiction League in May 1938. He even invited a few SF fans to witness some of his home-made rocket tests in the Mojave Desert, near Devil's Gate Dam. Certainly, during the early-to-mid 1940s he rubbed shoulders with pulp SF writers Robert Heinlein, Anthony Boucher and Cleve Cartmill as well as Williamson and Hubbard.

The May 1946 issue of *Amazing Stories* carries a noteworthy image on its back cover. Here, James B Settles illustrates the idea of a 'satellite space ship station'. Two red rockets are shown streaking away from a large docking station in the inky blueness of space, with a third rocket seen nosing towards it. There's nothing extraordinary about the rockets, with their pointed tips and tailfins. But the station itself, presumably orbiting the Earth, is another matter. It is long and cigar-shaped, with sleek rounded ends.

Here, a year before the Arnold story is distributed across the AP news wire, a modern archetype is taking shape at the semi-unconscious end of the mass media spectrum. In a space of shared fantasy usually reserved for images of semi-naked girls, primitive giants, titanic machines and rockets, the flying saucer is already emerging.

So, do flying saucers exist? Jung was right to say that flying saucers are psychosocial projections. I'd go further and say they also have a super-terrestrial aspect, not in the sense that they come from distant stars, but in the sense that they manifest cosmic energy. They are not empirically verifiable, but they are phenomenologically real.

Flying saucers are modern-day occult entities. Their stylings come from the fantasies of scientific materialism, just as John Keel intuited. The process is really no different from the way that the stylings of demonology – with all its wands, cups, robes, drugs and sombre chanting – come from a deformation of the Roman Catholic liturgy.

L Ron Hubbard's stroke of genius was to incorporate flying saucers into occultism when he created the space opera-style doctrines of Scientology. I'm not going to linger on the religion's demiurge Xenu, evil dictator of a Galactic Confederacy. His story has been well documented (not least in an episode of the cartoon show *South Park*). Instead, I'll sample a quote from *Have You Lived Before This Life?*, Hubbard's 1958 anthology of church-audited past life confessions from London initiates:

> The next episode is that I am called to a briefing room in a space-ship by a commander. There, by means of a projector beaming on the solar plexus and sex-organs, I get an implant with orders for an individual scouting or perhaps bombing mission in a saucer-type craft.

'the sign promised to him'

The Order of the Golden Dawn has four chief tools in its kit of ceremonial magic – the Air Dagger, the Fire Wand, the Water Cup and the Earth Pentacle. It's worth considering the pentacle – a kind of ceremonial disc – in some detail.

John Dee's pentacle is displayed in the British Museum. It is a disc-shaped slab of wax imprinted with a medieval logo composed of two circles, a pentagram, and three heptagons. Dee knew the design as the 'seal of God's truth' (which no doubt contained an element of special pleading before Christian authority). The names of various occult entities (known to Dee as angels) are also written on the disc. A magician uses this kind of seal to bind occult entities once they had been summoned.

Let's look a bit more closely at the magician's pentacle. According to Crowley, the disc can be fashioned from precious metal as well as from wax. It should be eight inches in diameter and half an inch thick. The artefact is effectively a Satanic variation on the sacred paten or 'diskos', the small gold or silver plate used to hold the bread which is to be 'transubstantiated' into the body of the Christian deity during the Catholic mass.

All four magickal tools (and more) are mentioned by Jack Parsons in his writings about the Babalon Working he conducted with Hubbard in March 1946. Out of them all, I certainly find the pentacle the most interesting. Parsons describes it as a three-inch diameter 'disk of copper' bearing the seven-pointed 'star' of Babalon, the whole painted in blue and gold (the brand colour palette of the Golden Dawn).

Once Parsons had summoned Babalon with his wand, he was instructed to direct the occult entity to his disk for storage. This devotional object was to be 'daily affirmed,' in the expectation that it would become a kind of portable generator of focused cosmic energy. What happened to this 'disk of Babalon' (as I call it)? I'm tempted to say that it became the template for the visions of flying saucers reported across America during the summer of 1947. Somehow, word got out.

Once an occult entity has been summoned and bound for a time to a magician's will, it must be banished. There is no evidence to suggest that Parsons or Hubbard banished the demon they had invoked during the Babalon Working. When an occult entity is not banished, then it is believed to persist as a kind of free-floating disembodied projection in the cosmic energy field closest to Earth (like the after-image that persists in one's field of vision once a powerful originating stimulus has been removed).

Parsons was a notoriously careless magician. Members of the Agape Lodge regularly performed banishing rituals after his invocations, sensing that 'troublesome spirits' had collected in the house on South Orange Grove Avenue. They believed that if an occult entity is dislodged from its home in the stars but not sent back, then it seeks re-embodiment. All sorts of suggestible people can then be exposed to the likelihood of accidental possession. The science-fiction writers who hung out with Parsons may well have found their imagination haunted by an occult entity said to be leaking from his disk of Babalon. It was perhaps a short step from here to the gaudy covers of *Amazing Stories* and *Astounding Science Fiction.*

'Howard Robard Hughes'

The gematric identification of the Beast with Howard Robard Hughes in the *CEW* text perhaps goes no further than noticing that there are six letters in each of his three names – 666.

'to discover the truth'

Jack Parsons died from his injuries after an explosion at his home laboratory in Pasadena on June 17th 1952. He was living in the coach-house of the property he had sold in 1946. His wife, Cameron, said she was not in the house at the time. She claimed to have gone out to get some supplies for their planned trip to Mexico the next day.

The Los Angeles police found that Parsons' death was an accident. He was working for the local Bermite Powder Company and had explosives in his house. The police figured that he accidentally dropped a coffee can filled with mercury fulminate (used as a trigger for igniting powder charges) and that it exploded in his face.

As soon as the news was reported, the rumours began to circulate. His wife thought he had been murdered. Her later associate, Kenneth Anger, claimed that the murder had been ordered by Howard Hughes, in revenge for Parsons' theft of 17 confidential technical documents from Hughes Aircraft in 1950. Still others speculated that Parsons had been employed by Hughes Aircraft on a secret gravity control propulsion research programme before his dismissal for theft. They said he had been killed by a US Air Force Office of Special Investigations team because he was about to go public with his knowledge.

Occultists preferred to speculate that Parsons was killed as the result of a failed attempt to cross the abyss of the 10th Aethyr in a Thelemite ritual gone wrong. It was remembered that he characterised Cameron, the elemental mate he invoked with his partner Hubbard in 1946, as 'an air of fire type'. A fire elemental is technically known as a salamander, an occult entity who was thought able to live in fire. It was also noted that fire was a constant motif in the trance-like utterances of the Babalon Working Parsons conducted with Hubbard. At one point in the ritual, Hubbard promised Parsons that he should 'become living flame'. Part of Parsons' house caught fire during the ritual. Occultists think that the lab fire in 1952 was a kind of consummation of the Babalon Working.

Perhaps they're not so wrong. It's said that every successful invocation of an occult entity needs a sacrifice. If the Babalon Working was successful, then it was successful for Hubbard, not for Parsons. What started out as a Thelemite ritual in which Parsons was the magician and Hubbard the medium became a Scientological ritual in which Hubbard was the magician and Parsons the sacrifice. Hubbard himself couldn't have been more explicit about the nature of Babalon: 'She feeds upon the death of men.'

Hubbard's 1947 novella 'The End is Not Yet' is about a man who is haunted by a version of himself from a parallel world, a man whose sacrifice helped to found a great new civilisation. Is there a hint here of Hubbard's feelings towards Parsons? He had, after all, set him on the path to self-destruction while stealing his occult formulae in order to found a new religion. The early pages of the novella talk of 'a meeting or two at Caltech', the technology institute with which Parsons had been associated as a rocket engineer. And the cover image of the August 1947 issue of *Astounding Science Fiction* in which the story first appeared shows a handsome figure strikingly similar to photographs of Parsons – a man with dark wavy hair, upwardly slanting eyebrows and the hint of a pencil moustache. The man appears as the ghostly double of another man, who wears a hat and carries an imposing red book stamped with an occult logo. Hubbard himself?

One of the doctrines of Scientology is reincarnation, which promises another life beyond the 'second death' mentioned in the Book of Revelation. If I imagine Parsons anywhere after his death, it's in the version of Heaven conjured up by Hubbard in a 1963 Scientology bulletin. He describes it thus:

The gates... are well done, well built. An avenue of statues of saints leads up to them. The gate pillars are surmounted by marble angels. The entering grounds are very well kept, laid out like Busch Gardens in Pasadena...

Need I add that Busch Gardens, a 38-acre pleasure park with manicured lawns, exotic plants, walkways and painted statues, was located on South Orange Grove Avenue, right next to Parsons' own home. Hubbard must have contemplated it many times during the six months he lived with Parsons in the mid-1940s.

'Cay Sal'

Cay Sal is an island in the Bahamas, lying about 60 miles south of the Florida Keys and 30 miles north of Cuba. Howard Hughes bought a 99-year lease on the island in 1957.

Hughes made Cay Sal available to the CIA so they could spy on Cuba after the Communist dictator Fidel Castro had taken over the country in 1959. The island also became important as an operational base for various Cuban exile militias sponsored by the CIA. According to a *Miami Herald* report of August 25th 1963:

Cay Sal has served a dual purpose, as a rendezvous and arms storehouse for exile raiders, and, for anti-Castro refugees, the first stop to freedom, a gateway similar to the Berlin Wall to anti-Communist East Germans.

'Bill Gay'

Gay first went to work for Howard Hughes in 1947. He was hired at the age of 27 to run the Hughes Tool Company headquarters at 7000 Romaine Street in Los Angeles. Hughes instructed him to employ only fellow Mormons. Hughes always trusted Mormons. They didn't drink, smoke or take drugs and they kept their mouths shut. Gay added Howard Eckersley, Levar Myler, Kay Glenn, George Francom and Wilbur Thain to the staff. According to Hughes biographer Charles Higham:

Almost all of Hughes's Mormons were like Disneyland employees in later years: clean-cut, slim, athletic, Aryan, crewcut, immaculately groomed. One reason for having them take his various starlets around for shopping was that they wouldn't go to bed with the girls; another reason was, that, in a few instances, Hughes could have sexual access to them.

When Hughes was ensconced on the top floor of the Desert Inn in Las Vegas between 1966 and 1970, it was the Mormon mafia who attended to his every whim day or night. Their home state of Utah was right next door to Nevada. They controlled access to the progressively ailing Hughes. Increasingly, they began to intercede between Hughes and his chief of staff Bob Maheu.

According to *Age of Secrets*, Gerald Bellett's biography of Hughes associate John H Meier, Gay set up the computer software company Hughes Dynamics in the 1960s without the knowledge of his boss. One of the main tasks of Hughes Dynamics was to help the Mormon Church computerise its genealogical records. The church was devoted to researching the family trees of its members because – according to official doctrine – the dead could be retrospectively baptised into the Mormon faith.

In 1970, Hughes fired Maheu, quit the US and went into tax exile. He gave Gay, his lawyer Chester Davis and Hughes Tool vice-president Raymond Holliday nominal authority over his

Las Vegas hotel and casino holdings. By the end of 1972, he had sold the Hughes Tool Company and Raymond Holliday had gone with it. That left Bill Gay in sole charge of the holding company that remained on Romaine Street in Los Angeles. Gay felt secure enough in his position to name it the Summa Corporation (when Hughes wanted it named after himself).

With Hughes out of the country, Gay also found himself a seat on the executive committee of the Howard Hughes Medical Institute in 1971. This was the tax shelter where Hughes Aircraft stocks had been parked since 1953, with Hughes as the sole trustee.

Mere weeks after Hughes' death in 1976, a will surfaced in the Salt Lake City, Utah headquarters of the Mormon Church. It parcelled out much of the Hughes estate in units of one sixteenth and included an allocation to the Mormon Church as well as to aides such as Gay. The bulk of the estate – a full one quarter – was willed to the Howard Hughes Medical Institute. However, the 'Mormon Will' was judged to be a forgery and struck down by a Nevada court in 1978.

For years after Hughes' death, there was a bitter struggle among his aides for control of the Howard Hughes Medical Institute. In 1984, a Delaware court appointed new trustees – including Bill Gay – to the Institute. They sold off Hughes Aircraft for $5.2 billion and used the proceeds to expand the institute's activities. By the time Gay retired in 2006, the institute had established a major role for itself in the funding of genetic research.

'Mormon'

The Church of Jesus Christ of Latter-day Saints, just like the Church of Scientology, is a distinctively American religion founded in occult ritual. In each case, the origin story of the religion features a possessed medium and a failed magician.

Joseph Smith, the founder of the Latter-day Saint movement, reckoned he was possessed by an occult entity named Moroni in upstate New York in 1829. Over a three-month period, from April to June, Smith saw visions in a 'seer stone', a rounded polished stone about the size of a small crystal ball. His practice was to dip his face into a top hat enclosing the stone and read aloud the written messages which flashed up on it. His scribe was Oliver Cowdery, a school-teacher interested in folk magic and the use of divining rods.

This whole shady effort was posited by Smith as a translation of an original magical text written in occult characters. Smith claimed that the magical text was transmitted to him by the angel Moroni, but that it was originally authored by an ancient prophet named Mormon who had lived in America in Biblical times. It was Cowdery's hand that wrote the Book of Mormon in English, under guidance from Smith.

Smith had managed to find work as a treasure-seeker before getting into religion. He had used his seer stone to identify where treasure might be buried. Something of this practice obviously survived into his skrying with Cowdery, because he insisted that he had found the original Book of Mormon as a set of 'golden plates' buried in a box under a hill.

On April 6th 1830, with the Book of Mormon printed and on sale, Smith founded the Church of Jesus Christ of Latter-day Saints with himself as First Elder and Cowdery as Second Elder. Cowdery was excommunicated in 1838 when he objected to Smith's habit of pulling young women into his personal orbit, seducing them, marrying them and adding them to his harem.

Smith, like Hubbard after him, had a tendency to attract trouble. In 1844 he was imprisoned for treason. The jail was stormed by a vigilante mob and Smith was shot and killed.

It was left to the practical and energetic Smith disciple Brigham Young to organise the Mormon Church on a sound footing. He led his followers on a trek to Utah, founded the state capital Salt Lake City and settled his church there in 1847. If Smith was the medium and Cowdery the failed magician in the original Mormon working, Young was the successful magician who went on to incorporate the Church of Jesus Christ of Latter-day Saints as a legal entity.

According to the logic of demonology, where every spirit-raising demands a sacrifice, it was Smith whose mortal remains were dedicated to Moroni and Young who benefitted from the angel's immortal legacy. Smith, like Jack Parsons after him, was killed. Young, like Hubbard, lived to tell the religious tale.

'a composite of recorded memories'

After a near-fatal plane crash in 1946, Howard Hughes disappeared from the world. As Paul Virilio notes in his book *The Aesthetics of Disappearance*:

The life of this billionaire seems made of two distinct parts, first a public existence, and then – from age 47 and from then on for 24 years – a hidden life. The first part of Hughes' life could pass for a programming of behaviour by dream and desire: he wanted to become the richest, the greatest aviator, the most important producer in the world, and he succeeded everywhere ostentatiously; overexposing his person, avid for publicity, for years he inundates the Western press with his image, with tales of his records or conquests of women. Then, Howard Hughes disappears. He is in hiding until his death.

Hughes died on a plane flying to the US from the Acapulco Fairmont Princess Hotel in Mexico. A death certificate was filed in Houston, Texas on April 8th 1976, listing 'chronic renal failure' as the cause of death. He had been in seclusion for decades before that, surrounded by his hand-picked Mormon valets, living out of hotels, manifesting himself to the public only as a voice on the phone.

Hughes' disappearance from public view had inevitably given rise to many rumours. It was said that his 1972 sale of the Hughes Tool Company, which had been in his family since 1908, was forced by his Mormon bodyguards, who were by now keeping him prisoner. Another rumour was that the body evacuated in 1970 from the Desert Inn penthouse in Las Vegas and flown to the Bahamas was not an ailing Hughes on a stretcher but a frozen Hughes in a cryonics chamber. Yet another story was that in 1957 he was kidnapped by shipping magnate Aristotle Onassis from his bungalow at the Beverly Hills Hotel in California, imprisoned on a Greek island and replaced by a double. The idea that the second half of Hughes' life was somehow faked is an enduring myth. Indeed, there are some who believe his death dates back to the disastrous 1946 Beverly Hills plane crash in which he was very badly burned. These conspiracy theorists say that Hughes never staged a miraculous recovery as official reports claim, but was instead replaced by a pliable doppelganger.

It's tempting to think of Howard Hughes after his disappearance from public view as a kind of occult media entity. His preferred medium of possession was the telephone or the hand-written memo. And he could be conjured by anyone with the right access codes.

His chief of staff Bob Maheu spoke to Hughes only on the phone and worked as his representative on earth for over 15 years. Mormon confidant Bob Gay gained power of attorney over the Hughes portfolio of Las Vegas hotel properties in 1970. This was when the Mormon mafia of Hughes attendants closed ranks around their dying pope to form an opaque ministry of petitioners.

This didn't stop fraudsters and tricksters from attempting to hack the Hughes entity. In 1971 the novelist Clifford Irving forged Hughes' signature on a McGraw-Hill publishing contract and scored 765,000 dollars for the old man's autobiography. Irving's ghosting of Hughes was deemed to be a hoax when seven reporters staged their own live telephone conference with Hughes in 1972. Sitting in a semi-circle around a speaker-phone, listening to a disembodied voice which spent much of the time vouching for its credentials, the reporters seemed to be engaged in some kind of electro-acoustic séance.

The announcement of Hughes' death in 1976 triggered another rogue manifestation of the occult entity which bore his name. A hand-written will with Hughes' signature was discovered in the offices of the Church of Jesus Christ of Latter-day Saints in Salt Lake City, Utah. Mormon gas station attendant Melvin Dumarr said he had deposited the will there after it had been given to him by a man in black soon after Hughes' death. The 'Mormon Will' left one sixteenth of the Hughes estate (156 million dollars) to Dumarr and the Mormon Church each. A Nevada jury ruled the document a forgery in 1978.

Even so, Dumarr gave a good performance and many believed him. He said he had picked up a tramp at the side of Route 95 on a cold night in the Nevada Desert in 1967, not far from the Cottontail Ranch whore-house, and given him a ride to Las Vegas. As he was dropped off at the back of the Sands Hotel, the tramp revealed himself to be Howard Hughes and said he'd never forget Dumarr's act of kindness. Dumarr contested that a share of the 'Mormon Will' was his reward for acting the Good Samaritan on that lost night in the desert.

'Richard Nixon landed in Dallas'

It's true that Nixon was in Dallas the same day that Kennedy got shot in 1963. But he had been some distance away from Dealey Plaza, the kill site, attending a client board meeting at the Baker Hotel. He had flown into Dallas two days before the assassination, on the evening of Wednesday 20th November. And he got a plane from Dallas back to New York some hours before Kennedy's own arrival at Love Field. The paths of the two men never crossed. In fact, Nixon was evidently so traumatised by Kennedy's assassination that he couldn't exactly remember when he first heard the news about it, giving at least two separate accounts.

'human experimentation'

In the early 1980s, Acquired Immune Deficiency Syndrome (AIDS) emerged in North America. Public health scientists had observed the spread of Kaposi's sarcoma, a previously rare form of skin cancer, among gay men in San Francisco, Los Angeles and New York City. They initially named this disease Gay-Related Immune Deficiency (GRID). In 1982, they changed the name to AIDS, in order to indicate that this disease was not confined only to the gay population. In 1984, they discovered that AIDS was caused by the infectious spread of a virus, subsequently named the Human Immunodeficiency Virus (HIV).

How AIDS spread was understood quickly enough. But where it came from and when it originated remained obscure. There was room for scientific debate about the origin of HIV. There was even more room for conspiracy theories. In other words, in the 1980s, at the height of the revived Cold War between the US and the USSR, the HIV virus became an occult entity of its own.

If there was one place where Soviet technology surpassed that of the Americans in the Cold War, it was the domain of information warfare. According to KGB defector Oleg Gordievsky in *Instructions from the Centre: Top Secret Files on KGB Foreign Operations 1975–1985*, Service A was the branch of the KGB responsible for secret propaganda operations abroad. Its techniques included the forging of official documents, the weaponisation of rumour, the corruption of information and the spread of disinformation.

The idea that AIDS was created by the Pentagon as a biowarfare weapon is a KGB invention. It can be traced to the planting of an anonymous letter (attributed to a 'well-known American scientist and anthropologist') in an obscure Indian newspaper, the *Patriot*, on 17th July 1983. The letter juxtaposed two true pieces of information. First, there were the known facts about AIDS, including the hypothesis that it was caused by a virus. Then, there was the revelation, gained through a Church of Scientology Freedom of Information Request, that the US Army had conducted bacteriological weapons research at Fort Detrick, Maryland between 1943 and 1969 – and that this had included the field testing of simulated bacterial agents on the unsuspecting population of San Francisco in September 1950. The letter then went on to introduce its falsehood – the claim that Fort Detrick had secretly ignored President Nixon's 1969 order to shut down its bacteriological weapons research and that it had gone on to discover AIDS by analysing disease-creating viruses collected by American scientists in Africa.

The letter bears all the hallmarks of a KGB Service A disinformation campaign. It follows the 'montage' principle of propaganda theorised by Soviet film-maker Sergei Eisenstein in the 1920s. As he says in his essay 'A Dialectical Approach to Film Form', montage is 'an idea that arises from the collision of independent shots' where 'each sequential element is perceived not next to the other, but on top of the other'. (This technique was later adapted for literature by Burroughs and Gysin as the 'fold-in' in *The Third Mind*).

True information about AIDS and true information about covert biowarfare experiments are placed next to each other in the text of the letter, but are placed on top of each other in the act of reading. The idea that AIDS is a secret US Army bioweapon arises spontaneously in the reader's mind as an act of dialectical synthesis. The falsehood about scientists collecting viruses from Africa is hardly required as a confirmatory nudge. The AIDS disinformation piece virtually conceptualises itself.

It seems to me that the author of *CEW* has fallen prey to a Soviet disinformation campaign with his AIDS conspiracy theory. I'm not surprised. The dialectical approach to mind control is particularly insidious. At its most effective, the operator's propaganda story is experienced by the target as their own spontaneous creation rather than as an externally engineered fabrication. As a result, they are that much more attached to it. Indeed, they will often make it their business to discover further pieces of information that support what they have come to see as their own theory.

So it is with the *CEW* text, where the idea that AIDS is a secret US Army bioweapon is supported by the juxtaposition of two pieces of true information about the US Health Department in the 1970s – first, its sponsorship of cancer research in vacated biowarfare labs at Fort Detrick, and second, its funding of hepatitis B vaccine trials among gay men in New York.

It's easy to play the AIDS disinformation game. If I were to get involved, I might juxtapose the following two pieces of true information – first, the heavy involvement of the Howard Hughes Medical Institute in microbiological and genetic research, and second, the similarity of Howard Hughes' skin lesions in his later years to AIDS-related Kaposi's sarcoma. Someone superimposing these two facts in their mind might easily synthesise the entirely false idea that Hughes was the 'patient zero' of the HIV outbreak, that he had been the victim of a life extension drug treatment gone wrong in one of his own labs and spread the virus through his multiple sex partners and Mormon valets.

It should be obvious by now that the intelligence operator and the target of a disinformation campaign have a structural affinity with the pair workings of black magic. The author of the AIDS letter in the *Patriot* in 1983 is like a magician summoning an occult entity – in this case, the spectre of a mysterious and fatal new disease created by the US military-industrial complex – which goes on to possess the body of a gullible media audience. It doesn't take much for conspiracy theory zines, cable TV infotainment shows and religious radio broadcasts to spread this powerful idea. Indeed, it persists only as the result of a vicious psychological repetition compulsion.

'persistence of Christian belief'

Human embryonic stem cell research has proved controversial in the US and elsewhere because it necessarily involves the destruction of human embryos. The position of the Roman Catholic Church on this matter is that the abortion of an embryo is an act of murder (because the human soul is present from the conception of life in the womb). This belief has formed the basis of the anti-abortion movement in the US as well as the moral objections to stem cell research.

The Howard Hughes Medical Institute has played a leading role in the development of human embryonic stem cell research. Might this have something to do with the persistent involvement of leading Mormon Frank Gay in the affairs of the Institute? The Mormon doctrine of reincarnation suggests that old souls are reborn into new human bodies at the moment of birth. The Mormon Church, unlike the Roman Catholic Church, holds that human embryos do not have souls. As a result, it has no position one way or the other on human embryonic stem cell research. Genetic cloning is a moral possibility left tantalisingly open to Mormons.

'new Heaven'

In the Mormon creed, there is no need for Heaven to descend on Earth, as in the Book of Revelation. There is not even any need for spaceships to ferry human bodies between Earth and the capital of some Galactic Federacy, as in Scientology. Instead, the Earth will become its own spaceship and travel directly to the throne of God in the middle of the galaxy. How is it possible to believe such a thing?

The answer lies in the sacred Book of Abraham, which was dictated by Mormon Church founder Joseph Smith to his scribes Oliver Cowdery and W W Phelps in 1835. Much of this book is a retelling of the Book of Genesis from the Old Testament. In Smith's version of the myth, it was the Gods (in the plural) who created the Heavens and the Earth. They also created the first man Adam and placed him in the Garden of Eden.

At the beginning of the world, according to the Mormons, time had yet to start. Or, to put it more precisely, time was still running on an older clock. As the Book of Abraham says: 'Now I, Abraham, saw that it was after the Lord's time, which was after the time of Kolob; for as yet the Gods had not appointed unto Adam his reckoning.' The name Kolob refers to a star, which Mormons believe is 'nearest unto the throne of God'. And the reason why the Earth was originally on Kolob time, according to Mormon elder W Cleon Skousen, is that it was created right next to Kolob

It was only after the Gods had created the Earth that they moved it from the vicinity of Kolob to its present location. And when the Apocalypse comes, so the Mormons believe, the Gods will pluck the Earth from its orbit around the Sun and return it to Kolob.

Mormon scholar Eric Skousen (son of W Cleon Skousen) identifies Kolob as Sagittarius A*, a black hole whose signature is observable from Earth with a radio telescope. Astronomers place Sagittarius A* at the heart of the Milky Way. For Mormons, the galaxy has a divine centre and the universe is justified.

6

Narratology: Liveblogging the End-Times

Field Notes on a Residency

Jenkins skipped the last workshop. He said he had a sick child to mind. Trinh, Novichkov and Gupta, however, were all back in the computer science department meeting room. They were here to think about the world constituted by narratology. Haubenstock sat in the corner, next to his tripod and video camera. Rausch finally arrived. Haubenstock put aside his copy of *Private Eye*.

One of the ways we orient ourselves in the world is by telling stories, I said. Ontology is a function of narratology. The scientists looked at me. I began to pace. In its various manifestations from the Russian Formalists onwards, narratology has depended on the value of separation and distance. Narrative cannot exist without there being a gap between here and there, now and then, you and me. I paused. A gap between the medium and the message.

Marshall McLuhan, said Gupta, delighted that he had caught the reference. In the electronic age, the medium is the message. Right, I said. That's a proposition Virilio would accept, but also lament. He argues that with the advent of telecommunications in 'real-time', people have lost any sense of distance between the world out there – I pointed to the small window with its dismal view of the Solent City campus – and the world in here. I tapped my GPS-enabled smartphone, which was lying on the table next to my laptop.

I flipped up a photographic image on the wall-screen behind me. An artwork by Peter Kennard. It showed a blazing oil-field in the desert, with bursting flames and thick plumes of smoke, and a white guy in shirt and tie standing before it. He held out his phone in front of him. He was grinning. He appeared to be taking a selfie.

Who's that? asked Trinh. Tony Blair, said Gupta. The UK's old prime minister. Oh yeah, said Novichkov. Blair was a cheerleader for the Iraq War in 2003. More than that, said Haubenstock, suddenly alert. He sent in the troops. Trinh's eyes narrowed as she stared more closely at the image. Good photomontage, was all she finally said.

Certainly, I said. It reminds me of Virilio's book on the first Gulf War of 1991, where he argued that here was a war fought through media vectors operating at light speed. The American air strikes on Iraq featured both GPS-enabled 'smart' missiles and television-guided artillery. My hand cut through the air. Obviously, I said, there were cameras in the nosecones of the missiles. It helped with targeting. But then the cruise missile footage got added to the live transmissions of embedded reporters on the 24-hours news networks. And so the first Gulf War was turned into a stream of real-time TV images.

Audiences throughout the world were transfixed by the first Gulf War, I said. And let's not forget those audiences included the embedded reporters, the soldiers and the American generals. The experience was similar for everyone. The real-time image annihilated the gap between being-in-the-world – here, I nodded to Rausch – and what we might call being-in-the-media. There was no distance, no separation between them. Which meant there was no basis for a coherent story about the war to be formulated. People watched it on CNN as it happened. But they didn't really understand it. And afterwards they quite easily forgot about it.

That was just the start of it all, said Haubenstock. Imagine what CNN could do with footage from an autonomous cruise missile, a bomb that makes its own decisions about where to fly, whom to target, where to land. What you think about that, huh? he asked the scientists at the table. They politely ignored him.

Disaster response professionals don't talk about the capacity to frame a narrative, said Trinh. But they do talk about 'situational awareness'. Maybe it's a similar kind of thing. In both cases, there's an emphasis on distance and delay. She said that Panoptic Rescue, a disaster response organisation the scientists were working with, always waited 72 hours before sending a search-and-rescue team into an earthquake zone or a plane crash site.

Right, said Rausch. The data collected during the first 72 hours of any disaster is generally so bad it's useless. There's chaos on the ground and confusion in the media. There are rumours, myths, conspiracy theories and even, in some cases, deliberate misinformation. It makes it hard to contextualise the visual data coming back from the drones. He shook his head.

Understood, I said. How is it even possible to know what kind of disaster you're dealing with before the dust on the ground has settled? Is it an accident, sabotage or a terror attack? I said, quoting a line from Virilio.

Gupta mentioned the 7/7 terror attack on the London transport network in 2005. He'd been in London at the time, attending a conference. He remembered all the confusion there was at the start of the day. First, there was a BBC news report about a power surge knocking out electrical equipment at various tube stations. Then, stories popped up on internet blogs about an explosion onboard a tube train at Liverpool Street station. At that point, said Gupta, people at the conference were already exchanging anxious looks and muttering about suicide bombers. It wasn't until some long minutes later that the London Underground finally abandoned its story about the explosion being nothing more than a bang caused by an electrical short-circuit.

I'd also been in London that day, having a meeting with some arts admin people. It'd been surprising how quickly the talk had turned to conspiratorial fantasies and jokes about government-backed Islamic terrorists, false-flag operations and secret cabals of Mossad agents. It was actually quite unnerving.

Novichkov looked up from his laptop. He'd been thinking. The story of any disaster can be told only after it has happened, right? he asked. You'll always have better data at least 72 hours afterwards, said Trinh. Okay, said Novichkov. But here's the thing. With the end of the world, there is no 'afterwards'. How could there be? No accident investigation report of the end of the world could ever be written. There would be no time for it, no place for it.

Maybe the end of the world would be like living inside the 72-hour window of bad information with no way out, said Gupta. Nobody knowing for sure what was going on. Everything in doubt.

You've got it, I said, walking round the table. Virilio's book on the first Gulf War had originally been written as a series of newspaper articles. He had written about the war as it had unfolded. Like a war correspondent, said Gupta. Not really, I said. Virilio wasn't in the desert with CNN. He'd written about his experience of the war as he'd watched it on TV. Like a live-blogger, said Trinh. That's more like it, I said. Only it wasn't exactly live. Virilio had given himself a few crucial minutes to think about what he'd seen before committing his thoughts to paper. What he was really doing was documenting the impact of the information war on his mind and his memory.

So the story of the Apocalypse can only be told as a live-blog, said Gupta. An unfinished live blog at that, said Trinh.

Yes, yes, I said. Exactly. That was it. I looked up and thanked the young scientists. I said they had come up with some great ideas. Gupta smiled. Novichkov shrugged. Trinh was already packing her bags. Rausch had left the meeting room. Haubenstock switched off his camera, eager to get to the gym.

I was burrowing inside my laptop drive. I'd opened up my PDF of *Virilio: A-Z* and was running a search on 'Gulf War'. I found out a few things I'd forgotten. Virilio had described the first Gulf War as a 'world-war-in-miniature'. Its global dimension came from the fact that it had been covered live 24 hours a day for an audience all over the world. Its miniaturised aspect came from the fact that it could be seen in its entirety on a screen. Interesting. I picked up my phone.

Later that day, I was in the senior common room, slumped in front of the TV. Sky News was on. I became dimly aware of new developments in the story of a missing passenger jet. It had disappeared over the South China Sea three days before. But still, nothing was known about what had happened to it. Pilot error or terror attack? The question was still unresolved. Even after 72 hours.

What would Virilio make of this news story? Here was a Malaysia Airlines jet that had gone missing somewhere on the flight path between Kuala Lumpur International Airport and Beijing Capital International Airport. It had enough fuel to have ended up anywhere within a potential search area of hundreds of thousands of square miles. But no trace of it had been found, not even crash wreckage. An unknown event was unfolding in real-time, moment by moment, on the TV news networks and Twitter feeds of the world. What did it all signify?

I decided, on impulse, to live-blog my experience of the missing MH370 flight as it was reported in the world's media. I would consider MH370 as a proxy apocalypse, a stand-in for the end of the world. Live blogging the event would be like chronicling Virilio's 'global accident' as it happened. It would be a version of the Apocalypse in miniature. I got writing at once.

At the time. I thought the story of the missing aircraft would come to an end within a few weeks, after its wreckage had been found in the sea. Little did I know that MH370 would become a lasting mystery, still unsolved by the time the residency at Solent City University had finished. I would have to abandon my blog in the end.

Not until August 2018 would the Malaysian investigators publish their final report on MH370. And even then, there was no firm conclusion. The official verdict was that what had happened to MH370 was simply unknown.

Model of a Global Accident Blog: MH370 Disappearance

Tuesday 11/03/14: Malaysian Jet Disaster and Media Scapegoating within the First 72 Hours

The informal rule adopted by disaster response experts is that the first 72 hours of a major incident are clouded with so much bad information, that it's difficult to get a clear narrative fix on what has happened. This is certainly the case with missing Malaysian Airlines flight MH370, which vanished from the skies three days ago. The immediate reflex response of the media to the mysterious disappearance was to blame two passengers on the plane who were travelling with stolen passports. The assumption was that the men were Islamic fundamentalist terrorists who had hijacked the Boeing 777 in a repeat of the methods used in the 9/11 attacks, when commercial aircraft were effectively transformed into huge petrol bombs. Only as the 72-hour limit passed did Interpol confirm the two men were actually illegal Iranian migrants who were hoping to make a connecting flight into Europe. This didn't stop CCTV images of the two boarding the plane from being flashed around the world, though.

Search: Malaysia Airlines MH370: Stolen Passports 'No Terror Link' | BBC News | March 11th 2014

Friday 14/03/14: Response to Malaysian Jet Disaster Takes Crowdsourcing Past the Tipping Point

Malaysian Airlines flight MH370 disappeared from radar screens two hours after take-off on Saturday 8th March 2014. The Boeing 777 was travelling from Kuala Lumpur to Beijing with 239 people on board when it vanished. It's assumed that the plane has crashed into the ocean, but so far no trace of it has been found. To help locate the wreckage, the US company DigitalGlobe has uploaded some of their commercial satellite imagery to a crowdsourcing platform. Volunteers can scour 1,988 square miles of territory at the conflux of the Gulf of Thailand and the South China Sea and tag objects of interest using special icons – raft, oil slick, wreckage. When DigitalGlobe conducted a similar campaign after Typhoon Haiyan struck the Philippines in November 2013, there were 60,000 map views in the first 24 hours. With flight MH370, six million views were logged in the same time frame and the website crashed.

Search: Tomnod – The Online Search Party Looking for Malaysian Airlines Flight MH370 | The Guardian | March 14th 2014

Sunday 16/03/14: Imitative Magic, Accident Investigation and the Missing Malaysian Jet

When local shaman Ibrahim Mat Zin arrived at Kuala Lumpur International Airport to help look for missing flight MH370, his rituals were met with scorn and ridicule by educated Malaysians. 'China deploys satellites to search for the plane while Malaysia uses a witch doctor', as one said. However, Raja Bomoh Sedunia Nujum VIP (to give him his full title) is actually adopting the same paradigm which underpins accident investigation research – namely, imitation. It's only his methods that are different. Whereas an accident investigator uses computer simulations to test hypotheses, the shaman uses theatre to model possible outcomes. In his first ritual, the 'bomoh' used bamboo binoculars to look for the plane and a fish trap to catch it. In his next ritual, his three assistants sat cross-legged on a carpet and mimed flying through the air to rescue the missing plane – one man with a stick for a rudder, another with a basket for a wing flap and the third man with two coconuts for an engine.

Search: Witch Doctor Performs Ritual to 'Locate' Missing Malaysian Airline Plane | YouTube | March 12th 2014

Monday 17/03/14: Shamanic Ritual in Pursuit of the Missing Malaysian Jet Reconsidered as Performance Art

Raja Bomoh Sedunia Nujum VIP wanted to perform seven shamanic rituals at Kuala Lumpur International Airport to help locate the missing flight MH370. Malaysian government ministers were amenable so long as the state-sponsored religion of Islam was not disrespected. However, after his first two rituals became a rather embarrassing sensation on YouTube, the bomoh was discouraged from returning to the airport. Why the official disquiet? Perhaps it's simply a matter of taste. The 80-year-old shaman was dressed in an old-fashioned suit and tie, his props referenced Malaysia's past (fishing, agriculture) while his bamboo binoculars and 'flying carpet' schtick were lifted from the corny old Malaysian movie *Laksamana Do Re Mi* starring 50s matinee idol P Ramlee. Styles have changed. The British shaman Marcus Coates, for example, uses animal head-dresses and operates in a performance art context.

Search: Marcus Coates | TateShots | YouTube | March 23rd 2009

Tuesday 18/03/14: Missing Malaysian Jet Considered as a Media Black Hole

Accident or terror attack? When Malaysian Airlines flight MH370 disappeared from civilian radar screens over the sea, it reappeared in public consciousness as an 'unknown quantity', a ghost aircraft, the object of rumour, speculation and prayers. What is astonishing is that it has breached the informal yardstick used by disaster response teams – the one that says an 'unknown quantity' lasts only 72 hours before it gives up its secret. It is well over a week since MH370 vanished and still no one knows what happened. This is a long time in terms of the 24 hours news cycle. As a media event, MH370 is already so comparatively ancient that it has generated its own distinct epochs of interpretation. It has even begun to recede into the realms of pop myth.

Search: Malaysian Plane Mystery Copies Comic Story of Hijacked Jet Which Landed on Remote Island | Daily Star | March 17th 2014

Thursday 20/03/14: Shamanism Meets Conspiracy Theory in the Case of the Missing Malaysian Jet

There is a vast anthropological literature on shamanism and it is always worth taking seriously the explanations performers give of their own rituals. All shamanic belief systems depend on the idea of a supernatural world in which the objects and entities of the natural world have their spiritual counterparts. The shaman is able to work at the interface between these two worlds in a trance state, manipulating symbolic objects in order to create equivalent transformations in the spirit world which themselves bleed back into the world of real objects. So what does Raja Bomoh Sedunia Nujum VIP say has happened to flight MH370? In his vision, he saw the plane's ghostly double plunging down after a black eagle flew over it. The ghostly plane was then flown to the hidden island of the 'Bunian' people, the elves of Malaysian folklore, where the passengers and crew are waiting to be rescued. Visible beneath this mythological tracing is the story of a hijacking.

Search: Did Malaysia Airlines Plane Escape in the 'Shadow' of Another Jet? | Mashable | March 17th 2014

Friday 21/03/14: Missing Malaysian Jet Considered as an Electromagnetic Trace Object

Malaysian Airlines flight MH370 has been missing since 8th March 2014 and has still not been found. It was seen taking off from Kuala Lumpur International Airport at 00:41 local time and was due to hove back into view at 06:30 as it landed at Beijing Capital International Airport. In the interval, it was scheduled to lead a shadow life, in the usual way, as a radar trace handed over from one Air Traffic Control (ATC) system to the next. This interval has now expanded from six hours to 13 days. Malaysia Airlines initially announced at 07:24 that the jet had disappeared from Subang ATC radar at 02:40, but later revised this time to 01:22. The craft slipped from Malaysian military radar at 02:15 and its final 'ping' was picked up by the London-based Inmarsat satellite at 08:11. Since then, the plane has shown no signs of electromagnetic life. Only a renewed human sighting is now capable of confirming its return to existence. MH370 has become lost in the fog of time.

Search: The Philadelphia Experiment | IMDb

Saturday 22/03/14: #prayforMH370 and the Kuala Lumpur Airport Memorial

When flight MH370 disappeared after taking off from Kuala Lumpur International Airport (KLIA), a culture of remembrance began to spring up in affected regions of the world. There were messages of hope shared on Facebook and Instagram, hashtagged prayers were circulated on Twitter and interfaith vigils have been held in Malaysia uniting Muslims with Christians, Hindus and Buddhists. At the epicentre of this outpouring of support for the missing passengers and crew was the huge 60m-long banner at KLIA's Observation Desk, crammed with thousands of hand-written messages, post-it notes, drawings and signatures, surrounded by cards, placards and crowds of students, older people and children. Here, perhaps, is the humble emergence of a global interfaith vernacular that makes use of public locations, everyday materials and simple messages.

Search: Malaysia Airlines Flight MH370: Prayers Continue as Search and Rescue Teams Scour the Globe for Missing Airliner | International Business Times | March 19th 2014

Sunday 23/03/14: Flight MH370 Considered as a Metaphysical Event

For Paul Virilio, the accident as a philosophical idea tracks back to Aristotle, who in his *Metaphysics* conceived of it as a property which has no necessary connection to the substance of a thing. So, a plane crash is an obscene chance event which interrupts what should be the inevitable spread of air travel around the world. Virilio deconstructs Aristotle to claim that the accident – or, at least, an accident waiting to happen – is always the necessary property of a thing. So, when a jet airliner like the Boeing 777 is invented, the potential for a complex event like the disappearance of flight MH370 is also created. Here, Virilio comes close to the atomist physics of Lucretius, who argues that a complex event is the result of an infinitesimal deviation in spacetime, much like the swerve-off course which Malaysian military radar revealed flight MH370 had taken before it disappeared.

Search: Michel Serres | The Birth of Physics | Amazon

Monday 24/03/14: The Crash of Flight MH370 Is Officially an Algorithmic Event

When flight MH370 shut off its transponder, it disappeared from Malaysian radar and was declared missing. Before the disappearance could be called a crash, the possible locations of the plane had to be computed. An Inmarsat comms satellite first picked up an automated signal from the plane's satcomm link at 02:11, receiving eight hourly 'pings' in total, before the last at 08:11. Based on the time it took the pings to reach the orbiting satellite and the angle of their elevation, Inmarsat calculated there were two corridors the plane could have flown along. The northerly corridor stretched to Central Asia, the southerly corridor swept into the Indian Ocean. Inmarsat checked their data against comparative data drawn from the trajectories of actual aircraft on relevant routes and narrowed MH370's last known location to just three per cent of the area of the southerly corridor. These findings were accepted by the Malaysian government, who at 22:00 on March 24th 2014 declared that the plane had crashed into the Indian Ocean, with all lives lost. MH370 RIP.

Search: In Full: Malaysia Airlines Flight MH370 Passenger List | South China Post | March 8th 2014

Tuesday 25/03/14: The Search for MH370 Debris Considered as a Mourning Ritual

Now that flight MH370 has been declared lost in the Indian Ocean, the search for the remnants of the crashed plane splits into various epistemological dimensions. There is the reasonable certainty, based on a mathematical inference concerning the plane's speed, flight path and fuel volume, that everyone on-board has died. And then there are the unreasonable hopes shared by the families of those on-board that their loved ones might still be alive. When there are no bodies to identify, it's easy to believe that death has not occurred. Meanwhile, the search in the Indian Ocean proceeds from a perception of quasi-objects that have an almost hallucinatory intensity. Pieces of fuselage supposedly lurk in the grain of satellite images, unreal images of safety belts and cargo pallets are conjured by spotter planes zooming over the sea, while ships crawl towards designated coordinates wishing to verify the ghostly sightings. Only when all the fragments of knowledge are assembled into a new whole, can mourning hope to have an end.

Search: 'The Science Of Ghosts' - Derrida in 'Ghost Dance' | YouTube | January 27th 2007

Wednesday 26/03/14: MH370 Families Considered as a Political Avant-Garde

Two thirds of the passengers on flight MH370 were Chinese. The families of these 154 people descended upon the Metropark Lido Hotel in Beijing during the time of the plane's disappearance and installed themselves in one of the conference rooms. Here, they watched the daily media briefings from Kuala Lumpur on a jumbo screen, held meetings with Malaysia Airlines officials, staged protests against the Malaysian government, chanted slogans, demanded answers and even threatened to go on hunger strike. The international media crowded in on them with cameras and microphones and relayed their anger, grief and incomprehension to the world. Hostages to the logic of a story over which they had no control, the families were informed of the MH370 crash by text message and finally mobilised themselves to march on to the streets of Beijing under the uneasy eyes of riot police. Is this an example of 'people power' triggered by a disaster and amplified by the media? And are these 200 people rehearsing a transformation of consciousness which will be undergone by all seven billion of us at the Apocalypse?

Search: 1 Corinthians 15:22

Thursday 27/03/14: The Search for MH370 Debris Considered as a Moment of Awakening

The global spread of technologies which enable people to see, hear, know and act at a distance are considered by Virilio, in his more gnostic moments, as a kind of demiurgic recasting of the world. The will of humanity, applied to the world through the development of technology, is to become god-like – immanent in everything, everywhere, all at once. When this happens, and humanity is cocooned inside a worldwide web of manufactured perceptions and behaviours, like a jet pilot speeding far above the Earth, then there is no longer an outside able to orient our inhabitation of global space-time. The accident, by contrast, restores an awareness of the reality of the world. As spotter planes search for the debris of flight MH370 in a remote part of the Indian Ocean, they are engulfed in clouds, dodging rain and typhoons, frustrated by high-speed winds and currents, conscious that below them lies the vastness of an undiscovered and completely alien environment.

Search: Solaris | IMDb

Friday 28/03/14: MH370 Disaster Response and the Architecture of Command

How did the international response to the disappearance of flight MH370 fit with an understanding of strategic, tactical and operational levels of command? Strategic command was effectively based at the Sama-Sama Hotel near Kuala Lumpur International Airport, where Hishammuddin Hussein, a Malaysian government official who combined the roles of acting minister of transport and defence minister, issued daily media briefings to the world's press. Tactical command seemed to migrate from the control room of Inmarsat in London, with its huge screen displaying the locations of its various global satellites, to the Australian airbase in Perth which has recently been coordinating the search efforts in the southern Indian Ocean. Operational command lies with the planes and ships scouring the ocean wilderness for plane debris, marking locations with smoke flares and GPS-equipped data buoys. But this neat picture masks the grubby reality of an investigation plagued by international rivalry, military secrecy and bureaucratic incompetence.

Search: MH370 Puts UN Search Agency's Protocol to the Test | South China Morning Post | March 27th 2014

Sunday 30/03/14: Mh370 Crash Considered as an Instance of Negative Theology

Virilio suggests that if the thought that goes into the invention of the jet airliner is revolutionary, then the thought which emerges from a plane crash is 'revelationary'. A major accident is not simply the negation of a technology, it is also the exposure of an unknowability lying hidden within that technology, the flashing up of an obscure set of coincidences which is experienced with

the force of a transcendent epiphany. A crash is first understood as a 'way of negation' in which knowledge of the world is
stripped away and signs that are expected instead fail to arrive.
At 06:30 on a certain day, flight MH370 did not land in Beijing,
at 01:37 it had not transmitted its expected half-hourly ACARS
data, at 01:22 it did not appear on Ho Chi Minh City civilian
radar and at 01:19 the co-pilot did not use his call sign when he
said, 'All right, goodnight'. And yet this unknowability is only a
starting point for the production of an accident-prevention literature of re-specifications and re-affirmations about the technology in question. The disappearance of MH370 will no doubt
have implications for everything from aerospace engineering to
airport X-ray scanner design.

Search: Apophatic Theology | Wikipedia

Thursday 03/04/14: The Search for the MH370 Black Box Considered as a Psychoanalytical Fantasy

The final stage of the search for flight MH370 will be reached with
the salvaging of the plane's 'black box' from the Indian Ocean. The
black box comprises two devices – a Flight Data Recorder (FDR),
which measures the aircraft's performance, and a Cockpit Voice
Recorder (CVR), which captures what the pilots have been saying
for the last two hours before the plane's destruction. The trouble
is that the black box issues ultrasonic location 'pings' for a mere
30 days after an accident, that this limit has nearly been reached
and that these signals have a radius of only a mile. Even if the
MH370 black box is found, the CVR is likely to be less than clari-
fying, given that the critical event which triggered the accident
had happened six or seven hours before when the plane swerved
off-course. The black box, considered as a repository of the traumatic memory of an accident, compares with the 'primal scene'

of psychoanalysis. It has the magical allure of fantasy. What is perhaps required to understand the truth of an accident is instead a 'topoanalysis' of designated places – the Boeing engine factory, the Subang ATC tower, the Kuala Lumpur home of the pilot – which pays attention to the 'infra-ordinary' details of perception, activity and routine. It is a task worthy of an avant-garde novelist such as Georges Perec.

Search: Georges Perec | The Infra-ordinary | UbuWeb

Friday 04/04/14: Flight MH370 Conspiracy Theories and Digital Provenance

Nearly a month since it went missing, flight MH370 has still not been found. The Malaysian police are conducting a criminal investigation into the plane's disappearance, but they have admitted they might never discover why someone switched off its communications and diverted it thousands of miles off-course. They have considered various hypotheses – mechanical or electrical failure (eg fire on-board or decompression of the aircraft cabin), terror attack (eg bomb on-board or hijacking), human factors (eg pilot error or suicide). But nothing is proven. Into this void of interpretation pours an internet-accelerated stream of conspiracy theories (eg Freescale patent coup, Diego Garcia forced landing, shoot-down, cyber-hijack). Is this an example of the crowd-sourcing of alternative hypotheses to help investigators? Or is it a result of moral panic, social prejudice and undeclared special interests? What's needed is the tracing of the passage of each conspiracy theory back to its origin to evaluate its trustworthiness (eg the cyber-hijack theory derives from an ex-UK government adviser who runs her own risk management business).

Search: #mh370conspiracy | Twitter

Tuesday 08/04/14: Mh370 Conspiracy Theories and UFO Disinformation

Digital provenance traces the history of an internet meme in order to evaluate its trustworthiness. It's based on the use of provenance in the artworld, which documents the chain of ownership of an artwork in order to verify its authenticity. The artworld wants to prevent fakes from entering the market. So what about fake memes? Intelligence agencies have a history of planting false conspiracy theories on the media fringe in order to shroud various covert operations. For example, it's thought the US Air Force's Office of Special Investigations spread UFO rumours in the 1980s to hide early drone tests in plain sight. Is there any disinformation at work in the conspiracy theories surrounding flight MH370? We need to unpick the good information from all the bad information that's tangled up in the stories of MH370 being abducted by UFOs and aliens. Is the idea of a mid-air plane swap actually credible? Only if we discount the UFO story published the day after MH370's disappearance.

Search: UFO in the Radar Readings of Malaysia Airlines Flight 370 | ForbiddenKnowledgeTV | March 9th 2014

Thursday 10/04/14: MH370 Considered as a Precursor of the 'Global Accident'

The Australian ship *Ocean Shield* is scouring the southern Indian Ocean with a towed pinger locator and has picked up four signals thought to be from flight MH370's black box. The search area is narrowing. Just a few weeks ago, though, it extended into Central Asia, comprising a vast area of almost three million square miles – or over one hundredth of the planet's surface area. MH370 has always had an incipient planetary dimension.

The plane disappeared between Malaysian and Vietnamese airspace, there were 14 different nationalities represented on-board, while a total of 26 countries have participated in the search – including China, the US, the UK and Australia. The world's media has been drawn to the nerve-centre of the international search efforts in Kuala Lumpur while the unfolding event has been live-blogged on every continent. If the search area had expanded – rather than contracted, as it did – then up for grabs would have been a vision of the planet eclipsed by a premonition of its own mortification.

Search: The Sixth Extinction: A Conversation with Elizabeth Kolbert | National Geographic | February 19th 2014

Wednesday 23/04/14: Underwater Drones, MH370 and the High-Resolution Mapping of the Ocean Floor

The search-and-rescue vessels in the southern Indian Ocean have not detected any more pings for days. It's assumed that the batteries in flight MH370's black box have died. A US underwater Bluefin-21 drone has been shipped to one of the ping locations, a relatively small area with a radius of 10km. On each of its missions, the drone takes two hours to dive to a depth of 4.5km, where it scans the ocean floor in parallel lines for 16 hours, before returning to the surface. It takes four hours to download its data. Slowly, methodically, a sonar map of underwater terrain is being compiled. So far, no plane debris has been detected. But the mission is a reminder that whereas the planet's landmass has been comprehensively and accurately mapped, its ocean depths – accounting for about 70 per cent of its total surface area – have barely been charted. Satellite maps of underwater terrain are fuzzy while the completion of detailed sonar maps would require the kind of investment usually reserved for probes of Mars or Jupiter.

Search: Malaysia Airlines MH370: Searching in an Ocean of Uncertainty | BBC News | April 9th 2014

Friday 02/05/14: MH370 Crash Considered as an 'Inverse Miracle'

Virilio distinguishes between the 'local accident' which happens in a particular time and place and the 'global accident' which happens everywhere at once. A Boeing 777 disappears between Malaysian and Vietnamese airspace on 8th March 2014 and supposedly crashes into the Indian Ocean 17 days later, but the 'global accident' is more like what would happen if the Large Hadron Collider in Switzerland were to inadvertently spawn a baby black hole which then expanded to consume the planet. Virilio is a Roman Catholic and just as he calls the global accident an 'apocalypse', so he calls the local accident an 'inverse miracle'. For Thomas Aquinas, the Eucharist conserves the Aristotelian substance of bread and wine (its texture, its taste), while miraculously transforming what would otherwise be its obscene accidental properties (its potential rottenness, its potential sourness) into the flesh and blood of Christ. So too perhaps does an accident like the MH370 crash, with its incipient planetary dimension, offer a revelatory experience of the awesome demiurgic power of air travel.

Search: Malaysia Jet Mystery Unfolds as Asian Air Travel Booms | Haaretz | March 20th 2014

Thursday 29/05/14: The Abyss Stares Back at the Flight MH370 Search Team

Australian authorities have announced that the Bluefin-21 drone has completed its meticulous underwater search of the patch of the Indian Ocean bed where flight MH370 was thought to have ended up. No plane debris has been found. A US Navy expert has said that the four 'pings' originally detected by search teams at this spot might have been produced by the pinger locator towed by the Australian ship *Ocean Shield* (or even by the vessel itself). The noises mistakenly identified as black box flight recorder signals were probably ghost signals, electronic interference, dismal echoes of the search team's frantic desire to locate the black box before its batteries ran out. The sonar map of the empty ocean floor so painstakingly acquired by the drone now takes on another guise as the enigmatic record of a misguided faith in search-and-rescue technology. Three months after vanishing from the skies, flight MH370 has pulled off another disappearing act by vanishing from the seas. It now looks set to become one of those perennial mysteries only ever rediscovered by the media on a slow news day.

Search: Elvis Sightings | Wikipedia

Outro: Field Notes on a Residency

It was June 2014 when our Solent City University residency came to an end. Haubenstock and I packed our bags with some sadness. We closed the door on our campus dorm room for the last time. Outside, it was raining. We struggled with our umbrellas against the wind and made our way to the computer science building car park. It was late afternoon.

Earlier in the day, we'd had a meeting with Jenkins in his office. I'd shown him some of the written outputs from our workshops with his computer scientists. These were end-of-the-world scenarios composed in a variety of styles. He selected two of the more conventional scenarios to tie in with his drone research project. He liked the television apocalypse, which had terrorists with nuclear back-packs holed up in a skyscraper in Tokyo. He could imagine how surveillance drones might prove themselves useful in such a situation, possibly even as autonomous negotiators. He also liked the idea of simulating the different possible impacts of an asteroid striking the Earth. That might work well as a mixed reality game.

As we'd put on our coats at the end of the meeting, Jenkins had said he was looking forward to our film about the end of the world. I'd already written the script. I told Jenkins we'd gone for a theological perspective in the end. The working title was *Cold Earth Wanderer*. Jolly good, said Jenkins, pumping my hand vigorously, his mind already elsewhere. He thanked Haubenstock for filming the workshops and said it would be lovely if the department could get a nice, little 20-minute video package out of all the footage. Haubenstock flashed a toothy smile and said nothing.

As we drove slowly away from the campus, Haubenstock started ranting about Jenkins. There was no way he was making a

corporate video for that guy's fleet of robot killer drones. The computer science department could have the workshop footage. Free
of charge. They could do whatever they wanted with it. As long as
Haubenstock's name was not on it.

Haubenstock's indignant effusions continued the whole
drive to the Whitlock Gallery. We'd decided to stop by and see if
the gallery director was around. Haubenstock parked in one of
the spare bays. The building loomed above us. It had originally
been designed as a tidal research centre and its grand sweeps
and curves gave it something of a maritime dimension, like a big,
floating hulk.

We poked our heads round the door of the gallery. It was
dark. There was a lot of banging and knocking going on. Farmer
surfaced from the gloom and greeted us warmly. He led us deep
into the gallery, which was as dimly lit as an aquarium at an
amusement park. We're busy supervising the build of an installation for an upcoming show, he said. He took us on a tour of the
rubble and half-built walls, nodding to curators and carpenters
as he went.

The subject of our conversation inevitably drifted to the film
Haubenstock and I were due to exhibit at the gallery. Farmer said
he'd booked us a six-week slot in December/January. The grave-
yard slot, said Haubenstock. No, no, said Farmer. It's the hinge
of the year. The winter solstice and all that. Good things always
happen then.

Farmer asked us what our film was about. The birth of the
Antichrist, said Haubenstock. Farmer stopped walking. We were
by the toilets. The film will be shot among the Second World
War bunkers on the Atlantic Coast of Europe, I said. Like the
Wilson Twins and *Sealander*, said Farmer. No, I said, like Paul
Virilio and *Bunker Archaeology*. Virilio had got to the bunkers
first, I continued, way back in the 1950s. He'd photographed the
abandoned observation posts and armoured cupolas of Brittany

decades before the artists had arrived. The locals had thought he was a mad-man. Or a fascist, said Haubenstock. I smiled. Prophets are always dishonoured in their own land.

We started walking again. There's a big space to fill, said Farmer, holding out his arms. Have you thought about an installation at all? Sure, I said. We want to build a bunker as a viewing space for our film. I was improvising. Out of concrete? asked Farmer. He was frowning. No, said Haubenstock. Out of recycled plastic. Farmer nodded. Okay, okay. How much Unilever money do you have left? he asked. Enough to make the film. *Cold Earth Wanderer*, I reminded him. Farmer said we'd have to apply for public funds from Arts Council England to cover the costs of the exhibition. My heart sank. Another institution to placate, another application form to fill in.

Farmer said he had to dash. He had to make a quick phone call to Lady Minus. Something about a painting stuck at Customs. Haubenstock and I wandered out of the gallery into the slanting light of the Sun. Lovely man, said Haubenstock, whose judgements could often surprise. We left Southampton and drove back to Brighton.

Over the next few months, we made our film. I took the voice-over script I'd written and got it recorded at a studio in London. I spoke the words into the microphone. There was no one else to do it. We were running out of money. Haubenstock flew to Jersey and filmed the decaying bunkers on the island's north-west coast. He said they had more of a desolate feel than the 'Virilio ones', as he called them, on the French coast. Once back in Brighton, in his bedroom edit suite, Haubenstock synched up the landscape footage with my voiceover, throwing in some archive footage and found imagery along the way. Haubenstock's collages always had a jagged, brutal feel. They carried the weight of a judgement made from some secret, inaccessible part of the culture. His instincts were very pure.

Meanwhile, I was spending long hours filling in the Arts Council England application form. I consulted with Farmer on the phone. He said he was sure we'd get the funding. It was a mere technicality. I finally got the form done and despatched it to the relevant bureaucrats.

In September, I attended the annual general meeting of Jenkins' drone research project team. It was the second meeting in a scheduled total of three and was held at a conference centre in Surrey. Jenkins and his team presented the results of their computer algorithm research to their backers, including British Aerospace. I also did a turn on the platform. I showed a few inoffensive stills from *Cold Earth Wanderer* and talked in general terms about how a dronecam might make a film one day, all by itself. There was scattered applause.

In October, we received a 'no' from Arts Council England on our bid for public funds. Farmer immediately cancelled our planned exhibition at the Whitlock Gallery. He sent us a one-line email. Angleton, to his credit, invited us to show *Cold Earth Wanderer* to his Virilio students at Chilton School of Art.

And so it was that Haubenstock and I made our way back to Southampton on a cloudy grey day in December. We got to the art school in the late afternoon and parked in the shade of a cedar tree. Angleton was there to meet us. Before playing our film in the screening room, he made a short speech about its connection with Virilio. His students seemed to enjoy watching it. They asked intelligent questions. And Haubenstock gave funny and illuminating answers. He was in his element.

After it was all over, Haubenstock and I found ourselves sitting in the art school canteen. It was raining outside and the night was drawing in. The foam in our coffee cups was cold. I never want to make another film again, said Haubenstock. It just isn't worth it. The Unilever residency had left him exhausted and in debt. Our career in the art world is petering out, he said. I'm getting old, nothing seems to work out, my life's been a waste. His worried little face shone in the gloom.

Things aren't that bad, I said. There's no reason we can't go on. But, deep inside, I knew something had changed. We were done.

Unidentified Fictional Objects appear in the spaces in between established genres and disciplines including fact and fiction, theory and practice, past and future, science and sociology, art and academia.

We believe that stories can be both provocative and engaging, especially when they use new methodologies and modes of communication to challenge current distributions of power and knowledge.

We seek objects that may (or may not) resemble science fiction, critical utopias, creative dystopias, speculative writing, weird fiction, weird non-fiction.

We publish things (print, digital, plus) of varying lengths and call out to writers and readers who no longer wish to be constrained by categories.

UFOs speculate, reinvent, weird and undo economies, societies, environments, identities and sexualities. They appeal to students and their teachers, friends, and relations (human and otherwise).